A SHOT OF MURDER

Whoever heard of a honeymoon on which the bride waited in Paris while the groom took a trip on the Orient Express — with a strange woman in his compartment?

Rocky and Jane Rockwell did. There had already been one murder on their Atlantic crossing, and it looked like more to come — particularly since the woman on the train was using a gun for a ticket . . .

The action was fast and furious, and before Rocky and Jane got back to honeymooning, they had unearthed enough excitement and adventure to last them a lifetime. . . .

by JACK IAMS

Author of
WHAT RHYMES WITH MURDER?
and
DO NOT MURDER BEFORE CHRISTMAS

A Shot of Murder

JACK IAMS

Author of:
WHAT RHYMES WITH MURDER?
DO NOT MURDER BEFORE
              CHRISTMAS
DEATH DRAWS THE LINE
GIRL MEETS BODY
and others.

WILDSIDE PRESS

FOREWORD

Part of this book is laid behind the Iron Curtain, and since I spent several months in Warsaw as a guest of the American Embassy, I should like to make it clear that everything that happens in the story is strictly imaginary and is not based on any inside information that may have come my way. On the other hand, such information as did come my way would suggest that none of the book's happenings is impossible, or even improbable.

As far as the physical aspects of the Iron Curtain are concerned, I have tried to present as authentic a picture as I could. The background of the sanitarium sequence is reasonably accurate, but the events that take place inside this institution are, once again, purely speculative. However, if only to show how conscientious I am, I have discussed the possibilities involved with the distinguished authority on anesthesia, Dr. E. A. Rovenstine, and I have tried to stay within the limits of scientific likelihood. I would like, very spontaneously, to thank him, and, much less spontaneously, to thank Shapiro, Bernstein & Co., Inc. for permission to quote from the song "Side by Side," on page 205. While I'm about it, I might as well give credit to Francis Scott Key for excerpts from another song which appears on page 179 and page 180.

CHAPTER ONE

THE QUEEN JADWIGA moved placidly down the North River, which on that June afternoon was a bright blue. On the deck below, the ship's orchestra was playing "Happy Days Are Here Again," and I wondered how it sounded to such passengers as were leaving America for Poland and points east for good and all. As far as I was concerned, it sounded fine, largely because of the golden-haired girl standing beside me at the rail.

"Now there," this girl said, "is something that's going to look awfully, awfully good to us coming back."

Among tugs and ferries and flatboats, the coppery green of the Statue of Liberty sparkled in the sunlight.

"If we ever come back," I said.

"Goodness!" cried the girl. "What a nice, cheerful thing to say."

"Just a roundabout way of rapping on wood." I grinned down at her. "You didn't think I meant it, did you?"

"I wouldn't know." Her blue eyes remained reproachful.

"And as for the Statue of Liberty, she can't hold a candle to you, going or coming."

The girl frowned, though not with displeasure. "I happen to take the Statue of Liberty very seriously," she said.

"So do I. All hundred and fifty-one feet of her. That's not counting the pedestal. The pedestal's a hundred and fifty-five feet, which makes a total of—let me see. Five and one are six, nothing to carry, five and five—"

"How in the world do you know that?"

"I was reading that guide to New York in the hotel last night."

"Well!" exclaimed the girl. "I suppose you were bored."

"I always like to improve my mind."

"I see," she said and sighed. "I guess I'll just have to get used to it."

I put my arm around her and she rested her blond head on my shoulder. She was a lissome girl, not very tall—about one twenty-eighth as tall as the statue—and her name was Mrs. Stanley Rockwell, a fact so new I could scarcely grasp it. Until recently she had been a Miss Jane Hewes.

Her eyes glanced up at me. "Having fun?"

"Just a minute. One to carry, three. Three hundred and six feet all told. You're darned right I am."

"So'm I." She snuggled a little. "I never thought it would happen."

"I did. From the minute you got your hooks into me."

"I don't mean getting married," said Jane Hewes Rockwell. "You're quite right about that. I mean the trip."

"It isn't exactly the trip I'd have planned."

"Mm, no, but it's better than Niagara Falls."

"We may think pretty tenderly of Niagara Falls when we're in those salt mines."

She lifted her head to look at me. "I do wish you'd stop saying things like that."

"All right. I guess it's because I've never been to Europe before. Let alone back of any Iron Curtains."

"I think it's romantic," said Jane. "Any old body can go to Paris or Bermuda for a honeymoon. It takes imaginative people like us to pick Warsaw."

"Imaginative and broke."

"Yes, but people who read it in the society column needn't know that. If we were in the society column."

"Good gosh," I said and snapped my fingers. "I haven't shown you the paper yet, have I?"

"Paper? What paper?"

"Our paper. I got it at the out-of-town newsstand this morning. Forgot all about it. It's down in the cabin. I'll get it."

"Hurry," said Jane. "I don't want to say good-by to America by myself."

By "our paper" I meant the Riverside, Ohio, *Record*, of which I was city editor in the normal way of things but for which I was now on a rather fantastic assignment—an assignment I had dreamed up as Jane's and my only hope of an ocean honeymoon.

I went down the companionway to the veranda deck, where a steward was already dispensing steamer chairs and rugs, on down to the promenade deck, and down again to the long polished corridor that led to our cabin. Most of the milling people I passed were chattering in languages I couldn't recognize, and such English as I heard was heavily accented. It gave me a strong sense of being already in foreign parts, and for a boy from a small Ohio city—well, eighty thousand—it was a tingly feeling, and one not quite devoid of uneasiness.

I got the paper and went back upstairs. I mean above. The *Queen Jadwiga* had passed through the Narrows, and the respective shore lines of Brooklyn and Staten Island were widening and dwindling. There was something irrevocable about the way they opened up, which I didn't exactly like; then I saw something else that I liked considerably less.

A man was standing beside Jane at the rail, close beside her, and apparently pointing out some distant object of interest. As if casually helping her to look in the right direction, his arm moved lightly around her waist, even while I watched. Jane edged away, and he edged a little closer.

I cleared my throat loudly, and they both turned. The

man let his arm drop indifferently, and gave me a cool smile. He was about my height but fleshier, with thick, damp lips.

"Well?" I said.

He shrugged. "Well what?" He didn't seem to have any particular accent.

"This is my husband," said Jane.

"That's nice," the man said. "See you around." He smiled again, put his hands in his pockets, and strolled off.

I watched him go, forcing back a desire to kick his plump behind. "Who's your friend?" I asked Jane.

"Really, Rocky, you needn't sound sore at me. He just came up and started to talk."

"Why didn't you tell him to peddle his papers?"

"Well, I certainly didn't encourage him."

"He didn't look discouraged."

"He's not the type that discourages easily," said Jane. "And I don't propose to have a honeymoon quarrel over a shipboard wolf."

"Neither do I, but—"

"All right, then. Count ten or something."

I made myself smile and started to count.

"And speaking of peddling papers," she went on, "let's see the *Record*. That's what you left me a helpless prey for, wasn't it?"

"Uhuh. Let's get out of the wind."

We walked together to a bench, back of the deck-tennis nets an attendant was setting up, and sat down. I unfolded the paper and spread it on my knees.

Jane whistled. "I didn't realize they were going to play it up like this."

"They've got to. If they didn't play it, there'd be no sense doing it."

The black eight-columned streamer said:

RECORD LAUNCHES HUNT FOR MISSING SINGER

And beneath it:

Tackles Mystery Of Disappearance
Of Local Athlete's Fiancée
Behind Iron Curtain

There was also a large photograph of a pretty, dark-haired girl in a low-cut evening gown. Her name, as the caption pointed out, was Nita Romaine, and if she hadn't happened to vanish in the course of a night-club tour in Poland, Jane and I would have had to take the *Maid of the Mist* instead of the *Queen Jadwiga.*

CHAPTER TWO

JANE HEWES AND I had promised each other we'd put off getting married until we had enough money scraped together for (a) a down payment on a place to live and (b) an honest-to-goodness honeymoon. Then one day in May, after we'd been engaged for several months, we looked at the bankbook and we looked at each other, and next thing we knew, we were down at City Hall.

It was a very quiet wedding, with J. H. Breen, my managing editor, as best man—this was largely a matter of tact, but I was pretty fond of the old boy at that—and with our society editor, Mrs. Pickett, as matron of honor. This was not a matter of tact—Mrs. Pickett had told us flatly, ahead of time, that she did not consider the marriages of city editors as worthy of mention in her column, which she conducted with an autocratic hand. She added, by way of amelioration, that if she herself were ever to marry again, D.V., she would consider it beneath her professional notice, and the groom could like it or lump it. Her first husband, incidentally, had lumped it many years before.

Mrs. Pickett did, however, exert a certain influence on our post-nuptial plans. It happened that Mrs. Pickett was going to Europe that summer, and that gave Jane and me ideas, especially Jane. She figured that we owed ourselves a real fling before we settled down in Ohio. That suited me, but how, I asked, were we going to manage it?

"How does Mrs. Pickett manage it?" Jane came back.

"Mrs. Pickett isn't married, for one thing."

This was twenty-four hours after the ceremony, and Jane had looked at me coldly. "Are you complaining?" she asked.

"No, but—"

"If Mrs. Pickett can do it, I don't see why we can't."

I saw, but at the time I didn't argue. Mrs. Pickett made these hegiras every five years or so, taking leave of absence without pay, and financing the expedition with savings and also with articles that she sent back, at space rates, about the places she visited and, in particular, about any local society folk who might be summering abroad. J. H. Breen approved because he felt it gave the paper class to print articles from Our Special Correspondent in Paris or whatever.

But J. H. Breen, I knew perfectly well, would never approve of my doing the same thing. The only possible chance would be if some story came up like a local girl trying to swim the Channel, and I even went so far as to get out the clippings on such swimmers as Riverside boasted but none of them looked like Channel material. Meanwhile, I had to watch Mrs. Pickett bustling happily about with travel folders and letters of introduction and consultations as to whether or not a woman of her age— she was in her late forties, large and earthy—should or should not wear a Bikini bathing-suit on the Riviera.

Then along came the story of this night-club singer, this Nita Romaine, disappearing somewhere in Poland. At the time, of course, I had no notion that it could have the slightest connection with my young life, and the main reason that the story made page one all over the country lay in Miss Romaine's sultry good looks as reflected in the glossy publicity poses which her New York booking agent happily scattered in all directions. In fact, there was a faint aroma of press-agentry about the whole business, I thought, but a couple of congressmen saw a chance to lambast the State Department, and anti-administration papers demanded that Something Be Done, and a fair amount of journalistic dust was kicked up.

Perhaps the briefest way to explain how Jane's and my honeymoon got involved in all this is to quote from the story that J. H. Breen and I cooked up—to be held for release until I actually left town—and which Jane was reading with skeptical fascination that afternoon on the *Queen Jadwiga*. It started out in three columns of fourteen-point type:

Following the Record's *exclusive revelation last week that the missing Nita Romaine is the fiancée of one of Riverside's best known athletes, this newspaper has decided to undertake its own investigation of this Iron Curtain mystery on its own initiative and at its own expense.*

I had to chuckle at that last phrase—J. H. had insisted on it, and I wasn't arguing; not after the gallons of sweat I'd shed in talking him into an enterprise from which he had shied away, at first, like a cart horse from a steeplechase jump.

City Editor Stanley Rockwell is already on his way to Poland where he will apply his years of journalistic ex-

perience to digging out the facts behind a situation that seems to have stumped our State Department. It should be added in fairness, however, that the State Department has promised this newspaper its fullest co-operation.

In fact, the State Department had leaned over backward to co-operate. The press officer to whom I talked in Washington pointed out that where the Department's hands were tied by international protocol, I could rush in where consuls feared to tread, and maybe take some of the editorial heat off the administration. And if I got in trouble, it would be my own trouble, and not the U. S. Government's—"Be sure you remember that," he had added. Anyway, he had rushed through my application for a passport, for Jane and me, and had instructed the American Embassy in Warsaw to apply what pressure it could to obtain a Polish visa, and fast. The visa had looked to me like a stumbling-block, and both the press officer and I were surprised when the Polish Government came through, not only with an order to its Consulate General to grant me a visa at once, but with a pledge of all possible assistance. "It's too good," the press officer observed worriedly. "I don't like the looks of it."

As was revealed in these columns, the vanished American singer was to have been married upon her return from her European tour to Leslie N. ("Les") Baldwin, former star halfback of the Riverside North High School football team, captain of the basketball team, and high scorer for two years in the Tri-City League.

Mr. Baldwin, who joined his country's armed forces in time to see action in the Bulge and who since the war has been employed in his father's hardware store on Bridge Avenue, told the Record *that he first met Miss Romaine when she was on a USO tour in the spring of 1945. They continued to correspond and in the months that followed, their friendship ripened into love, and finally flowered in their engagement.*

That wasn't exactly the way Les had put it, but it would do. I remembered the morning he had come into the *Record* office, a couple of days after the story first broke. He was a husky, good-looking youngster of about twenty-five, but that day his freckled face was wan and he bit his nails distractedly as he told me his woes.

He had produced a snapshot of Nita Romaine, one that showed a pretty, laughing, snub-nosed girl whom I scarcely recognized as the svelte charmer of the publicity poses. "I took this one myself," he had said, almost apologetically. "I'm no photographer, but it's more like her, to me, than these pictures in the newspaper."

Then he had sprung his idea. The State Department, it seemed to him, wasn't doing anything except sending notes; the newspapers weren't doing anything except yapping at the State Department; the Poles weren't doing anything, period. And so he, Les Baldwin, was, by golly, prepared to do something. He wanted the *Record* to send him to Poland.

It obviously wasn't feasible, but it gave me my own idea—that the *Record* should send *somebody* to Poland, and it was going to be me.

To recapitulate the known facts, briefly, Miss Romaine was engaged to tour Europe with a cabaret company organized in Paris and known as La Dixie Revue, although the singer was the only American in the group and does not come from Dixie. Her original home was in Brooklyn, N. Y. The company had been playing at a night club called the Monte Carlo in Kraków, Poland's second city, and upon the conclusion of its engagement was to have flown by Polish plane to Warsaw. Miss Romaine disliked flying, it appears, and had told her fellow artists that she would take a train and join them later. When the specified train arrived in Warsaw, Miss Romaine was not aboard. That was thirteen days ago, and nothing has been heard of the dark-haired beauty since. The proprietor of the Monte Carlo told representatives of American wire services that he had personally escorted Miss Romaine to the train in Kraków. He could offer no further details.

Other members of the troupe, who have since returned to Paris, told reporters that Miss Romaine was a talented, wholesome girl who rarely drank and even more rarely had any dates. It was recalled, however, that on several occasions after the performance at the Monte Carlo, Miss Romaine was met by a limousine and uniformed chauffeur. No one thought to obtain the number of the car, but it has been pointed out that in present-day Poland, limousines and chauffeurs are virtually limited to members of the government and foreign diplomats.

That bit must have hurt Les, but it had to be printed— it was the nearest thing there was to a clue.

The Record *does not promise its readers that it will solve this mystery. But it does promise them that it will give a full and revealing account of a sincere and able American newspaperman's efforts to shine an honest light into the dark crannies that lie behind Europe's Iron Curtain.*

That paragraph had been my own idea, except for the words *and able,* which J. H. had kindly inserted. The way I figured, this was a legitimate newspaper stunt, a sound piece of promotion, but in my heart, I felt that I had as much chance of solving the mystery of Nita Romaine as I had of breaking into Mrs. Pickett's column.

CHAPTER THREE

WE COULD HAVE FLOWN, of course, and perhaps we should have, but the Polish Consulate General offered us an immediate berth on the *Queen Jadwiga*—possibly as propaganda for the line—and when you figured possible delays in flying weather and the uncertainty of transport between Western Europe and Warsaw, the difference in time wasn't much. I'll have to admit that our desire for an ocean honeymoon was a predominant factor, but there were others. The *Jadwiga* was considerably cheaper and she would take us straight to Poland—she stopped at Calais, Copenhagen, and Gdynia—without a lot of borders to cross. Our idea was to do what could be done about Nita Romaine, then head west for Paris and a real honeymoon of a week or so.

"A real one," Jane had said, "as distinct from a wild-goose one."

We also thought it would be fun to meet Mrs. Pickett in Paris. She had already taken off in a majestic flurry and would be in Paris for a month, she had told us, at the Hotel Lutetia, which I had carefully written down. "It's on the Left Bank," she had added blithely. "Bring your beret."

So there we were on the *Queen Jadwiga*, which turned out to be a surprisingly comfortable, well-appointed ship. I had had vague expectations of a floating Communist cell, dark and sinister and hushed, and instead there was a concert on the veranda every afternoon, and dancing and movies on alternate nights, shuffleboard, deck tennis, horse racing, and a swimming-pool; fine food, two well-stocked bars, and a multitude of stewards and stewardesses to look after such of our needs as we were able to communicate.

Our fellow passengers were preponderantly middle-aged or elderly, mostly American of Polish or Scandinavian extraction making long-saved-for visits to their homelands. The atmosphere was more that of a Minnesota grange meeting than of any nest of Red intrigue. It was inevitable, in view of the general dearth of youth and beauty, that Jane's share of both should attract the unattached male complement.

In particular, the man who had spoken to her that first day out continued to press attentions that he must have known weren't welcome to Jane and were singularly annoying to me. He was a New Yorker, it appeared, a textile salesman by the name of Barrage, and he was one of these people that just can't be insulted. A dozen times Jane would refuse to dance with him, then suddenly he'd be out there on the floor, trying to cut in. Occasionally, this maneuver succeeded through sheer surprise, and then he would clamp himself to her like a limpet, until he practically had to be amputated.

Another of Jane's more assiduous partners was a young-ish Pole, a courier, I learned, for the Foreign Office. He certainly wasn't my idea of a Communist underling—he was good-looking, blond, bubbling with jokes and laughter, beautifully mannered, spoke near-perfect English, and loved to dance, anything from jitterbug to mazurka. His name was Wiktor Lepski, and whatever intentions toward Jane he may have nursed in his heart, he gave the impression of being completely satisfied to dance and talk with a lovely woman.

Also, unlike Barrage, he implied pleasantly that I was acceptable company on my own hook, and quite often he and I would have a couple of cocktails together while Jane was dressing for dinner. (The men didn't dress, but the women at least changed and primped.) One evening, the fifth or sixth day out, we were having our second Martini in the boat-deck bar, into which the fading sunlight drifted, and jokingly I asked him if he might not land in trouble for getting so matey with an imperialist American.

He smiled. "I might. I don't mind the risk."

"Are you being watched?"

He continued to smile, but he let his eyes move left and right to make sure no one was near our table. "Yes," he said. "Of course."

"Do you know by who?"

"Whom, please. You must not corrupt my little English."

We both laughed. "By whom, then?"

"I know one of them. But I am supposed to know him. He is my—what is the word?—my contact. I do not know the others."

"Are they watching me, too?"

"I would think so. Undoubtedly your mission is known to them."

"Well, it's not meant to be any great secret."

"I know. And perhaps that is a mistake." He still smiled but his voice was serious.

"Are they among the officers?" I asked.

His smiled widened and he shook his head. "One cannot sail a ship with politics. What if your country should insist that all ship's masters be Democrats? Do not many of them come from Maine?"

I grinned appreciatively. "You've got something there, Vic." (There's no sense my spelling what I called him with a W.)

"Thank you, Rocky. We have the same problem. No, those who watch are not among the officers. With the possible exception of the assistant purser. I am not quite sure about him."

"But, Vic," I said, "you work for the government. Aren't you a Communist?"

He frowned slightly, and I felt I shouldn't have asked

him. "Put it this way, Rocky," he said. "I am a loyal Pole. And, if you should need me, I am also a loyal friend. Meanwhile, here comes your charming wife." His smile returned and he rose gracefully.

The sea stayed flat and blue, a good thing no doubt. Jane developed a taste for the polka and I for vodka, both unshared, and we learned to say "thank you" in Polish by thinking of it as *Jane'll kill ya,* which simplified the benighted Slavic spelling of *dziekuje.* By and large, it was a wonderful voyage, marred only slightly by the drooling attentions of Barrage, on whom I enjoyed practicing "thank you."

Wiktor Lepski turned into one of those shipboard friends you feel you have known for a long time, although, after that one conversation in the bar, the subject of politics was not brought up.

On the eighth day out—the day before we were due in Calais—he approached me as I stood on the top deck watching a game of shuffleboard. He was grinning and his first words were, "Laugh, I am telling you a joke. But listen carefully."

He lowered his voice, as if not wishing his anecdote to be overheard by ladies. "Tonight is the Captain's dinner. There will be much to drink until very late. But you, you must not drink very much. You must stay very sober. Very alert. I have heard something. Now laugh."

He slapped me on the shoulder and burst into a guffaw. I tried to do the same, not altogether successfully. "A good one, yes?" he said more loudly, and strolled casually away.

The rest of that day he was careful to avoid me, or to speak to me only when several others were present.

He was certainly right about the Captain's dinner. Vodka and champagne were on every table and there was a great deal of toasting back and forth. The dinner itself was enormous and elaborate, winding up with sculptured ices lit by candles and borne en masse into the darkened *salon*. For the gala dancing afterward, Jane and I were invited to join the Chief Engineer's table, and whatever the Chief's salary was, a good part of it must have gone on champagne that night. Certainly I couldn't afford to keep up with him, even on an expense account. Paper hats and streamers were passed around, and pretty soon the big lounge was looking like an unusually merry night club. Jane waltzed with the Captain, tangoed with the Chief, and twirled through some singularly robust polkas with Wiktor. She even consented, in a glow of good feeling, to dance once with the objectionable Barrage, who brought her back to the table looking as if he'd at last swallowed the canary.

It was hard to keep sober and alert in that genuinely joyous atmosphere—an atmosphere that Slavs seem to have a genius for creating—but I managed. Now and again, the Chief would try to fill my glass and demand, "Whatsa mat?" I said I wasn't feeling very well.

Around four in the morning, the orchestra played "Now Is the Hour," then "Good Night, Ladies," and the party, in theory, was over. But the Chief was in high fettle and decided that everybody at his table should go down to his cabin for a nightcap. I didn't feel much like it, but the word had gone round that in another hour, at dawn, we would catch our first glimpse of land—the Scilly Islands, off the tip of England—and that struck me as something that I ought to stay up and see. Besides, Jane was having such a good time that I hated to play wet blanket.

So the half dozen of us at the Chief's table trooped out of the emptying, streamer-littered lounge and down into the bowels of the ship to his comfortable quarters. To my annoyance, Barrage came along. He had been hovering over our table when the invitation was sweepingly given and blithely included himself. But I was too absorbed in peering through the Chief's porthole, into the faint beginnings of a gray gloom, to think much about him.

The nightcap was cherry vodka, a little too sweet, and the crowded room was stuffy. Jane put her glass down untouched and her face was suddenly tired. "I'm turning in," she said.

"Don't you want to see land? Only half an hour more."

"I want to, but I'm out on my feet. You stay."

"No, no, I'll come with you."

"No, please. You want to see land and I want you to."

I did want desperately to savor this first sight of a foreign shore, and our cabin was on the far side. "Okay," I said. "I won't be long. Got the key?"

"Uhuh. I'll leave the door on the latch." She patted my arm affectionately and slipped away.

Outside the porthole the soupy gray was growing lighter. I thought I could make out a dim shore line and I began to feel excited. It was too big a moment to have happen in a smoke-filled, noisy room, with a phonograph blaring jazz. I glanced around and realized, uneasily, that I was among strangers. I wished Wiktor had been there. However, nobody seemed to be paying any attention to me, and I eased myself quietly out of the cabin and into the corridor, empty and silent.

The fresh air of the boat deck felt wonderful. Just as I got to the rail, the gray murk dissolved, like a lifting curtain, and through it appeared a long, low coast, green and white and reddish-brown. I took a deep breath and thought to myself, *Well, son, here you are.*

I stood there in a mildly ecstatic mood for several minutes, until it occurred to me that tomorrow was another day and there'd be nothing ecstatic about my approach to it unless I got some sleep.

Just as I turned to leave, I saw a door open, perhaps fifty yards along the deck, and what looked like the figures of three men lurched through it. In the haze and shadow I couldn't be sure, but they looked like three drunks come up to see land. They seemed to have their arms around each other, or maybe they were carrying something, it was hard to tell.

For some reason, I thought of Barrage and remembered that there had been no sign of him when I left the Chief's cabin, and suddenly I couldn't get back to Jane fast enough. I half ran through the deserted boat-deck bar, down the stairs, past the lounge where cleaners were mopping up confetti and streamers, on below to our own familiar corridor. It was almost dark, lit only by a dim light at the far end and the illuminated sign that said *Panoe*, i.e., *Men*.

Around the crack of our cabin door, a sliver of light showed. The door was locked. I tapped on it softly.

"Who is it?" came Jane's voice. It sounded tiny and tremulous.

"Me."

The key turned and the door opened, slowly, suspiciously. Then, "Oh, thank heaven," she exclaimed.

I slipped inside and locked the door behind me. Jane was in a dressing-gown and her face was ashy.

"Darling," I said, "what's happened?"

"I don't know," she whispered. "Something queer. I'm frightened, Rocky."

I put my arm around her and drew her down beside me on the lower bunk. "Tell me," I said.

She tried to smile. "Maybe I'm just being silly. Did you see your islands by the way?"

"I did. Go on."

"Well, I got to the cabin all right and I started to undress. Then I heard footsteps coming down the corridor.

23

They stopped outside. I thought it must be you. It had to be. Then the door opened a little. It was dark in the corridor and at first I couldn't see who it was. Then I recognized that horrid, lascivious face."

"Barrage?"

She nodded. "He stood there for a second, leering at me. I was in step-ins and bra, just taking off my stockings. He said something like 'oh, boy,' and started to come in. Then it happened. I saw something move behind him, and then he wasn't there any more. Somebody closed the door, and I could hear shuffling sounds outside, like people trying not to make any noise. I didn't dare look out. Then I just had to. I couldn't stand the suspense."

"Yes?"

"Anticlimax, I'm afraid. The corridor was empty."

"I don't know if that's an anticlimax or not," I said thoughtfully. "I can't think of anything better than an empty corridor at that point than, say, the United States Marines."

"As far as I was concerned," said Jane, "it *was* the U. S. Marines. In the nick of time."

"It's possible. At least, it's possible that a couple of crewmen suspected what he was up to and followed him. Still, I wonder—"

"What are you wondering?" she asked. Her voice was worried.

"Darned if I know," I said and patted her shoulder. "Let's just put it down as a case of the wolf who cried 'boy' once too often."

CHAPTER FOUR

SUNLIGHT WAS POURING through the porthole when I woke up, and my watch, in the little hammock by the upper bunk, said eleven o'clock. I stuck my head over the side and saw that Jane apparently had just awakened, too. She was stretching and yawning luxuriously. Through the porthole, between blue layers of sea and sky, a green coast line was visible.

"Hey, look," I cried. "That must be France."

Jane's answer was smothered in another yawn.

"What?"

"I said isn't that nice."

"Aren't you excited?"

"I'm not sure yet. I think I had too much champagne. Uh, darling?"

"Yes?"

"Did something awfully peculiar happen after the party or was it a dream?"

"If it was a dream, we both had it."

"About Barrage?"

"Uhuh." .

"Oh dear." She sighed sleepily. "I hate the thought of having to face him."

"Maybe you won't have to. He may be in irons. I hope so, anyway."

The top deck, when we got up there, was crowded. People whom we hadn't seen since we sailed had emerged from queasy beds to gaze on the lovely sight of land. You could see England, too, more clearly, in fact, than the green line of France. Steep white cliffs were plainly visible, broken now and then by the clustered red roofs of villages. Staring at them, I forgot about Barrage and everything else.

"Ouch," said Jane. "That's my toe."

"Later. We'll talk about your toe later."

"Ouch. You did it again."

I came back to earth and smiled apologetically. "I'm terribly sorry, dear. I'm afraid I—"

Then I stopped. Through the milling passengers, Wiktor Lepski was coming toward us, walking fast. He came straight up to me and seized both my hands.

"Rocky!" he exclaimed. "Thank God." He held my hands for a moment, as if making sure I was real.

"Didn't you think he'd survive the big night?" asked Jane.

Wiktor gave her a curious side glance. "Some people didn't think so," he said. "Some people still don't think so."

"You mean they think he's a zombie?" said Jane cheerfully.

"A what?"

"A zombie. The walking dead." She stopped as if the phrase had chilled her lips. "B-r-r-r. I take it back."

"As well you might," said Wiktor sternly. "It is not a matter about which to joke." He turned to me. "When did you leave your cabin?"

"Ten or fifteen minutes ago."

"Good," said Wiktor. "Because they"—he gave the word a delicately sinister flavor—"they still think they succeeded."

"In what?"

"No matter. The important thing is that they have not yet seen you. Unless in the last few minutes. That makes no difference because they will not dare do anything just now. We shall be in Calais in an hour. There will be a pilot coming aboard. There will be French officials; they can do nothing. But you must leave the ship at Calais. Understand?"

I blinked at him. "Leave at Calais?"

"Yes. Have you a French visa?"

"Yes, but—" In the back of my head was a dim suspicion that somehow I was being sidetracked.

"But nothing. You must do it."

"Look, Vic," I said, "are you suggesting I give up this whole expedition? Because if so—"

"I did not say that," he interrupted. "If you wish, there are trains and planes from Paris to Warsaw. It may still be dangerous for you, but to continue on this ship, that is not danger, it is suicide. Have you not looked at the passenger list?"

"Casually."

"Have you not noticed that only a handful of passengers will continue beyond Copenhagen for Gdynia? Have you not noticed that you and your charming wife are the only Americans among that handful? It is an overnight journey from Copenhagen to Gdynia. An overnight journey in a small, strange, hostile world. You would not see the morning."

Jane's fingers were tight on my arm. "We'd better do what he says, Rocky."

"But hang it all," I said, "what have 'they' got against me? There's no secret about my assignment. Do they think I'm somebody else or what?"

Wiktor glanced around. In the big, babbling crowd, we were apparently unnoticed. "I do not know," he said quietly. "I know many things, but this I do not understand. There is something very strange about your assignment as you call it. I will try to find out. But first, you will leave the boat at Calais? It is a promise, yes?"

I turned to Jane. Her eyes were fixed on me, wide and strained. "Don't you see what he means?" she said. " 'They' still think they succeeded. 'They' thought he was you."

I stared back. That brief and hazy scene on the boat deck, those three lurching figures, rushed vividly into my mind.

Wiktor was looking from one to the other of us. "Of whom do you speak, Mrs. Rockwell?" he asked.

"Can't you guess?" said Jane. "Who else would have

27

followed me to my cabin?"

Comprehension entered Wiktor's face. He bit his lip to keep from smiling. "It is not funny," he said, "but I cannot help it."

"Vic," I said, "what happened to him?"

"If he was the man," said Wiktor, "he was dragged from your cabin to the deck and—" His hands described an upswept arc. "Now will you promise to leave at Calais?"

I nodded, reluctantly.

Wiktor was scribbling something on a bit of paper. "When you get to Paris," he said, "you will call this number. You will ask for M'sieu Verdun. It is a little joke—Verdun, Victor. That will be I."

"You?" I said blankly. "I thought you were going to Warsaw."

"There has been a change. I have received instructions by wireless only this morning. There may be some connection, who knows? Now you must go and get your disembarkation cards." Once more, he shook both my hands, then walked rapidly away and lost himself in the crowd. It had been a warm and friendly handshake, but I couldn't help wondering if I was making the right move.

"And in Paris," Jane was saying, "we can track down Mrs. Pickett. We won't feel like babes in the wood any more."

"Darn it," I said with a touch of resentment. "She's just as much of a babe in the wood as we are."

"Not she," grinned Jane. "She's aged in the wood. Shall we see about those landing-cards?"

CHAPTER FIVE

FRANCE, AS SEEN through the far end of the cavernous customs shed at Calais, did not seem quite as desirable a country as it had from the *Queen Jadwiga*. The immigration officials and baggage inspectors were palpably unable to speak the language that I had been given to understand in high school was French. Jane seemed to be communicating perfectly with smiles and pretty gestures, which was understandable perhaps, but gave me that husbandly feeling of being outsmarted with a hairpin.

Farther down the long wooden counters, I caught a glimpse of Wiktor Lepski sliding with easy aplomb through the formalities, then strolling away with a couple of men who had apparently come to meet him. A black automobile was waiting for them.

Once we were on board the boat train for Paris, life began to hold better things. We had a compartment to ourselves, which offered certain advantages to honeymooners, but they were offset, more or less, by the traffic up and down the corridor outside. There was one dark little man in particular who seemed to pass by considerably oftener than circumstances warranted, and the more I thought about it, the more familiar he seemed, and yet changed.

"Penny for your thoughts," said Jane. "A franc, rather."

"A franc's too much. A sou."

"How much is a sou?"

"I'm not sure. Five centimes, I think. Anyway, it's what the French give for thoughts."

"All right. A sou for them."

"Don't you see that sign? *Ne pencher en dehors.* That means don't think out loud."

"Nonsense. It means don't stick your neck out."

"Same thing."

"Ha. So you're thinking about another woman."

"I'm thinking about that little guy who's peeking in here right this minute."

She turned quickly, just in time to catch a glimpse of

him sliding out of sight.

"What about him?" she asked.

"I'm trying to think where I've seen him before."

Jane wrinkled her pretty nose and thought. "It's those store clothes," she said. "He was probably a passenger, in slacks and jerseys and things."

"I can't see him in slacks and jerseys. I seem to see him in white for some reason. By gosh, that's it! White jacket. He waited on table in the bar."

"Is that anything to worry about?"

"I guess not." I was worrying though. I remembered what Wiktor had said—that "they" were not among the officers. And if I were going to plant some "they" on a ship, I'd certainly plant one of "they" in the bar.

Another hour of pleasant countryside went by, green fields and splashes of poppies, lanes of poplars, occasional glimpses of placid rivers and people fishing. The dark little man didn't reappear.

"Look," cried Jane suddenly. "There's Sacré Coeur!"

The great white dome soared against the pale-blue sky, and Paris was upon us.

As we passed through the platform gate into the huge and sunlit bustle of the Gare du Nord, a furtive creature in a cloth cap tried to sell me some postcards. He reminded me of the little man on the train, and I looked around several times as we walked behind our blue-smocked porter through the big, strange station. But there was no sign of our shadower, if that's what he was.

"Shall we call Mrs. Pickett's hotel?" asked Jane.

The helpless feeling I had had in the customs shed was coming back. "Why don't we just go there?" I said.

"Suppose she's not there and they don't have any rooms?"

"I'd rather risk that than get all tangled up on a phone."

"I thought newspaper men were weaned on phones."

"Not in French."

The porter who had our bags—Jane's two, my one, and a typewriter—on a dolly said, "Taxi?"

There was a good, simple word a man could understand, and it settled the discussion. *"Oui,"* I said firmly. It was the first word I'd said that anybody seemed to grasp, and I began to feel confident. I felt still more confident when the cab driver to whom we were entrusted nodded and repeated, "Hotel Lutetia," after me without suggesting that I was a backward child. In fact, I was so full of assurance that I loftily added, *"Vite."*

The driver's eyes gleamed happily. He gave a blare of his horn, and the shabby little cab leaped out of its place in front of the station and sailed full tilt into what looked like decidedly hostile traffic.

"You and your *vite*," gasped Jane, rocking against me. "What's the word for 'slow'?"

"I forget."

"No *vite*," yelled Jane. "Nix on the *vite*."

The driver glanced around disappointedly and slowed down. If anybody was trying to follow us, I thought, he'd have had the devil's own time with that explosive start. I took a look through the rear window. Another cab had pulled away from the station rank just behind us and was roaring down the inclined drive. In the whizzing confusion of the avenue into which we now skated, I lost sight of it.

It was a lovely drive, once we got used to it, in the late afternoon's paling light. We crossed the Seine just above the Louvre, catching a glimpse of that wonderful vista that sweeps from the lush, green Tuileries all the way up the glittering Champs Élysées to the far-off Arc de Triomphe.

"Where are we?" I murmured to Jane.

"Dreaming. We're in a dream."

But behind us, into the dream, another taxi came over the white bridge, slowing as we slowed, turning as we turned.

We entered a stately boulevard, full of taxis and buses and cars and people, and when we drew up in front of the Hotel Lutetia, gay with orange awnings against its creamy stone façade, it was impossible to tell if any particular cab had followed us. A bellhop pattered down the steps and opened the door.

I helped Jane to the pavement, which felt queer to our sea legs. "Better tell 'em to hold everything," she said, "until we've looked around."

I cleared my throat. *"Attendez,"* I said. *"Nous allons—"*

"Yes, sir," said the bellhop. "Okay, sir."

I wasn't to be put off. *"Eh, bien,"* I said. *"Alors."* We went up the steps and into the lobby.

It was a comparatively small lobby and felt friendly. Behind the marble desk a clerk in a black cutaway leaned forward on his hands and said, "Ah, good evening, m'sieu, m'dame."

Confidence flowed over me. I tried to give the impression that I was speaking English only because the clerk spoke it so nicely and I didn't want to hurt his feelings.

"We are friends," I explained, "of one of your guests, a Mrs. Pickett. We desire to see her, and, also, since she has recommended your hotel so highly, we hope to obtain a chamber."

"I see," said the clerk.

"My husband no speak so good the English," said Jane. I kicked her gently in the shin.

"About a room," the clerk replied, "that can be arranged, fortunately. But this Mrs. Pickett of whom you speak. We have no Mrs. Pickett staying with us."

"That's queer," said Jane. "I'm almost certain she had

a reservation."

"She always stays here," I added. *"Toujours."*

"I do not know that name," said the clerk. He turned to a list of indexed cards on a board. "We have a number of Americans with us, a Mr. and Mrs. Lightfoot, a Mr. and Mrs. Jamison, a Miss Lovejoy, a Mr. Hankins, a Mr. and Mrs.—"

"Wait a minute," said Jane. "What's Miss Lovejoy like?"

The clerk smiled slightly. "A lady of uncertain age, madame, rather large, full of *esprit.*"

"That sounds like her," said Jane. "Especially the *esprit.*"

"It sounds like her," I agreed, "but why?"

"I'm sure I don't know," said Jane. "Is Miss Lovejoy in?"

The clerk glanced at the mailboxes. "No, madame. Miss Lovejoy seldom comes in until quite late. She prefers to take her *apéritifs,* and to dine, in more Bohemian surroundings. She is frequently to be found at the Café de Deux Magots. Perhaps you know it."

"I've heard of it," I said. "Isn't that where the Existentialists hang out?"

"I believe it is," said the clerk with a hint of disapproval. "Shall I have you shown to your room?"

"S'il vous plaît."

"We've got to pay the taxi," said Jane.

"If you wish," said the clerk, "I will arrange for that and have the sum added to your bill."

Which struck me as a splendid idea.

Our room was large and old-fashioned, with red-curtained windows that looked out on an endless series of roofs. The fading sunlight slanted across the chimney pots, glinting here and there on towers and spires. The wallpaper was flowered and there was a crimson spread over the brass double bed. Beside the bed was a telephone.

"What about calling Wiktor?" asked Jane.

"Oh, damn," I said. "I'm trying to pretend we're on a plain, everyday honeymoon tonight."

"A plain, everyday honeymoon? I like that!"

"You know what I mean."

"I certainly don't. Anyway, he said to call him as soon as we arrived."

"I know."

"So go ahead and call him."

"Would you like to do it?"

"No."

I sighed and picked up the phone. "Have you got the number?" Jane opened the little book and showed it to me. "*Allo,*" I said into the phone. "*Allo, allo.*"

"Yes, sir?" said the operator.

"Alesia seven five three two, please."

The burr in the phone sounded like any phone. It went on sounding like that. There was no reply.

"Anybody else you'd like to call?" I asked Jane. "I handle these French phones pretty well."

Jane gave a little snort. "Let's go look for that café."

"Wouldn't you like to take a bath?"

"I would, but Rocky, darling"—she made a helpless little gesture—"it's no good pretending we're a pair of happy honeymooners. Don't think I didn't see you keep looking around in the taxi. I'm nervous as a cat and you are, too."

"Nervous or not," I said, "I'm going to change my shirt."

"Well, hurry up about it."

"Don't the Existentialists wear some sort of costume? Green spectacles and zoot suits or something? Or am I thinking of the bebop people?"

"If you're thinking of a disguise," said Jane, "I'm against it."

"I just want to be in the swim."

"You almost were last night." Then she suddenly gave a squeak. "What's that?"

Something white was moving slowly under the crack of the door. The triangular corner of a folded sheaf of paper, it looked like. Inch by inch, it protruded, then stopped.

"I'd better see what it is," I said, trying to sound calm.

"Pick it up with your handkerchief," said Jane.

I placed my handkerchief over the white corner and tugged. The folded sheets slid easily under the door. It was the European edition of the *New York Herald Tribune*, compliments of the *maison*.

CHAPTER SIX

THE DESK CLERK said the Deux Magots was at St. Germain des Près, which we could easily reach by Metro—he said "subway" and I had to correct him—or we could walk it in some twenty minutes. We decided we'd walk. It was a pleasant stroll, through the blue beginnings of dusk, and the Place St. Germain was pleasanter yet, overshadowed by the solidly graceful church. There were cafés all around with bright awnings, but the Deux Magots was the biggest and most populous, and its name was plain to see on the awning's edge.

The crowded terrace yielded no sign of Mrs. Pickett. We walked around it twice to make sure, then, feeling agreeably tired, sank into wicker chairs at one of the few unoccupied tables.

A waiter came up and gave the stained marble top a flip with a damp cloth.

"What'll it be?" I asked Jane.

"*Apéritif?*" said Jane hopefully.

"That's not enough. You have to be more specific."

"I'll have whatever you have."

I tried to remember what Hemingway's newspapermen drank. The waiter coughed. "*Deux Pernods,*" I said.

"Doesn't that do funny things to you?" asked Jane.

"I hope so." The waiter had already gone. "*Une cigarette?*"

She took one, grinning. "The old *boulevardier* himself."

"Yes," I said. "I've always felt I could do my best thinking at a café table."

"Then do some," said Jane. "Think about Mrs. Pickett. Suppose she isn't Miss Lovejoy. Then what?"

"We're no worse off."

"Wouldn't it suggest that something awfully queer has happened to Mrs. Pickett?"

"Maybe there's some other hotel that sounds like Lutetia."

Jane looked in her little book. "She spelled it for us herself."

"Maybe we're at a hotel that sounds like Lutetia."

"It was on all the towels."

The waiter came back with two glasses, a bucket of ice, and a siphon. He put ice in each glass and squirted soda, producing a milky effect. I took a deep swallow.

"You're supposed to sip," said Jane. She sipped delicately and made a face. "Licorice. I'm allergic to licorice."

I scarcely heard her.

"What's the matter?" she asked. "Are you allergic to something, too?"

"Yes. Him."

Beyond the café's glow, in the pavement's dusk, stood the dark little man from the *Queen Jadwiga*. He was staring at me, and yet not quite at me, rather through me, as if I were inanimate.

Then quickly he walked toward us, among the tables, his eyes still fixed somewhere beyond. He swerved slightly as he reached us, just enough to tilt the table, sending our glasses, ice, and siphon to the floor.

"Ah, *mille pardons*," he cried in a voice that rang with Old World regret. He stooped, as if making a helpless, rueful attempt to remedy matters, then straightened suddenly, his face darkening with rage. He let out a stream of angry French. I caught the phrase *"sales Américains"* and I realized what he was up to—trying to make the people around us think that I had started something. Even as he sent his epithets at me, I felt his foot kick me sharply in the shin, and I half rose with an involuntary yelp. He gave me a shove that sent me halfway over backward, far enough to crash against the nearest table. Two men sitting there rose with angry exclamations.

I turned, trying to mutter apologies, but the little gadfly hurled himself upon me, then just as quickly hurled himself away, backward, into still another table, with still another shattering of glass. It looked, certainly, as if I had struck him, and the people into whom he had careened lifted him to his feet with evident sympathy. He was yelling now, yelling for help and police, and among his frantic yappings, I caught again the *"sales Américains."*

Jane had leaped to her feet and inadvertently aided the enemy's cause by backing into a peaceful family group. The whole terrace was in an uproar, which the dark figure continued to whip up with the skill of a stage director. He flung himself at me again, and I tried to pinion his arms, to immobilize him long enough to let people see I meant no harm. But that only sent him into a fresh frenzy and he wriggled loose, scattering chairs and all the while appealing to the crowd, and to heaven, to witness the outrageous behavior of the American *cochon*.

The proprietor was on the scene now, waving his arms and shouting, and a moment later a policeman descended upon our seething group, his arm under his blue cape uplifted with a white stick in it. But he couldn't figure out whom he should swat apparently, and blew a whistle instead. I saw my tormentor's foot go between the gendarme's legs, and the blue uniform suddenly toppled among the overturned tables. Two more policemen came roaring up on bicycles, and in the midst of the swirling confusion, I became aware of fingers pointing at me, the proprietor's, the little man's, the prostrate cop's, the surrounding customers'. Even if I'd spoken French like Sarah Bernhardt, I couldn't have got my case stated just then.

More policemen were arriving, in a flurry of capes, of waving white sticks, and the vortex of the maelstrom was unmistakably wearing my shoes. Hands were clutching at my collar, at my sleeves.

Then a sudden booming voice rolled over the terrace like King Canute's, only more successfully. It was speaking French, but it was plainly an American brand of French, and just as plainly it belonged to someone who didn't propose to be ignored. All around me, people fell back, including the policemen, and like Moses advancing into the Red Sea, appeared the large and robust figure of Mrs. Pickett.

She looked at me and all she said was, "Well! I might have known it." Then she turned to the proprietor and, in the momentary hush, unlimbered a few remarks.

"*Oui, mademoiselle,*" said the proprietor humbly. "*Oui, Mademoiselle Loovejoie.*"

The policemen stood still, nonplused. Mrs. Pickett offered a few more comments. I caught the words *bons amis* and gathered that Mrs. Pickett, or Miss Lovejoy, was giving us a build-up. Then she turned to me. "What started all this?" she demanded. "I've got a lot of other questions but they'll come later."

I looked around for my recent assailant. He was no longer in the thick of things; then I saw him, backing furtively into the outskirts of the circle around us. "That guy," I began, but even as I pointed, he edged still farther into the shadows, turned suddenly and ran, melting instantly into the sidewalk crowd.

"What guy?" asked Mrs. Pickett.

"He's gone," I said. *"Il est parti."* Then I thought of the phrase I wanted. "He was an *agent provocateur."*

The phrase was well received. People around me began to nod and murmur sagely, recalling the events leading up to the fracas. The gendarmes shifted uneasily and looked at one another.

"You mean he deliberately started a row?" asked Mrs. Pickett.

"That's right. Apparently he wanted to get me into a jam."

"How superfluous," said Mrs. Pickett. She turned once more to the proprietor and rattled off a few more cheerful sentences, smiling and spreading her hands. The proprietor smiled and spread his hands. Then he shook hands with me, bowed to Jane, beckoned sweepingly to the waiters, and indicated to the policemen that they should all come inside for a drink.

Mrs. Pickett benignly watched the general restoration of good fellowship. "I told him to buy the cops a round," she said to me, "and that you'd pay for the spilled drinks and breakage."

"Darn it," I protested, "it wasn't my fault."

"Maybe not," said Mrs. Pickett soothingly, "but it's what we rich Americans are supposed to do. Anyway, you can put it on your expense account."

"That's going to look fine on my expense account. Breakage in café, drinks for police."

Mrs. Pickett smiled dreamily. "Maybe you won't boggle at mine in the future," she said. "Why don't we all sit down?"

CHAPTER SEVEN

THE WAITER brought an extra chair for Mrs. Pickett and another round of *apéritifs* was ordered, Mrs. Pickett advising vermouth *cassis* for Jane. In the humming tranquillity that returned to the terrace like moonlight after an April rain, I had a chance to note, with a raised eyebrow, our society editor's appearance.

For one thing, her hair, which she had always worn in a fierce bun, had been cut and, I suspected, touched up. A Glengarry cap sat firmly astride it. She wore the sensible tweeds she used for outdoor social events back home, but under the jacket, instead of a discreet shirtwaist, burgeoned a militantly red turtle-neck sweater. Even so, the august dignity that could reduce our local dowagers to tears remained with her.

"Now then," she said, heaving a comfortable sigh, "suppose somebody tells me what this was all about."

"First," said Jane, "will you tell us why you are masquerading as Miss Lovejoy?"

"Masquerading!" repeated Mrs. Pickett with an expression of outrage that didn't quite hide a trace of sheepishness. "That happens to be my perfectly legitimate maiden name. Masquerading, indeed!"

"You might have told us beforehand," said Jane severely. "We almost didn't find you."

"It escaped my mind," replied Mrs. Pickett. "Besides, I'd just as soon it didn't get around back home. People might not realize that it's only for passport purposes."

"They certainly might not," I said.

"Quiet, Stanley," said Mrs. Pickett. "May I ask why you are in Paris breaking up saloons instead of carrying out the assignment on which you have been sent at great expense?"

"For once," said Jane, "he's got a pretty good excuse."

"I'll decide that when I've heard it," returned Mrs. Pickett. "Well?"

I glanced around at the neighboring tables. Everybody seemed absorbed in conversation, and anyway, there was nothing secret about my side of the story. So I proceeded to unfold it.

Mrs. Pickett considered and sipped her vermouth. "The whole things sounds like a ruse to me," she said presently. "A ruse to scare you into getting off the ship. This fellow you call Vic—I'm inclined to suspect he was part of the plot."

"He danced divinely," said Jane.

"Oh," said Mrs. Pickett. "Excuse me. I apologize for having falsely accused him."

"He really seemed very trustworthy," I put in, partly trying to convince myself.

"Did you dance with him, too?"

"I thought this was a serious discussion. I seem to be wrong."

"Oh, come off your high horse," said Mrs. Pickett cheerfully. "Of course it's a serious discussion, but we might as well enjoy it. Let's have another drink."

She tapped on her glass for the waiter. "Now," she went on, "let's assume that there really was a concerted effort to do away with you. What sense would it make?"

"I don't propose to defend the project," I said, "but it makes sense to this extent—that somebody is awfully anxious to keep me from investigating the disappearance of Miss Nita Romaine."

"And who would that somebody be?" asked Mrs. Pickett.

"The Polish Government?"

"That would be the logical guess."

"Very well," said Mrs. Pickett. "Let us suppose that this Nita Romaine was a secret agent of some kind whom the Polish Government saw fit to dispose of. So they stand off the American Embassy and the whole State Department, and all of a sudden they learn that Mr. Stanley Rockwell of the Riverside *Record,* who has never been abroad and speaks no known languages, is on his way to clear everything up. 'Oh my gosh,' they say, 'this is the one guy we've got to stop at any cost.' That makes sense, does it?"

"Certainly," said Jane loyally. "And he speaks lovely French. You should have heard him say *vite* to the cab driver."

"Anybody who says *vite* to a Paris cab driver should have his head examined," said Mrs. Pickett. "And so should the Polish Government, if my hypothesis is correct. It seems to me perfectly obvious that if the government were really mixed up in this, it would welcome you to Poland with open arms and make sure you didn't find out a damned thing. The last thing it would want, in the circumstances, would be your mysterious disappearance from a Polish ship. Think it over."

I thought it over, while the waiter replaced the glasses. "Have you any better explanation?" I asked, feeling nettled.

"Not at the moment," said Mrs. Pickett. "Let's consider this little dust-up here in the café. What was the purpose of that, d'you suppose?"

"To get me arrested, presumably. And out of the way for twenty-four hours or so."

"What good would twenty-four hours do them?"

"I don't know—unless—" I sat up. "Unless it was to keep me from getting in touch with Vic."

"Were you planning to get in touch with Vic?"

"I'm supposed to call him as soon as possible."

"Why didn't you tell me? Have you called him?"

"I tried. There wasn't any answer."

"Well, try again for pity's sake. There's a phone inside."

I felt Jane's eyes watching me mockingly. "Very well," I said with dignity and went inside. Two of the policemen were still drinking at the zinc bar, and they lifted their glasses with red-faced joviality as I passed. I found the phone booth with no trouble and was relieved to find it a dial phone. There was a coin slot, but none of the coins I had in my pocket seemed to fit. Presently one of the policemen came over to the booth and managed to explain that one did not insert a coin in the slot, one purchased a token from the cashier and utilized that for the purpose. I was duly humiliated, but at least I hadn't had to ask Mrs. Pickett.

So I started over again and dialed the number. Almost immediately there was an answer. *"Allo?"* said a voice.

"Monsieur Verdun, *s'il vous plaît.*"

"M'sieu qui?"

"Monsieur Verdun."

"Ah, M'sieu Verdun. *Un moment.*"

I waited. Then, to my great relief, a voice that was unmistakably Wiktor Lepski's came on the wire. "Who is speaking, please?" he asked.

"Rockwell."

"Ah, good. I have just come in. There was a little trouble getting here. No matter. Tonight I expect to find out some of the things we wish to know. If I am lucky."

"Vic," I said earnestly, "don't go taking any chances for my sake."

There was a faint chuckle. "Do not worry, my friend. You and I, we are but single pieces of a jigsaw puzzle. It is to my interest as well as yours to find the others. But it will do you no good to see me tonight. I will be very busy. So listen carefully."

"I am."

"Tomorrow morning, at nine o'clock, you will go to a little café in the Place d'Alesia. It is called the Café Montrouge. Shall I spell those for you?"

"Maybe you'd better."

He spelled them. Then: "There will be newspapers inside on a rack. You will choose the copy of *Figaro*— there is only one of each. Casually, you will turn to the *mots-croisés*—the, how do you say it? The crossword puzzle. There will be jottings on the margin. Among the jottings there will be a number and the name of a street. You will replace the paper on the rack. You will finish your coffee. Then you will stroll casually to that address. Do not ask anyone the way. Purchase an *indicateur des rues,* a street guide. When you reach the address, ask once more for M. Verdun. There. Is all that understood?"

I thought I heard the sound of a door slamming at the other end. Vic's voice changed. It became roguish. "So, little cabbage, tomorrow, eh? Ah, you cute little English chickadee. I wish it could be tonight. But, alas. And so tomorrow, eh, little one? Save me a kiss." He hung up.

I wondered, as I walked back toward the yellow glow of the terrace, who or what had interrupted him. Then I put such uneasy thoughts aside in the pleasant realization that I need do nothing about it until morning, that tonight I was free to enjoy Paris, in springtime and in love.

CHAPTER EIGHT

I WOKE AT EIGHT O'CLOCK and couldn't think where I was: The flowered wallpaper, the red curtains, the brass bedstead, all had the look of some broken-down boardinghouse. Then I remembered that it was Paris, and the room became picturesque and gay.

As I slipped out of bed, Jane stirred and yawned. "What time's it?" she asked sleepily.

"Eight."

"S'too early." She opened her eyes a little wider. "Where're you going?"

"I told you. I've got a date with Vic."

Jane blinked. "I don't think you ought to go alone," she said.

"In broad daylight, for pete's sake?"

"It might be a trap."

"Nonsense." I went over to the bed and kissed her. "I'll bring you up some breakfast when I get back."

"Suppose you don't come back. What'll I do about breakfast?"

"You have to wait for seven years. Enoch Arden law."

"All right," murmured Jane drowsily. "If that's the law." She was asleep again when I tiptoed out.

In the lobby, I bought an *indicateur des rues* and looked up the Place d'Alesia. On the map, it didn't look too far away, maybe a couple of miles, toward the southern edge of the city, near the Porte d'Orléans. I had plenty of time, and it was a fine dewy morning, so I set out on foot, pausing to look pleasurably into shop windows and, less pleasurably, to see if anyone was following me. But the uncrowded streets looked singularly innocent in the sunlight that sifted through green plane and chestnut trees.

The Place d'Alesia was a bustling square dominated by a tall and rosy church, opposite which the words *Café Montrouge* appeared on a striped awning. The terrace was almost deserted, and I sat down and ordered coffee and rolls; then with elaborate casualness, I asked for *un journal—Figaro*, perhaps? My high-school accent must have been working well that morning because all of these items arrived and I leafed idly through the paper, beginning to feel excited.

The crossword puzzle was on the back page, surrounded by news of bicycle racing. It had been partially solved, and the solver had presumably experimented with various combinations of letters in the margin. Only two of these combinations made words—they were *rue* and *Seurat*. Close by were scribbled the numbers *22* and *4th*.

It took me a minute or two to find the Rue Seurat on the map—it couldn't have been much smaller if it had been on the head of a pin. At least, though, it looked fairly near. I finished my coffee and took a quick glance at *Figaro's Dernières Nouvelles*. One item jumped out at me, an item with a London date line. The body of a man identified by a water-soaked passport as Rudolph Barrage, of New York, had been washed ashore on a beach of the Scilly Islands. That was all, but it was enough to turn the Parisian sunlight gray. Enough to make me want to turn right around and go back to the hotel and Jane.

Instead, a ten-minute walk through a tangle of streets brought me to the Rue Seurat, just where the map said it would be. It was narrow and ill-paved, lined with flat stone houses between some of which unkempt vines clambered over sagging walls. There was a feeling of decay in its empty silence, and I saw that a hundred yards away, it came to an abrupt dead end.

I didn't like the look of it, and I didn't like the idea that nobody would know where I was, just in case. A little way behind me was a shabby café with a sign announcing *tabacs* and a telephone. I turned and went back there.

An old woman, behind the zinc bar, gave me a token for the phone—mighty cosmopolitan I was getting—and I dialed the hotel. Surely, I thought, it wouldn't be double-crossing Wiktor to let Jane know where I was. Unless the phone in our room was tapped. If so, I could at least make it tough for anybody listening in.

"H'lo." Jane's voice was still sleepy.

"Hello, Ané-jay arling-day," I said.

There was a pause. Then, "Gosh, you certainly speak all languages."

"Just a precaution," I told her. "Look, if I'm not back in seven years, or even in a couple of hours, here's where I am. Umbernay enty-tway oo-tway. Orth-fay oor-flay. Oon-ay. Eurat-say. Got that?"

"Better spell that last one."

I did.

"I guess I've got it," said Jane. "It's a language I haven't brushed up on lately. And if you're not back, what do I do?"

"Whatever you think best. I just want you to know the locale, that's all."

"Rocky?" Her voice was anxious. "Has anything happened to make you suspicious?"

"Not a thing. I'm just getting cautious in my old age."

"Old age is what I want both of us to die of," said Jane. "Please be careful, darling."

"Will you make me wear overshoes next winter?"

"I just want you to last till next winter," said Jane.

I went back to the dead-end Rue Seurat. Number Twenty-Two was a flat-faced building of five stories, once painted a creamy yellow apparently, but weather-beaten now and flaked. The top floor had no windows, only a slanting skylight, and I remembered that by the French way of counting, that would be the fourth.

There was only one bell beside the heavy wooden door and I rang it. Nothing happened. I stepped back into the cobblestone street and took another look at the skylight. From the roof of the adjoining building, it would have been easy enough to step across to Number Twenty-Two and at least get a look through the grimy panes. I rang the bell again. No sound came from inside the house.

Maybe it didn't work, I thought, and tried the door. Sheepishly, I found it swinging open with a creaky groan, and I stepped into a dark and musty-smelling hallway. There was a staircase, steep and winding, unlit except for patches of gray that drifted through a small dusty window at each landing. As I climbed it, I became aware of a curious odor, reminiscent of a hospital, that grew steadily stronger. The gloom of the top floor was heavy with it.

I knocked on the door at the head of the stairs. At once, a voice said, "Come in." It wasn't an English or American voice, nor was it that of Wiktor Lepski. It had a guttural sound, Teutonic maybe.

I pushed the door open. In the pallid filter of the great skylight I saw a large room that at first looked bare, but its sparse furnishings were purposeful—a shelf of fat, dusty books, a sort of workbench against the far wall littered with test-tube racks and retorts and burners, a worn leather couch under the skylight, and, in the center of the room, a cluttered desk, from behind which a man blinked at me through heavy tortoise-shelled spectacles.

His head was extremely large, with thick features, and its top was almost bald, while scraggly gray hair curled around its edges and over his collar. He was pretty old—well past sixty, I judged. His eyes, behind the thick lenses, were bright to the point of feverishness.

"Well?" he said in a voice that was gruff but not precisely unfriendly. The *w* was almost a *v*.

"I am looking for Monsieur Verdun."

The bushy brows above his spectacles gathered. "I do not know any Monsieur Verdun," he said. Then he suddenly lowered himself a few inches and I realized with a start that until now he had been standing up. The body on which that great head rested couldn't have been much more than a dwarf's, and I saw now that his hands were

48

tiny, with delicately shaped fingers.

"Sit down," he said. His little hand gestured toward a straight-backed chair on my side of his desk. I sat down.

"What is your name?" he asked.

I didn't see any point in hiding it. "Rockwell. Stanley Rockwell."

The big head nodded. "I see. And you are seeking a Monsieur Verdun?"

"Yes."

"An odd name. Would it be perhaps a sobriquet?"

"I wouldn't know."

"Oh." He smiled slightly and pressed his little finger tips together. "And what did you wish to see this Monsieur Verdun about?"

"A private matter."

He continued to smile. "Verdun, eh? A victory of a sort. Would it not, perhaps, be the sobriquet of a Monsieur Wiktor? A Monsieur Wiktor Lepski?"

I did my best to keep my face blank. But it didn't matter. The head leaned forward and said in the voice of a rather brusque uncle, "You do not need to be mysterious with me. I know that you have met Wiktor Lepski on board the *Queen Jadwiga*. You have arranged to meet him again in Paris. You have telephoned him last night. This morning you have followed some uselessly complicated instructions to come to this place, which is my private office."

Somewhat numbly I asked, "Who are you?"

"I am Wiktor Lepski's personal physician. My name is Doctor Edelweiss. Wiktor Lepski"—he paused and tapped his temple— "Wiktor Lepski is not well. That is why he has been sent to Paris. For treatment."

"Where is he?"

Dr. Edelweiss's eyes followed mine toward a closed door in the wall opposite the skylight. Again he smiled.

"He is not here, if that is what you are thinking. He is under proper medical observation."

"Can you tell me where?"

"No. He must be strictly undisturbed. The hallucinations which he suffers—it is not good for him to tell them to others, nor is it good for others to hear." He looked hard at me as he spoke these last words.

"I see," I said. Then, casually, "Mind if I have a look in the next room?"

Dr. Edelweiss shrugged apologetically. "Unfortunately, I am conducting an experiment there which would be spoiled by the intrusion of light. Otherwise, I would not object."

I stood up. "Doctor Edelweiss, the last time I saw Wiktor Lepski, there was nothing whatever wrong with him, physically or mentally. If you are not willing to tell me where he is, I propose to report his disappearance to the police and to request that a search be made of these premises."

The smile on the thick lips was not a pleasant one. "Should you do so, young man, you would make a complete fool of yourself. The French authorities know me and they know the importance of my work."

"I'll risk it. I've made a fool of myself before."

"No doubt you have," said Dr. Edelweiss. "However, in the present circumstances, I do not wish you to make a fool of yourself. I wish you to remain here for a little chat with a friend of mine."

"Thanks just the same," I said, and turned toward the door by which I had entered.

The doctor's large head bobbed up a few inches—he was on his feet again, I assumed—then quickly and silently as a cat, he was around his desk and at my side. "Please," he said.

The word was a command, not an amenity. He had

something in his hand. It was a syringe. His thumb was poised on the plunger, the needle pointed toward me.

"I would not like to use this," he said. "It would be wasteful. So please sit down."

His spectacled eyes came only to my chest, his body was humped and frail. But I didn't feel like playing pat-a-cake with that syringe. I went back to my chair and sat down.

"That is better," said Dr. Edelweiss. On tiny feet, he pattered round to his place behind the desk. "The question is," he resumed placidly, "have you been an innocent dupe of Lepski and his hallucinations, or are you engaged upon some unwise errand of your own? Whatever is the answer, young man, I give you a piece of good advice. Go back to the United States at once. Go back before anything unfortunate befalls you or the young woman who is traveling with you."

"Look here, Doctor," I said, "are you sure you haven't got me mixed up with somebody else?"

"Quite sure," said Dr. Edelweiss.

"Then what the devil is this all about? What sinister motives am I supposed to have, anyway?"

"Let us put it this way," said the doctor. "When the proprietor of a china shop sees a bull coming, he does not pause to inquire as to the motives of the bull. Perhaps that will answer your question. Meanwhile, I believe my friend is approaching."

There were footsteps on the stairs. A moment later the door from the hallway was flung open, then, as I turned, it was softly and firmly closed. The newcomer had his back toward me, bent over the latch, and I realized that he was locking the door. Then he straightened and swung round, put his hands on his hips, and stared.

He was a man perhaps six feet tall, but of such a barrel shape that he looked shorter. He didn't look soft, though —his massive belly, even his jowls, had a hard solidity about them. Above the jowls, his face appeared brutally handsome, but I couldn't see much of it. The collar of the long black overcoat he wore despite the weather was turned up, and a black felt hat, with an unusually narrow brim, was pulled low over his forehead. Dark glasses covered his eyes and gave him a disconcertingly expressionless appearance.

He removed the hat, revealing sleek yellow hair that fell in back to the upturned collar. He placed the hat carefully on the leather sofa and, with a jerk of his head toward me, said something in what sounded like German.

Dr. Edelweiss nodded. He looked nervous.

"So," said the newcomer. He addressed me in slow, careful English. It sounded like the English I'd heard Poles use on the ship. "So, my friend, you are going back to the United States like a good boy, eh?"

"What makes you think so?" I asked with a flippancy I didn't feel.

The man's lips, which were full and rather sensual, tightened. He looked from me to the doctor and said something I didn't catch even the gist of. The doctor shrugged and said something in reply that sounded defensive. His so-called friend turned back to me. He looked angry but he kept his voice calm.

"I did not expect to argue with you," he said. "I do not wish an unpleasantness."

"Neither do I."

"Good. Then you will return, yes?"

"I've come a long way," I said. "I'd like a couple of reasons before I decide to go back."

"Reasons, eh?" He glanced at the doctor. "Have you not given him reasons, Edelweiss?"

"I have tried," said Dr. Edelweiss.

"I see." The two words had an ominous quiet. The man looked at me broodingly. "I do not dislike Americans," he said slowly. "I do not dislike you. I do not wish you any harm. But I will not have you, or any other American, interfering with my arrangements. You wish reasons? I will give you a reason."

He threw back his shoulders as if he had reached a decision, and started briskly across the room toward the inner door.

"*Nein!*" cried Dr. Edelweiss.

"*Tak, tak,*" retorted the other, striding on. He reached the door and his big hand gripped the knob.

The doctor let out one of the few German words I could recognize: "*Dumkopf!*"

The door opened. Beyond it was a small room with bare, white walls, into which bluish light drifted through tinted windowpanes. In the center was a long white table, and on the table lay Wiktor Lepski.

A sheet covered the lower half of his body. The upper half was bare. His face gazed sightlessly upward, the blue eyes open and glassy.

I sprang to my feet, which was a mistake because my knees went watery. I gripped the edge of the doctor's desk to steady myself.

"Take care," snapped Edelweiss. His little hand moved quickly toward the syringe that lay in front of him. His brows were still gathered in displeasure, but he could not resist a sardonic smile at my horror.

There was a smile on the other man's face, too, one of malevolent satisfaction as of having proved a point. He closed the door. "Now," he said, "have you reason enough?"

A bitter expostulation burst from the doctor's lips. I could only guess at its import but I was pretty sure it was something like, "You've had your fun, you fool, so now we're in a pickle. What do we do next?"

The other, for a moment, looked sullenly abashed. Then

he quickly recovered his cool arrogance and shrugged.

Dr. Edelweiss, evidently, repeated his last question.

The dark glasses rested on me, speculatively it seemed, then the man growled a few words and made a gesture that suggested the doctor could hold the baby.

Something like repugnance appeared in the feverish eyes behind Edelweiss's thick lenses. *"Nein,"* he said flatly.

"Ja," said the other one.

I didn't know whose side I was on. Neither one was likely to be in favor of my making a peaceful exit. At the same time, I got an impression of a conflict, not so much between two powerful wills, as between two men each of whom had a certain hold on the other. Personally, I'd have bet on Edelweiss, and I was surprised when he suddenly threw up his hands and said something that had the ring of, "Oh, very well, if you insist."

Dark glasses gave a low rumble of content at the outcome. And yet I had a feeling that he himself was not quite easy to the decision, whatever it was. And whatever it was, I didn't expect to like it. Maybe, I thought hopefully, they would just ask me to sign something.

Dark glasses cleared his throat. "Go to the coosh," he said.

"Go to the what?"

"The couch," said Edelweiss. He was busying himself in one of his desk drawers.

His friend looked annoyed at being corrected. "Go to it, coosh, couch, what you like," he said.

"Why?"

"Do not ask questions!" The words burst out of him in angry impatience. "Do what I tell you."

I glanced across the desk at Edelweiss. He wasn't looking at me. He had brought another syringe out of his drawer and was holding it experimentally to the light. The first syringe was still lying in front of him. I pretended to steady myself on the desk, then made a quick grab.

The tiny fingers, with the speed of a chameleon's tongue, landed on the desk ahead of mine.

"Stand away." Dark glasses was speaking harshly. "Raise your hands."

I looked around and raised my hands. He was holding a short-snouted automatic. "Please do not make things difficult," he said. "It will be very awkward for all of us if it becomes necessary for you to disappear entirely."

"It is awkward enough already," said Dr. Edelweiss. He came out from behind the desk, still holding the new syringe to the light. The big head wobbled on the little shoulders as he padded toward me. Dark glasses moved toward me, too, the automatic leveled. Slowly, I backed in the direction of the couch.

My feet passed through a blotch of shadow on the floor that I could swear hadn't been there a moment ago. Dr. Edelweiss glanced up with a sudden frown and I heard a scraping noise on the skylight. I looked up, too, and through the opaque glass saw a dark shape. It could have been anything, possibly a sheet of newspaper blown against the panes. But it was bigger than that.

Dr. Edelweiss looked questioningly at dark glasses. Dark glasses tilted his head and seemed puzzled.

It was worth a bluff. I looked up at the skylight and did my best to give a contemptuous laugh. "You fellows didn't think I came here alone, did you?"

They both stood still. Edelweiss's eyes were shrewd and thoughtful. Dark glasses slowly lifted the muzzle of his automatic toward the shadowy blob above.

"Don't," said Edelweiss. "Wait."

There wasn't long to wait. With a slow, rending rip, the metal framework of the skylight gave way, there was a loud shattering crash of glass, and a bulky figure plummeted like a wounded eagle from the jagged patch of sky to the black-leather sofa below.

It was Mrs. Pickett. She landed on all fours, bounced to the accompaniment of a rusty shriek of springs, came down again in a sitting position and gazed imperturbably around the room, straightening her Glengarry cap.

CHAPTER NINE

THE STUNNED SILENCE was broken by an anguished cry from the big man in the dark glasses. "My hat! You are on my hat!"

"I can't help it," said Mrs. Pickett. "Wait till I get my breath back and we'll have a look."

"But it is a brand-new hat! It is an expensive hat!"

"Goodness," replied Mrs. Pickett, "you don't think I aimed at your hat, do you?"

"Your hat is of secondary importance, my friend," began Dr. Edelweiss irritably.

"To you, perhaps!" retorted dark glasses. "Madame! Please to arise and let me see what you have done to my hat."

"Take it easy, Buster," said Mrs. Pickett. "I'll please to arise when I'm good and ready."

Dark glasses was breathing hard. He shook the muzzle of the automatic at her. "I tell you, arise. Arise immediately."

"Maybe you'd better, Mrs. Pickett," I put in. "I don't think this guy's kidding."

"Possibly not," said Mrs. Pickett, "but he's making a ridiculous fuss over nothing."

"Nothing!" cried dark glasses. "In my country, madame, a new hat is not nothing."

"Neither is it in mine," said Mrs. Pickett. "And you might as well put that gat away. It'll make a bad impression on my friends."

"Your friends?" repeated Dr. Edelweiss warily.

"Yes," said Mrs. Pickett cheerfully. "They should be here any minute now."

Dr. Edelweiss raised his head, listening. His eyes narrowed and he compressed his thick lips. He said something to dark glasses, then, as the latter hesitated, repeated it peremptorily. Dark glasses shrugged and crossed the room to the inner door. He paused there with his hand on the knob.

"I will expect you to pay for my hat," he said. Then he opened the door quickly, and closed it behind him.

Dr. Edelweiss, at the same time, had slipped back to his desk and dropped the syringes into a drawer, though I couldn't see which one. Then, quietly, he sat down in his chair. Only his fevered eyes indicated any discomposure. Had it not been for the shattered skylight, Mrs. Pickett and I might have been a couple of patients consulting a respectable physician.

I heard footsteps outside. The knob was tried fruitlessly. Then there came a rather timid knock.

"Shall I answer it?" asked Mrs. Pickett.

"No," said Dr. Edelweiss. "This is my office." He glared briefly, then rose the few inches to his full height and pattered across the stone floor. Through the closed door he called politely, "Who did you wish to see, please?"

A youthful sounding voice said, "Why, uh, I'm looking for a Mrs. Pickett."

"I am sorry," Dr. Edelweiss began, but Mrs. Pickett's boom rocketed past him. "This is the place, sonny. Open up."

"Who is it?" I whispered.

"Guy from the Embassy," said Mrs. Pickett. "I figured we'd better have somebody along with some authority. Knowing the kind of jams you can get into."

Dr. Edelweiss was unlocking and opening the door. As if a mask had been slipped over his large face, it assumed a look of benign professional interest. "Ah, good morning, sir," he said. "Pray come in."

A young man of about my age entered the room. He wore a neat blue suit and a bow tie, and his brown hair was smoothly parted. He looked around, trying to smile affably in spite of his palpable bewilderment. "Ah, there you are," he said to Mrs. Pickett. "Are you all right?"

"I think so," said Mrs. Pickett. "Though I haven't really tried myself out as yet."

The doctor was not to be put off his act. "So, sir," he said urbanely, "I am Doctor Edelweiss. Perhaps you have heard of me."

"Uh, no, I'm afraid not," said the young man. "Although the name is rather familiar, at that."

"Diplomat," said Mrs. Pickett to me. "Second secretary, I believe, or some such thing."

"Third secretary," said the young man, speaking past Dr. Edelweiss.

"You can't tell," said Mrs. Pickett. "You may be promoted for this morning's work. Or fired."

"Please," murmured Dr. Edelweiss, giving her a glance of the mildest, most amiable reproof. "Now, sir, what may I do for you?"

"Well," began the young man, "this lady—"

"Ah, you know these people?"

"Yes, that is, I have met the lady and—"

"How careless of me," said Mrs. Pickett. "This is Mr. Rockwell, the chap I was telling you about, and what was your name again?"

"Baird. Charles Baird. How do you do, Mr. Rockwell?"

"How do you do," I said, and we shook hands. It was like a dream in which a duel to the death had turned into a gavotte.

Dr. Edelweiss once more insinuated himself into the proceedings. "I must explain to you, Mr. Baird," he said, "that this lady is a stranger to me." He smiled. "As you can see, she has made a rather unceremonious entrance. But I must also explain, Mr. Baird, that such bizarre events are not altogether unknown to practitioners of my particular branch of medicine."

"I see," said Baird.

Dr. Edelweiss paused in simulated embarrassment. "Mr. Baird, I must ask you. How well do you know this lady?"

"Well, I only met her this morning," said Baird, "but I have every reason to believe—"

Dr. Edelweiss leaped at the opening. He stopped the young man with a delicately uplifted finger. "Ah, my dear Mr. Baird, that begins to explain matters. You see, dear sir, this other gentleman, this Mr. Rockwell, is one of my patients. And, while I do not normally discuss a patient's condition in his presence, I have no alternative in the circumstances. Sufferers of his particular type are prone to seek out fellow sufferers—which is understandable, is it not?—and I am very much afraid that this good woman is, well, you have seen her behavior for yourself."

Baird was considerably shaken, I could see that. He looked from the doctor's benign face to Mrs. Pickett, in her Glengarry cap and crimson sweater, sitting in a welter of broken glass, and then he looked at me.

"Baird," I said, "this so-called doctor is an unmitigated liar. I can prove it very easily. Simply by opening that door."

I caught Dr. Edelweiss giving Baird a regretful wink. "In that case," he said soothingly, "why don't you open it?"

"I damned well will," I said. I strode across the room and seized the knob. I half expected to find it locked, but it turned easily and I threw the door open.

Baird's face reflected the doctor's sad sympathy. He bit

his lip and passed a nervous hand over his hair. I blinked, then peered around the door into the smaller room. The long white table was there, but it was empty. The entire white-walled room was empty. There was no closet, no other door, no visible openings of any sort except the bluish windows.

"It is a sad case," I heard Dr. Edelweiss saying. "He seems to have been a rather intelligent young man."

For a delirious instant, I thought maybe Dr. Edelweiss had me pegged. Then I got a grip on myself. "Baird," I said, "the last time that door was opened, a man was lying on that table. A man whom I knew." I was careful to say "whom." Then I thought that that was just the kind of thing an insane man would be careful about.

"Is that so?" said Baird politely. It was plain whose side he was on now.

"Furthermore," I went on, "a moment before you entered this room, another man, a big man in dark glasses, went through this door."

"I can vouch for that," chipped in Mrs. Pickett.

Dr. Edelweiss spread small, deprecatory hands. "As I feared, Mr. Baird, the lady is obviously a fellow sufferer. I hardly need tell you that the man they describe is imaginary."

"Maybe so," said Mrs. Pickett, "but he left his imaginary hat behind him."

With a heave, she pulled out from under her the black slouch hat with the narrow brim, crushed flatter now that a zootsuiter's porkpie.

Baird glanced at Dr. Edelweiss.

"That is my hat," said the doctor.

Mrs. Pickett began to laugh. "Let's see you try it on."

Very stiffly Dr. Edelweiss said, "I do not propose to be instructed by my patients."

"I'm not a patient," said Mrs. Pickett. "I'm willing to

become one, though, if you can wear this hat."

She bounded, grinning, to her feet, and before Edelweiss could do more than utter a shrill protest, she plunked the remains of the black hat squarely on top of his huge bald dome. It sat like a bumblebee alighting on an egg.

"There," said Mrs. Pickett complacently. "Who's loony now?"

Dr. Edelweiss was speechless. He could only fume and splutter. He tore the hat from his head and threw it to the floor. Then he jumped on it, over and over, with his tiny feet.

"Tell you what, Doc," said Mrs. Pickett. "I'll go halves with you on a new hat for that friend of yours. If he's imaginary, so much the better. Meanwhile, I'd suggest getting the heck out of here."

Dr. Edelweiss stopped jumping. He stood still, his thick features contorted, then suddenly he made a swift dart toward his desk. I cut fast across the room and blocked him. He gave me a look of bitter despair through his thick lenses. His little shoulders sagged and his eyes turned dull. "All right, go if you are going," he said. "Don't stand there like a pack of fools."

We went.

CHAPTER TEN

"DEAR ME," said Mrs. Pickett as the three of us walked down the narrow Rue Seurat, "I forgot we had a taxi waiting." It was standing at the entrance to the dead-end street. "Who pays for it, I wonder."

"Who ordered it?" I asked.

"Really," declared Mrs. Pickett, "of all the ungrateful remarks! And from a man who's wallowing in an expense account, too. Next thing, I suppose you'll balk at buying

Mr. Baird a drink for his trouble."

"Not at all, I merely—"

"I really should be getting back," murmured Baird.

"Rubbish," said Mrs. Pickett cheerfully. "It's practically lunchtime." She stepped into the cab. "How about the Dome? All Americans have to go to the Dome at least once, and it's on everybody's way."

"Couldn't we stop at the hotel first?" I asked. "I'd like to report back to Jane."

Mrs. Pickett gave me a quizzical look. "Rocky," she said, "before you report back to Jane, I want to have a little talk with you. Seriously. The Dome is a splendid place for serious little talks."

Something in her tone made me uneasy. "It's just a question of putting Jane's mind at rest," I said.

"Why shouldn't her mind be at rest?" demanded Mrs. Pickett. "She knows I'm looking after you. *Café du Dome, s'il vous plaît.*"

As we rattled back toward the center of the city, Mrs. Pickett explained her abrupt descent upon Number Twenty-Two. It seemed she had looked in on Jane a few minutes after my fortuitous phone call and had instantly suspected some kind of a trap. "I felt it in my bones," she said—sufficiently so to enlist the assistance of the Embassy. "After all, we're both taxpayers," she added. "At least, I assume that you are." The Embassy had turned her over to Baird, who, I gathered, had the rough assignment of helping visiting firemen out of trouble, and the two of them had rolled off to the Rue Seurat. Mrs. Pickett hadn't liked the look of things, and when the concierge next door muttered darkly of queer doings in Number Twenty-Two, she had proposed that she utilize his roof. Baird was to remain below and force his way in if anything untoward occurred.

"Mind you," said Mrs. Pickett, "you never can tell what

might strike a diplomat as untoward, but falling through the skylight seems to have qualified. Ah, here we are. Lovely, lovely Montparnasse. Suppose we get ourselves settled and you can tell us just what was going on up there."

"I'll try," I said.

We found a table toward the back of the Dome's spacious terrace, and I told my story over vermouth *cassis*—"The cup that cheers but not inebriates," said Mrs. Pickett, "except that it inebriates a little. Bless it."

In the brightness of midday, in the lively hum around us under blue awnings, what I had to tell sounded unreal even to me. I had a feeling that Baird was looking at me queerly. "Well," I finished up somewhat defensively, "that's the way it was."

"Your friend Lepski," said Mrs. Pickett, "d'you think he was dead?"

"He looked dead. But I couldn't be sure."

"It might have been an act," said Mrs. Pickett. "I can't get over the feeling that this Lepski is part of the plot. If there really is a plot, and there seems to be. Of course, I never danced with him. What do you think, Baird?"

"I don't know what to think," said Baird. "If you really saw this man in the other room, Mr. Rockwell—"

"There's no 'if' about it," I said rather sharply.

"Sorry. But what do you suppose became of him?"

"I suppose there was a trap door or something like that."

"Know what I'll bet?" said Mrs. Pickett. "I'll bet that little gollywog of a doctor does illegal operations. And has an escape hatch in his operating-room in case of police trouble."

"Whatever," I said, "let's make good and sure that he has some police trouble. Pronto."

"Hmm," said Mrs. Pickett. "I wonder. What do you

say, Baird?"

"If Mr. Rockwell wants to go to the police, that's his affair," said Baird. "Personally, I'd advise against it. As far as the Embassy is concerned, I can tell you frankly that they won't touch it."

"Not with a ten-foot teaspoon," said Mrs. Pickett, "and I wouldn't either, in their shoes."

"You see," said Baird, "Paris has always been a sort of capital of Polish intrigue. In the days of Partition, before the First World War, this was the focal center of Polish patriotism. Today, there's reason to believe that it's a center of activity against the Red regime. And, presumably, the Red regime has its own agents here to check up on such activity. It's my guess, Mr. Rockwell, that you have stumbled out into a strictly internecine Polish imbroglio, and you're well out of it."

"Wiktor Lepski was my friend," I said stubbornly.

"Maybe," said Mrs. Pickett, "and maybe not. Your loyalty does you credit, Rocky, but use your bean. Whatever this Lepski is mixed up in, alive or dead, the last guy in the world he needs help from is a corn-fed editor out of Ohio who doesn't know intrigue from night baseball."

I had to grin. "You've got a point."

"Yes," said Mrs. Pickett, "and you've got an assignment. If you get yourself involved with the Paris police, you won't be out of here for days."

"Weeks, more likely," said Baird.

That did it. "Okay," I said, "I give up. What's my best way to Warsaw from here?"

The question sounded fantastic on my corn-fed Ohio lips. I half expected Baird to say two miles down the pike and bear left, you can't miss it.

He stroked his chin. "You'll be alone?"

"No. My wife will be with me."

Mrs. Pickett started to say something, then apparently changed her mind.

"I'd say your best bet was by train," said Baird. "You could go by plane, but you'd have to make arrangements with the military in Berlin and you might have a long wait. Whereas you could take the Orient Express this afternoon at a pinch."

"The Orient Express?" I liked the sound of that.

"It's a two-day trip," Baird went on, "but it would probably get you there quicker than gambling on planes. And it's more comfortable."

"I guess that's the pitch," I said to Mrs. Pickett. "I know Jane would prefer it."

She nodded, but she seemed to be thinking of something else.

"If you're really in a hurry," Baird was saying, "I can fix it up. The Express doesn't leave till five and the Czechs are fairly decent about transit visas—you can't get off the train, of course—and I can build a fire under the army for your pass through Germany. It's American Zone all the way. And the Embassy can always get a compartment."

"That's darned swell of you."

"It's my job. Got your passport?"

He examined it professionally. "Your wife's on here with you, eh? That simplifies it. If there isn't any hitch, I can have everything ready for you by four o'clock. But I'd better get started right now." Baird stood up. "I say, can't I contribute something toward *l'addition* here?"

"Nonsense, laddie," said Mrs. Pickett airily. "I told you that Rockwell's got money running out of his ears."

"Well—thank you."

"Thank *you*," said Mrs. Pickett. "You've been a brick, Baird. If they don't make you second secretary by next week, I'll write my congressman."

When Baird was gone, she was silent for a bit. We both sipped our dark-red drinks, she brooding, I waiting. Finally she looked up. "Rocky, this is a heck of a thing to say to a man on a honeymoon. But I don't think Jane should go any farther with you."

I couldn't think of anything to say. She was right, and I knew it. I'd been kidding myself, that was all.

"I don't know what it is that you've run up against," Mrs. Pickett went on, "but whatever it is, you can't expose Jane to it."

I nodded unhappily. "I guess I've been selfish in thinking I could."

"Well, it's an understandable sort of selfishness. And if it was a case of plain, ordinary danger, something you could face together like a forest fire or a bill collector, then her place would be by your side. But this is different. We don't know what direction it's coming from. It doesn't make sense. All we know is that someone, or group of someones, is ready to stop at nothing to keep you from carrying out this job of yours. The dear lord knows why, but it's a fact, and if Jane were to go with you, she would make you just that much more vulnerable. An extra heel, as it were."

I managed to grin. "I'm sure Jane would like that description."

"Jane wouldn't like any part of this discussion," said Mrs. Pickett. "You're going to have to talk her into it."

"Have you mentioned it to her?"

"Well, I did a little hinting around, and even at that, she went through the ceiling."

"That's all you and she seem to do these days."

"But in opposite directions," said Mrs. Pickett. "Anyway, the point for you to stress is that she'd be a definite hindrance to your success. That may bring her around."

"Think so? It isn't exactly true."

"Of course it's true. Even if these enemies of yours, whoever they are, couldn't get at her, they'd have you so jumping jittery about her that you'd never have time for anything else."

An unpleasant thought struck me. "Suppose she does stay behind," I said, "what's to prevent their trying to get at her in Paris?"

Mrs. Pickett smiled and patted my arm. "If anybody gets at your Jane in Paris, it'll be over my dead body. And having resumed my maiden name and bobbed my hair and lost eight pounds, I don't propose to see it dead."

CHAPTER ELEVEN

"An extra heel, eh?" said Jane.

"Mrs. Pickett's phrase, not mine."

"Did Mrs. Pickett put you up to this?" She was sitting on the edge of the brass bed and she looked at me squarely.

"Yes and no. She told me what I already knew in my heart."

"Oh, hell," said Jane despairingly. She got up and took a turn around the room. "Do you honestly not want me to go?"

"Darling, I want you to go more than—well, more than I want a Pulitzer Prize."

"Even a posthumous Pulitzer Prize? To be accepted by the widow who stayed behind?"

"You mustn't talk like that."

"That's the way you're talking. You keep telling me I'd be in danger, that I might be kidnaped, all sorts of moonshine."

"That part isn't moonshine. Taking hostages is standard Iron Curtain practice."

Jane paused in her pacing. "D'you suppose that's what

happened to Nita Romaine? That she's a hostage for somebody else?"

"It's a darned interesting angle."

"See how helpful I could be to you? New angles and everything."

"Darling, nobody's saying you wouldn't be helpful, but—"

"But I'd be a burden at the same time. A nice, helpful millstone around your neck. Is that it?"

"In a word, yes. Or in two words, *tak, tak*."

"You speak Polish as well as French, m'sieu?"

"But *oui*. Including seven dialects."

She came up to me and put her arms around my neck. "Oh, darling, I don't want to let you go alone."

"I don't want to go alone."

"But you're going to? You've made up your mind?"

"I'm afraid so."

"All right. I won't give you a bad time. But hold me for a minute. Tight."

I held her for a minute. Tight. Then she went to the bureau and powdered her nose. "It'll be one for the grandchildren," she said. "Where did you spend your honeymoon, granny? Why, children, I spent mine in Paris and your grandpappy spent his in Warsaw. We had the time of our lives. And your grandma bought a lot of expensive new hats."

"Oh, no!"

"Oh, yes," said Jane. "And she also had a very expensive farewell lunch."

"Which explains, chillun, why you've had to go barefoot all your lives."

It was an expensive lunch, too, at the Tour d'Argent, but worth it. Afterward, I had barely time to pack and get to Baird's office in the great white Embassy at four o'clock.

Baird had my passport on his desk, together with the

tickets in an envelope. "Everything's in order," he said, "unless the Reds have passed some new laws since this morning. Which they may well have." He paused and glanced up. "I was rather expecting you'd bring Mrs. Rockwell with you."

"There's been a change of plans. She's not going."

"Oh," said Baird. His eyes were curious but he was too suave to ask questions. "That raises the question of the double passport."

"Yes. I was going to ask you about that."

"It's a problem that comes up now and then. Has the passport been presented to the police?"

"Yes. The hotel did that for us."

"In that case, she shouldn't have any trouble. If by any chance she does, she can get in touch with me. Has she any friends in Paris?"

"She'll be with Mrs. Pickett."

Baird allowed himself to chuckle. "At least, she won't be bored," he said. "I don't know how Mrs. Pickett looked from your side of that skylight, but from my side, it was something."

"From my side, she looked like manna."

He continued to smile to himself for a moment, then went on. "Oh, say, about these tickets. I can get a refund on your wife's, but I'm afraid it's too late to cancel the compartment."

"It's my fault. I should have phoned you."

"Well, you'll be more comfortable this way. You won't have to double up with some bearded spy. Another thing, I wired the Embassy in Warsaw to reserve you a double room at the Hotel Polonia. That could be changed, I suppose, but it would be rather awkward."

"That's all right. I've been enough of a nuisance already."

"Brother," said Baird, "if you think you've been a nuisance, you ought to see a junketing congressman in action. Now then, if you'll just pay me for the ticket and the compartment, you'll be all set. The congressman, of course, wouldn't expect to pay."

I signed a traveler's check for a hundred dollars, and Baird gave me the change in dollars. "You'll run into exchange trouble on the train," he said, "but with these and some American cigarettes, you ought to make out. Which is more than you can say of Russian cigarettes and rubles."

As I started to go, he called me back. "Oh, by the way, I did some checking on that doctor friend of yours. Edelweiss."

I turned with lively interest. "Find out anything?"

"A little. He's existent, or somebody of that name is. The military had some dope on him. He was a German doctor that the Russkies found in Berlin at the end of the war, but he got away from them and into the American sector. At least, that was his story, and he begged the Americans to let him move to Paris. So the Americans turned him over to the French and that's the last anybody seems to have heard of him. There's no record of his living in Paris."

"Suppose he changed his name?"

"It's very possible. That German name wouldn't help him, and I guess the guy has to make a living."

"Why?" I asked coldly.

Baird laughed. "You may have something. Well, best of luck, old man."

We shook hands again, and I went out and down the huge marble staircase. The American flag in front of the Embassy looked awfully good as I left it behind.

It was after four-thirty when I reached the Gare de l'Est, through the great glass roof of which the afternoon sunlight poured upon a scene of cheerful and cosmopolitan bustle. Jane and Mrs. Pickett were to meet me at the gate of whichever platform it would be and were to bring my lone suitcase and typewriter.

I saw Jane first, standing quietly under a large figure *I* on a square blue sign. Under that were the words *Orient Express*—hard to believe I was boarding it, harder still to believe that I was married to, and leaving, that wonderful girl. She looked singularly lovely in the dusty light that drifted down upon her like a shaft from a cathedral window. Among the blue-smocked porters, the vendors of flowers and lemonade and paper books, her motionless beauty seemed almost unearthly.

But there was nothing unearthly about her companion, in tweeds and Glengarry cap. Nor about that booming voice—"About time you got here. Got your ticket? Know where you're going?"

I pointed to the sign. "Wherever it says up there." Then I took both of Jane's hands and we gazed at each other.

"Don't get soulful just yet," said Mrs. Pickett. "Let me tell you about your train. I've been making inquiries and I don't propose to have done so for nought."

Jane grinned at me. "By all means, Mrs. Pickett," I said, "tell me."

"Well, there's only one car that goes all the way through to Warsaw, and it's plainly marked, so you can't very well miss it. It's up there in the middle somewhere."

I followed her glance, past the grill and along the line of a dozen or so burnished maroon-and-blue cars, each bearing the proud legend of *Wagons Lits et Grands Express Européens.* "Where do the rest of 'em go?" I asked.

"All sorts of places," said Mrs. Pickett. "That's what I'm trying to tell you. Apparently the train divides like an ameba at Stuttgart, I think it is, and half of it swings south to Vienna and Bucharest. For pete's sake, try not to be on that half when it happens—though I don't suppose it would make much difference in the long run."

"What happens to my half?"

"It goes on to Prague, and at Prague your one and only Warsaw car is switched to another train that chugs into Poland, with luck. Think you can stick with it?"

"Is there a diner?"

"Restaurant cars," said Mrs. Pickett, emphasizing the distinction, "will be attached from time to time."

"Three times a day, I hope."

"I am sure that normal wants will be cared for," replied Mrs. Pickett. "There is also strong drink available, I understand. Brandy in France, slivovitz in Czechoslovakia, vodka in Poland, and beer every place. I trust you will exercise discretion. Though why I say 'I trust,' lord knows. Any more questions?"

"One. I always thought the Orient Express ran to Istanbul. That's where Marlene Dietrich and Hercule Poirot and all those people always go."

"It seems there are two or three Orient Expresses," explained Mrs. Pickett patiently. "I don't see why you couldn't find some of these things out for yourself. The one you're speaking of is properly called the Simplon-Orient. Yours is just the naked Orient. And the fewer romantic ideas you have about it, the better. Pretend it's the Delaware Lackawanna. Marlene Dietrich, indeed! A fine thought for a brand-new husband. You'd better be getting aboard."

I picked up the suitcase and typewriter.

"Let me take the typewriter," said Jane. "It'll make me seem useful. Oh, darling, I feel so useless to you."

"Not as useless as you'd be in Warsaw," said Mrs. Pickett. "Get along, the two of you. I know when I'm *de trop*."

We went through the gate and along the platform, crowded with departing voyagers and people seeing them off and embracing. Any number of languages were floating around, as were Homburg hats, military caps, chic veils, and even a couple of turbans. Jane clung to my arm, and I felt an awful sense of approaching loneliness.

"Here's your car," she said. "I suppose that means Warsaw."

An attendant in a purplish-brown uniform was standing by the entrance to the car marked *Varsovie* on a slotted sign. He seemed harassed and gave my tickets a cursory glance when I handed him the envelope. He would keep them, he said in halting English, and would we please to follow him. He took the bag and the typewriter. "I'll see where I'm located," I told Jane, "and come back for a proper good-by."

I followed the attendant along the corridor to a compartment halfway along. He slid back the door and put the bag in a rack above the brown-plush seat. He raised the top of a table in one corner to show me that it was a washbasin as well, closed it and laid the typewriter on it. Then he gave me a mildly puzzled look.

"Is madame not coming?" he asked.

Before I could answer, someone called him from down the corridor, and the attendant, with a sigh, scuttled off. I went back to the platform.

"You'd better stay aboard," said Jane. "I don't trust trains that leave at seventeen hours. You can kiss me through the window."

"I can't kiss you thoroughly through the window." I took her in my arms and held her, kissing her fragrant blond hair and her cheek and finally her mouth.

"Hurry back, darling, hurry back," she murmured. "And, oh, please, be careful."

Somewhere along the platform, a whistle blew. Slowly, reluctantly I released her, and hurried into the car. Opposite my compartment I leaned out of the open corridor window. Jane stood on tiptoe on the platform beneath, lifting her face for a final kiss.

As I bent my head toward her, she suddenly pulled back and her eyes stared past me, wide and faintly outraged. I blinked at her and turned.

Inside my compartment, the compartment that I should have been sharing with Jane, sat a self-possessed young woman, dressed in smartly simple black. Her legs were crossed, revealing a silken knee, and she was calmly lighting a cigarette.

Another whistle blew. I turned quickly back to Jane, but the train was moving, and my last glimpse was of those wide and troubled eyes.

CHAPTER TWELVE

THE TRAIN SLID with gathering speed out of the station and into the deep twilight of a tunnel. I remained in the corridor, unable to see more than a dim oblong where the door of my compartment was—at least, I had assumed it was my compartment. As the train burst out into the flowing roofs and trees and gardens of suburbs, the fading light of late afternoon revealed the young woman still sitting there. Her cigarette was lit by now and she took a deep puff and smiled at me.

I looked around for the attendant, but he was still busy apparently. I coughed. The young woman looked at me with cool interest. Under a skittish little veil, her face was noticeably pretty and of a creamy texture, with black eyes and painted mouth. But there was a kind of flexible tautness to it that was vaguely alarming, as if it could contort itself quickly and easily into rage or passion or cruel mirth.

I had visions of any one of these emotions making an appearance, but something had to be done. I stepped through the open door and said, *"Pardonnez-moi."*

"But certainly," said the young woman.

"You speak English?"

"Some. Not very well."

That helped, but it didn't tell me what to do next. I coughed again.

"Won't you sit down, please?" she said.

"Uh, thank you." I sat down on the brown plush beside her.

"You are American, yes?"

"Yes."

"I love the Americans. I love America."

"You've been there?"

"Ah, but yes. In Hollywood. In Hollywood, I have been in the movies. In France, also."

I was impressed. "That's very interesting," I said.

She accepted the tribute with a gracious inclination of her head. There was a silence. Evidently, she was going to let me bring up the subject of whose compartment it was. I reached in my pocket for a cigarette and couldn't find one.

"You wish to smoke?" she said. "Please." She snapped open a silver cigarette case and held it out to me. I took one. The tobacco was coarse and black and loosely packed. As soon as I lit it, I began to choke.

The young woman looked sympathetic. "It is a Gauloise Bleue," she said. "I am afraid you do not like it."

"I could learn to," I said, "but I've got some of my own. In my suitcase." I emphasized the last words slightly, hoping it might lead without unpleasantness to the topic of the compartment. But she merely maintained her look of bright interest. I got up and took the suitcase off the rack, pulled out a carton of Luckies and put the suitcase back. I took a pack out of the carton and left the rest on the washstand table.

"Will you try one of these?"

"Oh, but yes. With pleasure." She stamped out her Gauloise Bleue. "I love the American cigarettes," she said.

There was another silence. Someone walked past in the corridor, and she sat up quickly. "Would you please close the door?" she asked.

"Won't it be sort of stuffy?"

"Please." There was just a hint of command in her voice.

I slid the door shut. "See?" she said. "It is not stuffy. It is"—she sought the right word and found it with a happy burst—"cozy!"

The topic had to come up sooner or later. But my approach was still cautious. That imperious note hadn't reassured me any. "Are you going to Warsaw?"

"I do not know."

"Oh," I said. She smiled at my expression and smoked in silence. I waited a while, then asked, "Do you often get on trains without knowing where you're going?"

"No," she said. "Not often."

"It must be sort of awkward," I hazarded. "I mean, getting a compartment and so on."

"I have not booked a compartment. I have hoped to be lucky and find one. And I have been lucky. Have I not?"

The topic was up now, all right. It hung high. "I'm the lucky one," I said hastily. "But what I mean is—later on—I mean, you can't very well stay, can you?"

She stared at me in pure amazement. "I do not understand," she said. "You do not wish me to stay?"

"Well, I would, but—"

She leaned against me like a cat that wants its back scratched. I could feel her warm breath on my cheek. "You do not wish Griselde Miratour to stay?"

She smelled wonderful. I wriggled a little away from her and said, "Ordinarily, yes, but I happen to be newly married. It's—it's an embarrassing situation."

"Is it not?" said Griselde Miratour. She straightened up with dignity and busied herself in her small black handbag for a moment. "Whether it is embarrassing or not," she went on, without looking at me, "I propose to stay."

She spat the last words and turned. Her red-nailed fingers clutched a pearl-handled revolver. A grim smile appeared on her red mouth.

"You would not wish me to kill two people, would you?" she said.

"Two?"

"Yes. Two."

"Me and who else?"

She looked down at the little weapon and continued to smile, but dreamily now. "Someone," she murmured. "Someone who thinks he can play with the heart of Griselde Miratour. Someone who thinks she will be his plaything in Paris while he has another plaything in Poland. He will soon find out." She bent her head and kissed the pearl handle.

There was a tap on the door. Griselde Miratour looked from the little revolver to me. "Remember," she said. "I stay—or, bang!" She slipped the gun back into her bag and folded her hands demurely.

The tap came again, more impatiently. *"Entrez,"* I called.

It was the attendant. He had my ticket in his hand and he looked at Miss Miratour in meek bewilderment. She smiled at him brightly.

"I do not understand," he said in English. "I have the compartment booked for two but there is only one ticket here."

"Cheri," cried Miss Miratour, giving me a gaily rueful little laugh, "how stupid of me. I have kept my ticket

in my bag. I forgot to tell you."

She had a ticket, all right. The attendant looked at it and scratched his head. He knew something was fishy but he wasn't sure what. Then he said to me, "May I have your passport?"

"Why?" I asked.

"Because," he said, very patiently, "it will be quite late, after midnight, when we cross the border at Strasbourg. The French and American Zone officials being very sympathetic, it will not be necessary to disturb you if I have your passport. And I am sure," he added with the faintest hint of a leer at Miss Miratour, "that you will not wish to be disturbed."

I handed him the green passport and he opened it. He looked at the photograph of Jane, beside mine, and then he looked at Miss Miratour. "M'sieu," he began, but my new companion interrupted him with a loud but bashful titter.

"Oh, *cheri*," she cried, "we must tell him everything. He is a Frenchman, he will be kind, he will understand our beautiful *amour*. Will you not, dear friend?" She clutched with prettily frantic hands at the attendant's sleeve and half whispered to him in French. The attendant began to smile. With an impulse, Miss Miratour reached for the washstand, seized the carton of cigarettes, and pressed them upon the attendant. It was my last carton. The attendant smiled more broadly and winked. "*Eh, bien,*" he said. "When I was young—" He clucked, put the tickets back in the envelope which he placed inside the passport, tucked the carton of Luckies under his arm, and with another wink, bowed out.

Miss Miratour beamed at the door as it slid shut. Then she beamed at me and blew me a kiss from her finger tips. She reached into her handbag and brought out the revolver.

"I knew you would be sweet," she said. "I knew I would not need this. I am going to throw it away. Open the window."

I blinked. "What about the other guy?"

She clapped her hand to her face. "Oh, *mon dieu*, how I am forgetful. Of course, I must keep it for him. What a foolish girl you are, Griselde."

She returned the revolver to her bag, smiling and shaking her head at herself.

"When is this, uh, event supposed to happen?" I asked.

Griselde considered the matter. "I am not quite sure," she said. "It will depend somewhat on opportunity. But it must be done before we reach Strasbourg. It must be done on French soil. The French authorities will understand. I would not do it in one of these terrible Communist countries. One does not know what those dreadful people might do. They have no chic."

"I've heard a lot of anti-Communist complaints," I said, "but this is a new one."

"There is always a new one," said Griselde moodily. "They are absurd, these Communists. I am sorry, now, that I have had this beautiful and tragic affair with one of them."

"Is he a Pole?"

"I do not wish to discuss him any more. Do you know how to play gin rummy?"

The abrupt switch threw me for a moment. Then I said yes, I did, and Griselde promptly produced a pack of cards from her handbag. "Arrange the table," she commanded, indicating a collapsible shelf beneath the window, and there we were, in no time at all, playing a peaceful game of gin like a couple of commuters.

The express was running along the lush banks of a small, placid river, which Griselde said was the Marne. In the paling haze of near dusk, an occasional persistent fisherman drowsed in a motionless rowboat. Rows and clusters of white houses flashed past, and bright little vegetable gardens running down to the river.

After a while, around seven I guess it was, a discreet gong sounded in the corridor and a voice said that dinner was now being served. I asked Griselde how she felt about food, sounding to myself like a traveling salesman who had made a pickup between Columbus and Dayton.

Griselde shook her head. "He might see me," she said. "The element of surprise would be lost."

"Have you seen him?"

"A glimpse. He is in a single compartment three doors away."

I started. Somehow it hadn't occurred to me that the mysterious "he" was so close, though it stood to reason he would be in this car if he was Warsaw-bound. And if there was such a person.

"When do you plan to surprise him?" I asked.

"I have been thinking about it," said Griselde. "I think I will wait until we are nearly at Strasbourg. Then in the confusion, I may be able simply to leave the train there. It would save much complication and"—she paused and her eyes flickered at me—"it would save you the embarrassing situation."

"Why didn't you do it in the station at Paris? That would have been simpler yet."

"Perhaps," said Griselde equably. "But I like a little voyage by train sometimes. Go get your dinner, if you wish, and be sure you do not warn him, understand?"

In the deserted corridor I counted the doors. The third door beyond mine was partly open, the compartment behind it plainly empty. I peeked in. On the rack was a pigskin bag and a folded overcoat. On the seat lay a sexy French magazine and a hat.

It was a black felt hat with a narrow brim. It looked

new, but battered. It looked as if it had been mashed flat, then painstakingly thumped into shape again. It was a dead ringer for a hat I had last seen on the floor at 22 Rue Seurat.

Suddenly I felt scared. Scared and lonely. Darkness had closed in on the rushing train, and I had a sense of being helplessly swept through the night. If it really was dark glasses, and he knew I was aboard, I was trapped. People had disappeared from this train before. There had been that case in the papers not long ago of an American naval attaché from Bucharest, found dead beside the Orient's tracks.

But maybe he didn't know I was aboard. Maybe his presence was pure coincidence. And if it was, my best bet was to keep out of sight, and specifically out of the restaurant car, where presumably he had gone. My stomach could—

The lavatory door at the end of the corridor opened, and there he was, the massive chest, the yellow hair, the brutally sensual lips, and the dark glasses. He saw me at the same time, and one question was settled. He hadn't known I was on the train. His start of amazement was violent and genuine. Then he came down the corridor, moving slowly and breathing hard. He reached his own door and stopped, staring at me. I stared back. Neither of us spoke. Then with a smothered exclamation of what sounded like disgust, he stepped inside his compartment and slid the door shut with a bang.

There was no sense hiding now. In fact, the more people that saw me, talked to me, remembered me, the better. I went on through the corridor, and through the corridors of two more sleepers, to the restaurant car.

It was a fine French dinner, but I couldn't eat much. If dark glasses hadn't boggled at murder in the past to keep me from going to Warsaw, he wasn't likely to boggle now.

He would find out the number of my compartment easily enough—he might also find an unpleasant surprise in the person of Griselde. Or was she a plant? It sounded more reasonable than her own fantastic story.

I had a large brandy with my coffee and felt better. So much better that I had another one. Then I went back to the Warsaw car. The door of my unwelcome neighbor's compartment was still closed. The door of my own compartment was closed, too. Like a wet towel, the thought struck me that he might be inside, waiting for me. Well, nothing like finding out.

I slid the door back, and there was only Griselde, playing solitaire on the collapsible table. "Did you have a nice dinner?" she said. "Shut the door."

I shut the door and sat down and lit a cigarette. "I had quite a nice dinner. Also, I met a large Polish gentleman with long yellow hair and dark glasses."

Griselde studied the cards, looking for some place to play a four of spades. She found a five of diamonds and with calm deliberation placed the black card upon it. Then she said, "Did he enjoy his dinner, too?"

"I don't think he ate any."

"A pity. It would have been his last one."

I waited a moment. "Who is he?"

"You will find out when you read the newspapers." The thought seemed to please her. "Ah, it will make a great noise in the newspapers. There will be pictures of me everywhere. Unless"—she paused and frowned—"unless, of course, I escape. Shall we finish our game?"

"Have we time? Before you, uh—"

"But yes," said Griselde. "Plenty of time."

The attendant came by presently, and asked if we would like him to make up the beds. Later, I told him. We went on playing gin. The night streamed past, the clustered lights of villages, the lonely glow of a farmhouse. A dreamy unreality took hold of me, and I lost all sense of time.

There was another tap on the door. "Later, later," I called. I wanted to put off the bedmaking as long as possible.

The door slid open, hard and with a bang. The man in the dark glasses stood there. He was holding the same short-nosed automatic he had pointed at me that morning in Dr. Edelweiss's strange room.

"So!" he began; then he saw Griselde. His mouth dropped open, his hand shook, and the gun fell. I stooped for it fast, but his heavy foot aimed a kick at my face, almost absent-mindedly. He waved me back, without even looking at me.

"Griselde!" he exclaimed, then something in French, something amazed and angry.

She sat quite still, smiling at him, a strange tight smile. Her hands were moving quietly inside her handbag, as if she were in need of a handkerchief or smelling-salts. Then swiftly her hand came up with the little pearl-handled revolver in it. Her eyes blazed. Her voice came harsh and shrill, pouring out a torrent of French that included no verbs, only epithet after epithet. Then she fired.

The loudness filled the compartment and the air was suddenly acrid.

A thin, ragged line of red appeared on the man's broad cheek and trickled toward his mouth. He put his hand to his face, dazedly, slumped against the side of the door and very slowly slid to the floor.

"*Mon dieu*," cried Griselde. "What have I done!"

I took another look at her victim. "Nothing much," I said. "You grazed him, that's all."

She sat there for a moment, pressing her fist against her mouth. Then with a little cry she hurled herself across the compartment and upon the massive chest of the reclining figure. My first impression was that she had gone after him tooth and nail, then I realized that she was sobbing, that she was covering the fleshy face with kisses, one hand clutching feverishly at his shoulder, the other smoothing back his yellow hair.

He put his arm around her and his large fingers patted her back, soothingly. "*Ça va, ça va, petit chou*," he murmured. I think that's what he murmured. It was an endearment, anyway, and she came back with endearments of her own through her sobs.

I tried to see where his gun was, but he apparently was sitting on it.

The attendant appeared in the doorway behind them. "What has happened?" he exclaimed anxiously. I could hear voices in the corridor.

Dark glasses waved him away and said something guttural and peremptory. The attendant looked at me. I spread my hands in bewilderment.

Dark glasses said something that I took to mean, "Go away." The attendant shifted uneasily from one foot to another. The man's voice grew angry; then he seemed to think of something and uttered what sounded like instructions of some kind.

The attendant coughed. "Is it all right?" he said to me.

"Is what all right?"

"The gentleman wishes you to exchange compartments with him."

I stared, and then I began to laugh. I couldn't stop laughing. Dark glasses scowled at me across Griselde's shoulder. She herself turned a reproachful look that seemed to say I had no finer feelings.

"It's perfectly okay with me," I said to the attendant. "In fact, I think it's a fine idea. But first, you might tell me who the gentleman is."

"I do not know, sir," said the attendant. He glanced

anxiously in the gentleman's direction. "He is traveling incognito, sir." He stepped over the two forms and reached up to the rack for my bag. I picked up the typewriter and likewise stepped over them.

"You are a very lucky young man," said dark glasses, in a voice slightly muffled by Griselde's embrace. "If this lovely lady was not here, you would be dead on the floor."

"So would you," I said, "if her aim had been better."

The attendant closed the door and I followed him down the corridor.

CHAPTER THIRTEEN

WHEN I WOKE UP we were in a station, a great, gaunt, battered shell of a station with twisted iron girders overhead through which a soft, dark rain was dripping. On the platform outside my window a group of American GI's were lounging against a baggage truck, and it did my heart good to see them. I stuck my head out and asked them where we were, and they said Nuremberg.

All that morning, the train rolled through Germany, winding among dark green hills, and a little before noon we reached the Czech border. There had been no sign of Griselde Miratour or her cutie pie. We stopped for about half an hour at the control station on the German side, then we chugged slowly ahead, across the actual frontier. Nothing marked it that I could see, but throughout the train, you could sense a stiffening of atmosphere. This was the Iron Curtain, boys, this was it.

The Czech control station was a place called Cheb, as ugly as its name. The rain had stopped, and a hot sun beat damply upon an expanse of concrete platforms and corrugated tin roofs. A small army of officials in khaki uniforms swarmed aboard the train, and next thing I knew, three of them were turning my compartment upside down. They looked disappointed when they couldn't find anything wrong.

As they moved on down the corridor, I peered out to see what would happen when they reached dark glasses and Griselde. One of them pounded officiously on the door, but as soon as it opened, they instantly became all bows and smiles. A couple of minutes later, they came out again, looking relieved.

We stayed in that hot and barren Cheb for at least two hours. When we finally got going again, the very country-side seemed to apologize—it grew lovely and fresh, abloom with mountain ash, and on top of great and sweeping hills perched an occasional crenelated tower. Along about dusk, we rolled into the cavernous station of Prague, where there was another long wait and a great deal of shunting about. When we left, it was pitch dark, and I could see only that we were climbing through craggy hills. I had some dinner and went to bed.

I was awakened by a tapping on my door. It was still dark, and the dim countryside rushing past outside had a wild and mountainous look. My wrist watch said three o'clock. The tapping came again. "Who is it?" I called.

It was the attendant. I climbed out of my bunk and opened the door a crack. He was most sorry, he said, but would I mind going back to my own compartment until the Polish border formalities were completed? The incognito gentleman, he explained, could not possibly afford any irregularities in entering his own country.

"Damn it, he should have thought of that before," I said irritably.

The attendant looked unhappy and said nothing.

"If I do this," I went on, "I want to be told exactly who and what this guy is."

The attendant coughed. Behind him, a gruff voice said,

"You will not bargain. You will do as you are told."

I saw him, then, in the dimness of the corridor. He still wore the black discs over his eyes, and his overcoat covered a pair of violently flowered pajamas. There was a patch of sticking plaster on his cheek. What was more important was the presence of that same snub-nosed gun in his hand.

The door was open only a couple of inches. Fast, I slammed it, but he got his foot in ahead of me. At the same time he gave a sharp yowl of pain. I glanced down and noted with a grain of pleasure that the foot in the door wore only a thin carpet slipper. I stepped on it and he yowled again and jammed the gun through the crack into my ribs. "Come out," he snapped.

"Take it easy," I said with forced bravado. "You wouldn't dare shoot in front of a witness."

Quickly the attendant said, "Oh, yes, he would, sir. He would, indeed. There would be very little I could do."

"If there was even a little you could do," said dark glasses, "I would shoot you, too." He prodded me with the gun. "Hurry up. We are almost there. It would embarrass me to shoot at this time, but if I must, I will."

"Shall I take your bag sir?" asked the attendant.

"I guess so," I said. "What about the lady?"

"The lady does not concern you," said dark glasses. "Please hurry."

The attendant came in and got my bag. The train was beginning to slow down, and the outlines of pine trees emerged from the amorphous hills outside. I picked up my typewriter and followed the attendant into the corridor. Dark glasses, impatiently, stepped inside and slammed the door.

The door of the other compartment stood open. As I entered it, gingerly, the train ground to a halt, and through the window, I could make out a long, low building, white in the darkness, with a steep hillside above it. On the platform, blobs of flashlights scurried about like overgrown fireflies.

Griselde Miratour lay in the rumpled lower berth. The compartment was dark, but I was sure that her eyes were open. The attendant put my bag in the rack and closed the door. I sat down on the edge of the bed and lit a cigarette.

"Who is it?" said Griselde.

"Me."

"Oh," said Griselde. She was silent for a moment; then she began to repeat, "I hate him, I hate him, I hate him."

"What's he done now?"

"What has he done? How can you ask? For twenty-four hours, he is telling me how madly, passionately he adores me, and now, pouf! He throws another man into my arms."

"Well, not exactly."

Griselde sighed. "No matter, he goes away. And why? Because he is a coward. He is afraid to be found with me."

"Me and him both."

She ignored this. "And do you know why he is afraid? He is afraid the inspectors will talk. The gossip will get around. It will reach into high places. And then maybe he will lose his silly job. I hate him."

"Miss Miratour," I said, "what is his job?"

"I do not know. He is in the government, I think, but I do not know what his job is."

"What is his name?"

"Stanley."

"Now, wait a minute," I said. "You're getting confused. My name is Stanley."

She laughed. "His name is really Stanislaw. But in Paris, he calls himself Stanley. He likes to be very western when he is in Paris. The hypocrite."

"What is his last name?"

"I do not know," said Griselde. "In Paris, he is just Stanley."

There was a rap on the door, loud and authoritative. I opened it and three officials came in. Two were in khaki, the third in a tweed coat and Tyrolean hat. Apparently they were satisfied with the thoroughness of their colleagues at Cheb, or maybe they had been tipped off that this was a special case. Whatever, they finished quickly and went away. They were even mildly polite, and the man in the Tyrolean hat tipped it to Griselde.

"He was cute," she said.

"That was his hat. I'd be cute, too, in a hat like that."

"You are cute, anyway," said Griselde.

"Would you like to play some more gin?"

Again, Griselde sighed. "Later," she said. "After we have passed the Polish control."

"How soon will that be?"

"I do not know. Sometimes, I am told, it takes very long."

After the experience at Cheb, I didn't like the sound of that.

But I was agreeably surprised. We reached the Polish control ten minutes after leaving the Czech station—it looked like little more than a whitewashed chicken house in the overhanging shadows of the Carpathian peaks—and two officials, one in khaki and one in powder blue, came in. They were both affable and went through the formalities briskly. The one who examined the passport asked Griselde, with a hint of roguishness, if she were Pana Rockwell and Griselde said *"Tak, tak,"* she was. She said something else in Polish and the inspector laughed. The one in blue gave me a money declaration to fill out, and then they went away.

"They were cute, too," said Griselde.

"Suspiciously cute. Do you suppose your boy friend told 'em to go easy?"

"He is not my boy friend any more."

"Maybe he doesn't realize that."

Griselde shrugged.

"What were you and the cute inspector talking about?"

"Nothing. Just making a little joke."

"I didn't know you could speak Polish."

"Oh, yes. I speak a little of all languages. Besides, once I have made a film in Poland. At Lwow, which is a kind of Polish Hollywood. But different."

"I'll bet. Did you meet your boy friend—your ex-boy friend—then?"

"No, no. I have known him only in Paris. I did not meet any government people in Poland. Only artists."

"How were they? Cute?"

"Very," said Griselde. "Now I am ready to play some more gin."

She sat up and for a startled instant, I thought she was naked. Then I realized she was in a pink slip.

"Would you like to borrow my bathrobe?" I asked.

"I am quite comfortable. And quite respectable."

That was a matter of opinion, and I tried not to look at her bare shoulders as I dealt. But there was another reason why I found it hard to keep my mind on the cards. Something baffled me. If dark glasses really amounted to something in the Polish Government, and was anxious to the point of murder to keep me from entering his blasted country, why was my official path being made so smooth? All this horseplay with guns, it seemed to me, could have been avoided simply by arranging to have my papers found out of order. There was one possible answer—that dark glasses was involved in some personal imbroglio, conceivably with Nita Romaine, that he couldn't risk having brought to official attention.

"You are not paying attention," said Griselde.

"Sorry. Is that your jack of spades?"

"Yes."

"Gin."

"You are a beast," said Griselde.

It was growing light outside. The train was rushing again through mountains, thickly wooded but rising to rocky crags above us against the gathering gray of the sky.

There was a tap on the door. The low, harsh voice of dark glasses said, "You can go back now."

In a flash, Griselde was out of bed, the lace edge of her slip swirling around her slim legs. There was a sharp click as she slammed the bolt on the door. "Go away," she cried. "I never wish to see you again."

There was a shocked pause. Then, "Open that door."

"Never."

"Shut up. You, the American. Open that door."

"Sorry," I said. "This was your idea, you know."

"Open, or I will smash the door."

Griselde gave a mocking laugh. "O-ho, you will smash the door, eh? You who are so afraid of the scandal, you will smash the door? Oh, that is very funny."

"You will not think it is so funny."

"If you do not go away, I will scream."

Another pause, a thoughtful one. "You, the American. Do not let her scream."

"We'll both scream," I said cheerfully, "if you don't go away."

"You will be sorry."

Griselde laughed again, loudly and merrily. "Look at Stanley, the great lover," she cried, "standing in the corridor in his pajamas shouting, 'Open the door.' Oh, how everyone in the car must be laughing. Oh, how they will laugh in Warsaw. They will laugh in the Kremlin. How funny you must look, Stanley."

It was a well-taken point. I heard the soft pad of carpet slippers receding, and then there was complete silence in the corridor, except for the throbbing rumble of wheels. "Your deal," said Griselde.

CHAPTER FOURTEEN

THE SUBURBS OF WARSAW, which we reached in the early afternoon, appeared lush and green. Houses of white and pink were surrounded by cherry trees, heavy with fruit, and there were a great many sunflowers. Here and there was an occasional gaping ruin, but these provided little warning for the vast horror that the once great capital now flung up before our onrushing gaze: row after row after row of shattered, crumbling walls, thousands upon thousands of blank-staring windows, like eyes tortured past comprehension.

However, the station looked bright and new, and the open platform onto which Griselde Miratour and I emerged was cheerful and crowded in the sunlight. Petunias and geraniums dripped from baskets along the concrete walls, and a great deal of embracing and kissing was going on.

As we stood there looking around, a burly, blue-jowled man in what looked like a chauffeur's uniform—dark gray, with shiny puttees—came pushing through the crowd and made his way aboard the *wagon-lit*. A moment later he reappeared with a pigskin bag, and behind him came dark glasses, walking very erect, arms swinging. He wore his overcoat, but I noticed that he carried his hat in his hand, and I grinned. He stalked past us without the slightest sign of recognition. Heads turned as he strode down the platform, people got quickly out of his way and a little pool of silence moved in his wake, followed by a low, awed buzz.

"I should have shot him," said Griselde.

"Darn it, you did."

"I mean completely. Ah, well, somebody will shoot him one of these days. Perhaps you will."

"I don't want to shoot him. But I'd like to find out who he is."

"Why do we not follow him?"

"Okay. Why do we not?"

But we were embroiled for a moment at the gate, and reached the street beyond the waiting-room only in time to catch a glimpse of our quarry in the back of a long black sedan—a Russian Zis, though I didn't know it then—just as it pulled away.

Griselde ran across the pavement to the first of a line of tiny, shabby taxis. She called something to the driver, and I could see him shake his head. He was an old man with a blue cap. Griselde shrugged and turned to me.

"I have told him to follow that car," she said, "and he asks me if I am crazy, do I want all of us to be arrested."

The black sedan was roaring down the street jammed with horse-drawn carts, trolleys, and buses. Everything scuttled out of its way, and a white-coated cop at the next intersection sprang to attention. Then the sedan disappeared.

"I guess he's a big shot, all right," I said. "Ask the driver who he is."

Griselde spoke to the driver in Polish. "He does not know," she said. "He knows only that it is someone important in the government."

"I'll bet he does know."

"I am sure he does," said Griselde calmly, "but he is afraid. Shall we mount his taxi?"

"Mount it and go where?"

"Have you not engaged a room?"

"Well, yes, but—"

"At the Bristol? Or the Polonia?"

"The Polonia. Is that all there are?"

"For Americans and British, yes. Very well, we shall go to the Polonia." She spoke to the driver and, ducking her head, climbed into the cramped back seat. I got in beside her dubiously and yet aware that her company had its advantages. Then I forgot my own problems in shocked wonderment at the city through which the little taxi briskly jounced.

It was like nothing so much as inferno come to earth, and Griselde, who had known it before the war, provided an earthy Beatrice. She pointed out the one-time Ghetto—now a flat prairie of rubble—and the Old City, colorful once with gaily painted façades, now a mess of gaunt walls and caved-in roofs. In the Modern City, a lone skyscraper protruded from the wreckage like a huge dead tree from a mass of rotted undergrowth. Most of the shattered buildings were an ugly red, their stone facings lost to the brick beneath, producing a fearful sense of anatomy laid bare.

Yet even on that ride of perhaps fifteen minutes, I could feel a lively energy in the midst of all this ruin—everywhere construction was going on, men on scaffolds plastering, painting, laying brick, steam shovels at work, horse carts trundling in and out of rising structures; and in windows, even in crumbling shells, flower boxes blazed with bright defiance.

The Hotel Polonia was virtually untouched, a massive building of somber, weather-beaten stone, with big curtained windows and little balconies. A soldier with a Tommy gun was standing beside the plate-glass door, but he didn't pay any particular attention to us. A bellhop came out and got the bag and the typewriter, just like a bellhop anywhere else. The lobby was dignified and gloomy, with a couple of potted palms, a marble desk, a big, cold staircase, and a newsstand.

The clerk spoke English, and was expecting me. He had

a nice double room, he said, for Mr. and Mrs. Rockwell and he would pay for the cab. Everything would be taken care of until I could cash a traveler's check which, regrettably, the hotel couldn't do.

"Is it not nice?" said Griselde.

I cleared my throat. Griselde looked at me narrowly. The bellhop was waiting. So was the desk clerk. It was no time for a scene.

The room was large and not unlike the one Jane and I had occupied in Paris. There was a brass double bed and lace curtains. The clerk opened the door to a good-sized but dingy bathroom. "Everything very nice, yes?" he said hopefully.

"It is lovely," said Griselde.

"All Americans like the Polonia," said the clerk. "Maybe you do not know, but the Embassy was here in the days after the war. Some members of the Embassy remain here."

Griselde was looking at herself in the speckled mirror above the bureau. "Oh, my hair," she exclaimed. "Look at it. Will you kindly send the hairdresser to our room?"

"Yes, madame," said the clerk.

"And we should have something to drink, should we not? Perhaps champagne to celebrate our arrival?"

"I will send the *sommelier*, madame," said the clerk. "Will there be anything else, sir?"

"I hope not."

The clerk and the bellhop went away. Griselde stretched, luxuriously, then sank with a sigh into a flowered chair by the window. "This is very nice," she said.

"Miss Miratour."

"Yes?" Her voice was lazy but wary.

"You can't stay here."

"Oh, but yes."

"It's impossible."

"Nothing is impossible."

I took a nervous turn around the room. "But, Miss Miratour, I have explained to you that I am a married man. A newly married man."

"So?"

The telephone beside the bed rang. I gave Griselde an uneasy look and said, "It's probably the house detective."

"I do not know what that means," said Griselde.

"For once," I said, "I hope you find out." I picked up the phone.

A brisk American voice said, "Is that Mr. Stanley Rockwell?"

"It is."

"My name is Watkins, Walter Watkins. I'm the press attaché at the Embassy. We understood you'd be in today on the Orient."

I was agreeably surprised, not to mention flattered.

"Have a good trip?" he asked. "I hope your wife wasn't too uncomfortable."

"She didn't come. There was a last-minute change."

"Oh. Too bad. Still, maybe just as well. The main thing is that you're here, and I think you and I should have a chat as soon as possible."

"Fine," I said. "At your convenience."

"As a matter of fact, right now would suit me," said Walter Watkins. "I've got a lunch engagement at two-thirty—that's the local hour—but I'm free till then."

It was half-past one. "Okay," I said. "Shall I come over to your office?"

"You needn't," said Watkins. "You might have trouble getting here. I'll meet you at the hotel."

I glanced at Griselde, who had propped her feet on the window sill and was smoking unconcernedly. "No, no," I said, "I'll find your office all right."

"It just happens," said Watkins, "that my lunch date

is at the Polonia. It will really be more convenient for me to meet you there."

"Well—" There wasn't much I could do about it. "Shall we meet in the bar? I presume there's a bar."

"There is, but around this town, a bar isn't a very good place for a private conversation. I'll come straight up to your room. In fifteen or twenty minutes."

He hung up. I turned to Griselde. "Miss Miratour, you'll have to get out of here."

"Why?"

"Because a man from the Embassy is coming."

"You like the man from the Embassy better than me?"

"I'm prepared to. And that isn't the point. You can't be here when he comes."

She stared at me, and suddenly her lip began to quiver. "What do you expect me to do?"

"What did you expect to do when you left Paris?"

"I expected to kill somebody. I expected to be in jail by now." She sniffled and her eyes began to well up.

"They've got jails here. Go find one."

"How can you be so cruel!"

"I'm not cruel. If it's money you need, I'll pay for a room. Why don't you go to that other hotel you mentioned?"

"One does not just go to a hotel in Warsaw. One must have an official position."

"Well, you've got to go someplace."

"If I leave here," said Griselde with tearful solemnity, "it may mean death."

"Nonsense."

"Yes, to you it is nonsense. Not to me."

"Look, Miss Miratour, you knew perfectly well you couldn't stay with me."

"I did not know it. You deceived me. You are as bad as that other one."

Her eyes darted toward her bag. It was on the bureau, and I was closer to it than she was. She started to get up, and I moved quickly to the bureau.

"Give me my bag," she said.

"In a minute." I opened it and took out the pearl-handled revolver. There were a lot of other things in it, but I guess there are in all women's handbags. "Now you can have it."

"Thank you." The words were icily, tragically ironic. She stood up. "So you wish to get rid of me, do you?"

"Not exactly, but—"

"Very well. You will see." She lifted her chin, her mouth a tight, tremulous line, and stalked like Lady Macbeth into the bathroom. The door closed.

I didn't like it. Then there was a knock on the other door, and I opened it. A round-shouldered man in waiter's black and white stood there. He had a chain around his neck and he silently handed me a slip labeled "*carte des vins.*"

"You'd better come back later," I said. He didn't understand. I fell into the silly practice of enunciating very clearly and loudly. "La-ter. Come—back—la-ter." He stood there, blinking.

I sighed and looked at the card. Now that I thought of it, I could use a drink. The names on the card didn't mean much and the prices looked staggering. I recognized champagne, and that seemed to be five thousand something or other. Then I spotted vodka, and that was only one thousand, so I pointed to that, and he bowed and went away.

The bathroom door opened and Griselde came out. Her face was very white and in her eyes gleamed a strange and bitter triumph. She had a little bottle in her hand and she held it up. Empty.

"So you wish to get rid of me," she said. Her voice was shaking. "Very well. Do you know what these are? Sleeping-pills. I have taken them all."

With a high-pitched laugh, she hurled the bottle across the room and it shattered against the wall. She came forward, lurching a little. "Very soon," she murmured, "very soon you will be rid of me."

"Oh, my God," I groaned.

A sad, grim smile touched her lips. "So, now you are sorry. But it is too late." She swayed against the bed.

"Like hell it's too late." I grabbed for the phone. The girl on the switchboard gave me the clerk who spoke English. "Is there a doctor in the hotel?"

"A doctor? Is something wrong, sir?"

"My—the—uh, madame seems to be suddenly ill." Madame is a useful word that way.

"That is too bad, sir."

"Yes, it is. How about a doctor?"

There was a pause, as if he were thinking. "Do you wish an American doctor, sir?"

"Not necessarily. Any doctor."

"It happens, sir, that there is an American doctor staying in the hotel. If you wish—"

"Thank God. I certainly do wish. Send him up. Quick."

I banged down the phone and turned round to Griselde. She leaned against the bed, her eyes sad and faraway.

"You'd better lie down," I said. "No, you'd better keep on your feet. Here let me walk you around the room." I took her arm but she shook her head and clung to the brass bedstead. She looked as if she might crumple any minute.

There was another knock on the door, and I flung it open. A short man in a white coat and carrying a black bag came in.

"Doctor," I exclaimed, "thank heaven!"

The short man looked blank. "Dok-tor?" he repeated

in a puzzled way. He pointed to himself. *"Nie* dok-tor." He held up his bag and said a word that sounded like "frizzler." It was close enough for me to realize that he was a hairdresser.

Griselde gave a moan and sank slowly to the floor.

"Oh, lord," I cried. "Here, give me a hand."

He got the idea. He put down his bag, and together we lifted Griselde's limp body and laid her on the bed. The hairdresser ran an experimental hand through her now tumbled hair, then took a comb and scissors out of his bag. He looked at me questioningly.

"No, you idiot," I snapped. "Not now."

I heard someone else at the door and turned in quick relief. It was the man with the chain again, this time carrying a tray on which were two small glasses and a carafe. He looked stolidly from me to Griselde and said something that I took to mean, "Shall I pour?"

"No," I cried. "Not now."

He stood uncertainly in the doorway with his tray. Behind him, then, someone else appeared. It was a small, wispy man, middle-aged and wearing pince-nez. He, too, was carrying a black bag.

"Well, well," he said, "what seems to be the trouble?"

"Are you the doctor?"

"I am." He glanced in mild bewilderment at the hairdresser and *sommelier*. They looked at each other uneasily.

"She's taken a big dose of sleeping-pills," I said. "I don't know how many."

"Your wife?"

"Yes. No. Never mind. I'll explain that later."

The doctor clucked. "What kind of pills?"

"I don't know. Wait a minute, there's the bottle. There was the bottle." I scrambled to the corner where the glass fragments lay and found one with the label clinging to it. "Here we are."

The doctor adjusted his pince-nez and examined the label. "This isn't exactly in my line," he observed. "I'm a pediatrician." He pursed his lips and studied the bit of glass. "I can't make head nor tail of this."

With a sigh, he walked to the bed and stared down at the motionless form. Then he reached out and slapped her smartly on the cheek. There was a brief flash of life in Griselde's eyes, then they glazed over again. He slapped her once more.

"Let's get her on her feet," he said. "Try to keep her walking." He beckoned to the hairdresser and *sommelier*. "All of you."

The four of us, tugging and wrestling, got her off the bed and on her feet, a dead weight, ready to topple. The doctor busied himself in his bag. "That's it," he murmured to the rest of us as he fumbled around, "keep her up, keep her moving. Let's see, I must have something here that will do as an emetic. Yes, ipecac. That ought to do it. Let's get her into the bathroom."

We swayed, lurched, and staggered across the carpeted floor into the cavernous bathroom. "Hold her, boys," said the doctor. "I'll see if I can get this down her. It's not in my line, you know. Different with children. Haven't treated an adult in years. Never expected to. However— do my best—ah, that's the girl. That's it. Ah, that does it."

It worked. It worked quickly.

"Ought to be all right now," said the doctor. "But keep her moving. All of you."

The three of us walked Griselde around the room, hairdresser and *sommelier* each holding an arm, I in back with my hands on her waist. The doctor retreated backward in front of our Laocoön group, considering matters through his pince-nez.

"Jumping Jehoshaphat!" The exclamation burst from the open doorway. I saw a tall man of forty-odd, dressed in a dark pin-stripe suit and with a gray fedora on his head. There wasn't much doubt in my mind who he was.

"Mr. Watkins?" I said feebly.

He folded his arms and nodded. Apparently, after that one expletive, he could find no further words.

"Won't you take a chair— We've had a little trouble— In just a minute—"

"Shall I come back later?" asked Watkins.

Before I could answer, Watkins gave a sudden lurch, as if he had been shoved by someone in the corridor. Between him and the door jamb, a heavy figure shouldered its way and strode with a military snap into the room. He wore a gray uniform and black puttees. I knew I'd seen him before, but it took me a couple of seconds to remember. It was the chauffeur who had met dark glasses at the station.

He stared around the room, his eyes watchful, puzzled, but determined. He pointed to Griselde and said something aloud in Polish.

Griselde opened her eyes, and they suddenly looked normal, except that they were frightened. She shook her arms, and the *sommelier* and hairdresser let go. They also looked frightened. She slapped at my hands on her waist, and I let go, too. She took a couple of steps forward alone, and said something to the chauffeur. Then she turned her head toward me. Her voice was low and weak, but firm.

"He wishes me to go with him. You do not wish me. So what shall I do? I shall go."

"No, Miss Miratour, please, I—"

"He wishes me. You do not. I go." She turned back to the chauffeur and said something in Polish. With a kind of brutal gentleness, he took her arm and led her out of the room.

The hairdresser grabbed his bag and scuttled out after them. The *sommelier* gravely handed me a slip, which I dazedly signed and he went out.

The doctor said, "You staying in the hotel? I'll get in touch later." And he also went out.

Watkins of the Embassy gazed after them and then at me. "For a man who's been in Warsaw exactly one hour," he said, "you've certainly met a lot of people."

CHAPTER FIFTEEN

WATKINS CLOSED THE DOOR. He laid his gray fedora on the bureau, beside the handbag Griselde had left behind.

"Would you like some vodka?" I asked lamely.

"Don't mind if I do."

I tilted the carafe. "The glasses haven't been used," I said, handing one to Watkins.

He smiled. "I lived in the Polonia for a year and I'm not only accustomed to using any glass that's handy, but also to rooms full of peculiar strangers."

I returned his smile gratefully.

"Still," he went on, "I'm a bit curious as to who all those people were. That last chap who went out, he sounded like an American."

"Yes. He's an American doctor who's apparently staying here."

"Oh, that must be Clendenning. Did he say if he works for the International Service Committee?"

"No, he didn't have a chance to say much. Except that he's a pediatrician."

"That's Clendenning all right. I haven't met him yet, but I've heard a good bit about him. He only got here a day or so ago. Who were the others? That chauffeur looked like a government type. Acted like one, too."

"I understand he is. At least, he was at the station to meet a supposed big shot traveling incognito."

"Oh? What'd he look like? The big shot, I mean."

"Husky, heavy-set fellow with sleek blond hair. Somewhere in his forties, I'd guess. Wore dark glasses by way of disguise, but everybody seemed to recognize him. Scared of him, too."

Watkins frowned and rubbed his chin. "Hmm. A fairly common type from the description, but it does happen to fit— Well, let's not jump at any conclusions. Who was the girl?"

"That's going to be a little tougher to explain."

"You don't have to explain," said Watkins, "if you don't want to." He grinned.

"No, it's nothing like that. It's just complicated and somewhat implausible."

"Nothing's implausible on the Orient Express."

I liked this Watkins. I told him, as best I could, how Griselde Miratour had come into my life, out of it, and back in again. Watkins, who had settled comfortably in the chair by the window, listened and chuckled.

"That's not so darned implausible," he said. "Your Polish male is a pretty vigorous guy, in all departments, but if he happens to be in the government, he's got to be very careful how he plays around. If he's important enough to wangle himself an occasional trip to Paris, that's where he'd do his playing. In Poland, he never knows when the U.B. might be watching him."

"The U.B.?"

"The Urzad Bezpieczenstwa, if that makes it clearer."

"Of course," I said. "What else could it stand for?"

Watkins laughed. "Sometimes known as the Betsy Boys. The security police."

"Do the security police watch people in the government?"

"They sure do. As closely as they watch us, if not more so. These lads don't trust each other worth a damn. And rightly, I might add."

"This particular lad," I said, "would seem to have done some playing in Poland as well as in Paris. According to Miss Miratour, he tried to ditch her for somebody closer at hand."

"Risky business," said Watkins.

I hesitated. "This may sound silly, and it's just a hunch, but I've been wondering if it might be Nita Romaine."

"What?" Watkins sat up, frowning. "What in the world makes you think that?"

"As I say, it's just a hunch, and a very shaky hunch. But there was this angle of the black limousine calling for her, for one thing."

Watkins considered. "If it's the guy I'm thinking of—but it would be incredible. Still, I wish we could find out more about that limousine."

"That raises a point I'm not quite clear about. How much investigating have you been able to do?"

"Practically none," said Watkins. "The fact that the girl's an American citizen doesn't give us any right to muscle in on the local police jurisdiction. You see the position, don't you?"

"Officially, yes. But how about unofficially?"

Watkins shook his head. "It's not an important enough case for us to risk anything unofficial. There's a fairly constant stream of entertainers of all sorts of nationalities drifting back and forth across Europe. Frankly, the disappearance of a cabaret performer wouldn't justify the slightest action on our part that would jeopardize any of the objectives that we're here for. I hope that doesn't sound callous, but that's the way it is."

"I see."

"I hope you do," said Watkins earnestly. "Because I don't think the American newspaper reader does. That's why the Department is glad to have you here and wants you given all possible help. If you come a cropper, it won't do the Embassy any official damage."

"If I come a cropper," I said, "will the Embassy consider me as unimportant as Nita Romaine?"

Watkins grinned. "Depends on how bad a cropper you come."

"How about the American correspondents here? Haven't they done any digging of their own?"

"None that I know of. It happens that right now there aren't any full-fledged staff correspondents in Poland. Just local stringers. Now when Larry Allen was here for the A.P., he'd have gone out and sunk his teeth into this story. But not these guys. Furthermore, they're in somewhat the same position we are—they have their contacts and pipelines that might be endangered if they got too nosy."

"You sound as if you might have been a newspaperman in your day."

"A very sheltered one," said Watkins, smiling. "I was an editorial writer for the Baltimore *Sun* before I got into this. There's something else I ought to tell you about these local boys. They've heard, of course, about your coming, and they don't like it. If by any chance, you do dig up this story, it's going to make them look bad. So don't count on any co-operation."

"That makes it tougher."

"I wouldn't worry," said Watkins. "You're having a nice junket and you'll at least have some color stuff to send home. I've got a plan of action laid out for you, unless you have ideas of your own."

"The only idea I've got is a little more vodka."

"Thank you," said Watkins, holding out his glass. "Well, it seems to me that the place for you to start digging is Kraków. It may sound like looking for a lost coin in another room where the light's better, but Kraków will be a lot easier town to get around in than Warsaw. If only because the war left it in one piece. Also, the Communist grip is considerably looser there—people won't be quite so leery of talking to you."

"How do I get there?"

"That's where you get a break," said Watkins. "It happens that Doctor Clendenning is headed for a children's hospital just south of Kraków, and the Embassy is providing him with a car and chauffeur. He's leaving tomorrow, and there's no reason why you shouldn't go along with him."

"Fine. If it suits Clendenning."

"I imagine he'll be glad to have company. Meanwhile, there's a couple of formalities you'll have to go through. First, you've got to register with the police. We have a clerk who'll go with you. Second, you'd better report to the Foreign Office. There's a very affable chap there, name of Chelinski, who's assigned to deal with Americans. You'll like him, and he'll be helpful—though the plain fact is that he's strictly window dressing. As you'll discover when you meet his boss."

"I don't like the sound of this boss."

"Nobody does. His name is General Gritska—he acquired the 'General' in the underground—and he's a rough, tough piece of goods. Pretty suave, though, and speaks fair English."

"What does he do?"

"He's an undersecretary of the Foreign Office in charge of propaganda and press. When you read that a Foreign Office spokesman said some damned thing or other, that's he. There's a good deal of the Doctor Goebbels in him. You won't like him, but you'd be well advised to pretend to."

"Okay," I said. "When does all this happen?"

Watkins looked at his wrist watch. "It's pretty late to set anything up for today. Suppose we arrange it for you to go to the police bureau at eight tomorrow morning, see Chelinski at eight-thirty and General Gritska as soon afterward as feasible. Say nine. Then you and Doctor Clendenning can get away around ten, which should land you in Kraków comfortably in time for dinner."

"Isn't that pretty early?"

"No, they're early birds, these Poles. Most offices open at eight or even earlier. They knock off around three."

"Is that the new Utopia?"

"It wouldn't be to me," said Watkins. "In my Utopia, we sleep till noon. However, when in Rome— Does that suit you?"

"You bet."

"I'll see you in the morning, then—come to the Embassy a little before eight. One more thing. You'll very likely be shadowed while you're here. Your chauffeur tomorrow morning will almost undoubtedly be a U.B. agent. But you needn't worry about physical danger or anything like that. Good luck."

He rose and picked up his gray fedora.

"Wait a minute," I said. "Speaking of physical danger, I ought to tell you that one or two efforts have been made to keep me from getting here."

Watkins frowned. "Efforts? What kind of efforts?"

"Decidedly physical."

Watkins stared and put down his hat. "What are you talking about, man?"

I told him. Very briefly. I told him about Barrage and about Dr. Edelweiss and Wiktor Lepski. Watkins bit his lip. His face was serious and thoughtful.

"This puts a different light on things," he said slowly. "This suggests that somebody attaches a lot more importance to Nita Romaine than we have assumed. Ruthless as this government is, it doesn't risk the international stink of a newspaperman's murder without one hell of a good reason. By George, this has me worried."

"Maybe I should hunt up a rabbit's foot."

"It's not you that I'm worrying about," said Watkins. "Not right now. If Nita Romaine's disappearance is a matter of such concern, then she must know something— or know somebody—or even be somebody—that we've got to find out about."

He jammed on his fedora almost angrily. "Sometimes I wish I'd never left Baltimore. Well, we'll go ahead on the present basis unless something turns up. And for pete's sake, don't tell Clendenning about this."

"You mean he's not to be trusted?"

"From what I've heard, it would scare him to death. See you in the morning."

CHAPTER SIXTEEN

DR. CLENDENNING WAS NERVOUS enough as it was, without knowing his companion-to-be was a marked man. I found him in the Polonia bar early that evening, sitting in a booth with a carafe and glass in front of him. He recognized me and beckoned.

"Fetch a glass," he said. "Know what this is? Water. I'm a strict teetotaler myself."

His eyes, I noticed as I sat down, were unusually bright behind the pince-nez and his voice was slightly thick. The waiter brought a glass, and the doctor filled it.

"It tastes like vodka to me," I said.

"Precisely. But d'you know what vodka means?" He pulled a little yellow dictionary out of his pocket. "It means water. More precisely, it's an affectionate diminutive for water. Very understandable. Most lovable water I ever tasted." He emphasized this statement by refilling his glass.

"By the way," I said, "you are Doctor Clendenning, aren't you?"

He peered suspiciously. "How did you know that?"

"The Embassy told me you were staying here. My name is Rockwell. I'm a newspaperman."

"Oh," said Dr. Clendenning. "Please to meet you." We shook hands across the table.

"Apparently," I went on, "we're to be traveling companions tomorrow. I'm on my way to Kraków."

Dr. Clendenning thought about this. "Do you know Poland?" he asked.

"No."

"Or any Polish?"

"Just 'yes' and 'no' and 'thank you.'"

"And the diminutive for 'water,'" said Dr. Clendenning. He sighed. "It doesn't look as if you're going to be much help."

"I'm very sorry."

"Still, I suppose your company will be better than nothing. Frankly, Stonewall—"

"Rockwell. I'm usually called Rocky."

"I'm usually called Clen. Funny, neither of us uses first names. Funny, eh?" He put out his hand again for me to shake and upset his glass. "No matter," he said airily. "This stuff is cheap. Ought to be, too. Water ought to be cheap. Eh? Where was I?"

"You were saying my company was better than nothing."

"Now why in the world did I say that?"

"Just expressing an opinion, I presume."

"I remember now," he said, looking pleased with the feat. Then he looked worried again. "I was about to tell you that, frankly, I'm jolly well leery of this whole expedition. I've heard that these people—these Communists—frequently tempt strangers with young girls. I am a married man, Rockwell."

"So am I."

"Well, doesn't that worry you?"

"Not particularly."

"Perhaps you are a libertine. I am not." His eyes looked at me sternly, or as sternly as they could manage. "That young girl who was in your room today—who was she?"

"It's a long story. I met her on the train."

"Ha! One of their temptresses, no doubt. Was it fun?"

"Was what fun?"

"Being tempted?" He sounded wistful.

"Darn it," I said, "you saw how much fun it was."

"Now, now, you don't have to cover up with me," said Dr. Clendenning. "I'm a married man. And a teetotaler. I'm very highly thought of in my own community. My community is Philadelphia and I wish I were there right now. But I've agreed to spend a month in this hospital, so I suppose I've got to go through with it, temptresses, water, and all. Where is your wife?"

"In Paris."

"Mine's in Philadelphia. Thought I might phone her tonight. It's quite cheap, you know. Have you phoned yours?"

"No," I said, but it struck me as a first-rate idea. "How much would it be to call Paris?"

"I'm not sure. Millions of zlotys, but only a couple of dollars, I dare say. Why don't you call her? Instead of gadding about with a lot of temptresses."

"I think maybe I will."

"Wait till after dinner. It'll be cheaper then. What are you doing for dinner? Nothing? Splendid, we'll dine together. And drink a lot of water. You can tell me all about being tempted. I'll tell you all about Philadelphia. Give and take, that's the secret of—of—" He paused, trying to think what it was the secret of, and quite suddenly he

111

went to sleep. He reminded me of nothing so much as Alice's Dormouse.

He woke up in time for dinner, in the Polonia's huge and half-empty dining-room, but fell asleep again over coffee, and I finally had to help him upstairs. At least, though, I was grateful for his suggestion about calling Paris—I hadn't got it through my head that such amenities prevailed in this strange new world—and once the doctor was safely tucked away, I went to my own room and put in a call for Jane.

It didn't take long, maybe half an hour. The hotel switchboard did all the spadework, and suddenly the English speaking clerk's voice was saying, "We are ready with your call to Paris, Mr. Rockwell." There was only the slightest suggestion in his tone that he disapproved of a Mrs. Stanley Rockwell being in Paris and another one being registered in his hotel.

Jane's voice floated over the wire, clear and lovely as soft music. But it sounded strained. "Hello. Hello. Rocky?"

"Yes, darling. Me."

"What's wrong? What's happened?"

"Nothing's wrong, darling. Why should there be?"

"Why are you calling?"

"Because it's cheap and I wanted to hear your voice."

"You're sure?"

"Of course."

There was a little pause, then, "Thank God. I was so frightened when I heard them say Warsaw was calling."

"Why? Why should you be frightened?"

"I don't know. Just foolish, I guess. How was the train ride?"

"All right."

Another pause. "Who was that—that person in your compartment?"

"Oh, that." It was my turn to hesitate. "It was some kind of mix-up. It got straightened out. How's Mrs. Pickett?"

"Fine. Worried about you, though. So am I."

"Darling," I said, "don't be—"

Then I stopped. The door moved. I hadn't locked it, I realized then. It opened an inch, then an inch or two more.

"Rocky! Are you there?"

I couldn't answer.

"Rocky!"

The door opened wider. Griselde Miratour walked into the room. She was terribly pale and she moved a little unsteadily. "Go ahead with your call," she said. "Do not mind me."

"Rocky, Rocky!" Jane sounded frantic.

"It's all right, dear."

"What happened? I heard a voice."

"Uh, the chambermaid came in."

"She spoke English."

"Yes, they all speak English around this hotel. Lots of Americans here."

Griselde had walked across the room toward the little table on which still sat the tray with the afternoon's carafe and glasses. As she reached the table, she stumbled against it, and it went over with a crash.

"Rocky! What was that?"

"That clumsy chambermaid," I said. "She's just dropped the thunder mug."

There was a strangled sound as of hysterical laughter in the phone. "Darling, it scared me so. I thought it was a bomb or something."

"Stop worrying," I said, trying to sound severe. "I'm in a fine, civilized hotel. Tomorrow I'm going to Kraków in an Embassy car. With an American doctor. And—"

"Why do you need a doctor?"

"I don't need one, it just happens that—"

Griselde, who was leaning wearily against the bureau, said, "Are you going to talk forever?"

Jane said, "Is that still the chambermaid?"

"Yes, dear. Look, everything's fine. Go to sleep. And please don't worry."

"I'll try."

"Good night, dear Jane."

"Good night, Rocky."

I hung up and turned irritably to Griselde. "Damn it," I said, "I was talking to my wife. In Paris."

"I am sorry," said Griselde. The effort with which she spoke, the whiteness of her face, made me feel a brute.

"I didn't mean to be angry," I said. "You'd better sit down."

She shook her head. "I came for my handbag. I forgot it." It was still on the bureau beside her.

"You look tired. You ought to rest for a minute."

"Tired?" A scornful smile touched her lips, on which the red looked dry and flaky. "I am worse than tired. But I will not rest here unless—"

"Unless what?"

"Unless I can stay."

"Look, Miss Miratour," I said patiently, "there must be other rooms in the hotel."

"No, that would be no good. I would not be safe. They would come for me."

"Who?"

"He. He and his men."

"Who is he? You must know by now."

Again she shook her head. "I have found out nothing. I have been a prisoner in his flat."

"How did you get out?"

"I said I must have my handbag."

"Did he let you come alone?"

"No, But they will not dare come into your room." She gazed at me and her eyes grew pleading. "Oh, please, please, let me stay. I cannot go back to him. He frightens me. Oh, please."

Heavy footsteps sounded in the corridor. We stared at each other. Griselde's hand went involuntarily to her mouth.

"I have not locked the door," she cried. "Quick!"

I moved toward the door, but I wasn't quick enough. There was a sharp rap on it and simultaneously it opened. The heavy-shouldered chauffeur in the gray uniform and black puttees walked into the room. He pointed at Griselde, then jerked his thumb over his shoulder toward the corridor.

"No," cried Griselde. "Oh, no, no, no." She pressed back against the bureau. The chauffeur took a step toward her.

"Stop him," she called to me. "Stop him." Then, frenziedly, she plunged her hand into the bag. For a moment she looked blank, then recollection appeared in her face. "You have it," she cried. "You have my little gun."

I looked quickly at the chauffeur. He had stopped in the middle of the room.

"He does not understand," said Griselde. "The gun, where is the gun?"

I tried to think. Then I remembered. I had put it in the drawer of the bedside table on which the phone stood. It was only a few feet behind me. I backed toward it, trying to look unconcerned as the chauffeur's eyes followed me. I made a casual half-turn, then I opened the drawer fast and got my hand on the pearl-handled revolver. The chauffeur started toward me but I beat him to it. He stopped suddenly as I pointed the little muzzle at him.

"Tell him to get out of here," I said.

Griselde said something in Polish. The chauffeur laughed contemptuously.

I kept the gun on him and reached for the phone. The clerk who spoke English answered.

"There's a guy in my room," I said, "and I want him thrown out."

There was a short silence; then the clerk's voice came in unhappy embarrassment. "Mr. Rockwell, it is a man in a chauffeur's uniform?"

"Yes."

"I am sorry, Mr. Rockwell, but he is—there is nothing we can do."

"What do you mean?"

"He is— I cannot say it on the phone—he is special."

"Damn it, so am I."

"You do not understand. I cannot explain now. It is very awkward."

"It sure is."

"I am very sorry." There was a click and silence.

The chauffeur had been watching me with cold eyes, faintly bored, faintly amused. He spoke in Polish to Griselde, in a tone that said, "Sister, you can't win." Then he moved toward her.

"Shoot," screamed Griselde.

I didn't like it. But I had to do something. "Tell him I'm going to count three," I said. "If he hasn't gone by then— he's had it."

Griselde backed away from him, past the bureau, past the spilled tray, till her back was against the armchair by the window. He moved after her, slow and implacable. Griselde cried out something in Polish, and the man's face turned, scornfully daring me.

"One."

"*Jeden,*" said Griselde.

The man watched me.

"Two."

"*Dua,*" from Griselde.

He put his hands on his hips and faced me with a frank sneer.

"Three." My finger was jelly on the trigger. There was a crashing thud, but not of a bullet. Griselde had picked up the vodka carafe and brought it down with all her might on the chauffeur's close-cropped head.

It didn't quite do the trick. He reeled toward the bureau, but before he could brace himself, Griselde let him have it again, and this time he crumpled. Slowly, like a rock going over a cliff, he went to the floor and lay still. The black puttees stuck awkwardly out from his humped, gray-clad body.

CHAPTER SEVENTEEN

"At least, he's breathing," I said presently.

"So?" Griselde stared down at him. "Perhaps I should strike him again."

"Good lord, aren't we in trouble enough?"

She shrugged. "It was his own fault."

"Do you think that's going to make any difference to his boss?"

"His boss will not find out. Not for a little time."

"Darn it, he's certainly going to get suspicious when the guy doesn't come back. With you."

"He has gone to a meeting, a government meeting. They last very late, these government meetings. Sometimes all night."

"That's a help," I said. "But sooner or later—"

"Yes," admitted Griselde, "sooner or later." She brightened. "But you know what I think? I think he will be afraid to come to see what has happened. It would be a scandal."

"He must have some other boys he could send."

"I do not think so. This one, *évidemment,* he has been forced to take into his confidence. But he would not wish for others to know."

It was a comforting thought. "I hope to pete you're right," I said. "Meanwhile, what are we going to do with palsey here?"

"It is a difficulty."

"It sure is. Tell you what, I think I'll get that American doctor in."

Griselde frowned. "I did not like him so much. He gave me something nasty."

"He kept you alive, didn't he?"

"Yes, but we do not wish this one kept alive."

There was a certain rough logic there, but I didn't propose to debate it. I picked up the phone and asked for Dr. Clendenning's room. It took quite a while to wake him, and when he finally answered, his voice was muzzy and querulous.

"Doctor?" I said. "This is Rockwell. Could you come to my room? Something has happened."

"Couldn't it wait till morning?"

"Not very well."

A sigh. "Oh, dear—do I have to get dressed?"

"No. It's informal."

"Well, all right," said Dr. Clendenning.

We waited. Griselde sat down in the armchair and lit a cigarette. I walked nervously around the room. Beyond the curtained windows, I could see the vast, jagged expanse of ruin, with a faint light or so deep in the shadowy wreckage. There was a tap on the door.

"That you, Doctor?"

"Who else could it be?"

I opened the door and he came in, wearing a bathrobe over pajamas and carrying his black bag. He looked at Griselde and said, "Ah, the temptress again." Griselde stared back at him coldly. Then his eyes fell on the inert heap on the floor. "Great heavens," he exclaimed. "Who is this? Anyone I know?"

"I think you saw him earlier in the day. He is a chauffeur employed by—by a friend of Miss Miratour's."

"I see. Has he had an accident?"

"Yes. Would you mind having a look at him?"

"I keep telling you," said Dr. Clendenning petulantly, "that I am a child specialist. Why don't you ever ask me to look at some children?"

"I don't know any."

"Have you none of your own?"

"Doctor," I said, "some other time—would you mind—"

"Don't be impatient," said Dr. Clendenning. He lowered himself laboriously to one knee, and bent over the crumpled body. He lifted the man's wrist, automatically glancing at his own left wrist, though there was no watch on it.

"Hm, what's this?" he said. "A nasty bump on the noggin?"

I nodded, and Dr. Glendenning rose. "Looks like a mild concussion," he said. "You'd better tell me what hit him."

"We're not trying to hide anything from you, Doctor. This man came here to take Miss Miratour away against her will. In the course of events, she—that is, he was struck by the bottle you see there."

Dr. Clendenning looked from one to the other of us. "In other words, you're in a pickle?"

"Well—yes."

"I see," he said. "Then I'm getting the dickens out of here."

He started briskly toward the door. "Wait, Doctor," I cried, grabbing at the sleeve of his bathrobe. "We're fellow-Americans. We've got to stick together."

"Why?"

"We just do. I stuck with you, didn't I, when you fell

asleep at dinner?"

He hesitated. "What do you want me to do?"

"Well, I don't know exactly. I'd certainly like to get rid of this bird."

"I daresay the hotel has some arrangement for disposing of inanimate guests."

"I'd rather the hotel didn't get involved."

"Humph. You're willing enough to get me involved."

"Please, Dock-tor." Griselde's voice came with soft pleading across the room. "We are in terrible trouble, Dock-tor. Please."

Dr. Clendenning looked round at her with suddenly interested eyes. He wagged a roguish finger. "You think you can tempt me," he said.

"Please, Dock-tor."

"I can never resist the appeal of a woman in distress," said Dr. Clendenning. "So you want to get rid of this chap, do you? Why don't you just put him out in the hall?"

"Somebody would find him. And even if no one did, he'll probably come to in a little while and start raising the roof."

"Oh-ho," said the doctor shrewdly. "So part of the problem is to keep him unconscious, is it?"

"It would sure help if he could stay like this until you and I leave for Kraków."

Griselde started to speak, then changed her mind. Dr. Clendenning pulled thoughtfully at his chin. "This raises a rather delicate question of ethics," he said. "You see, I happen to specialize in children's anesthesia, and I have something here that would keep our patient comatose for quite a few hours. It's quite safe, and easily administered, but I'm not sure about the ethical aspect."

"Oh, Dock-tor, that will be wonderful," murmured Griselde.

"Ha," said Dr. Clendenning. "You notice she uses the simple future tense? No ifs or buts."

"You must not laugh at my poor English."

"I am not laughing," said the doctor. "I am admiring. What do you think, Stonewall? Would it be ethical?"

"Rockwell. And I'd say yes."

"Very well, then." He opened his black bag, then looked up. "I have another suggestion," he said, "as long as I seem to have become involved in this. There's a public bath down the corridor a way. They call it a *lazienka* or some such silly thing, but it's just an everyday tub. We could undress our friend here and simply leave him in the tub. Even if he recovers consciousness inconveniently soon, he might find it awkward to raise a fuss without any clothes."

"Sounds like a good idea," I said.

"Ah, Dock-tor," said Griselde, "you are so clever. You are cute, too."

"Thank you," said Dr. Clendenning primly. "Now then, young lady, you'd better step into the bathroom while we prepare the patient."

"I am not a child, Dock-tor. I do not blush easily."

"It happens that I do," said Dr. Clendenning. "Please go into the bathroom."

Griselde smiled at him and obeyed, and the doctor and I buckled to the task of getting the chauffeur's burly form undressed. He moaned and twitched a few times, and it was no joke to roll him over, but finally the job was done. Clendenning got a syringe out of his bag and knelt over him. Meanwhile I went through the pockets of the gray uniform. They yielded a crumpled pack of Polish cigarettes, some slices of sausage wrapped in brown paper, a clasp knife, and a worn wallet containing a number of greasy cards, one of which was apparently a driver's license. I put these things into a bureau drawer and piled the clothing on the floor of the old-fashioned wardrobe.

Dr. Clendenning stood up. "That ought to hold him for a while," he said. "I'll just make sure the coast's clear."

He peered into the corridor, then tiptoed out. Griselde called from the bathroom. "Can I come in now?"

"Not yet."

"This is very silly."

"Do what the doctor tells you."

Dr. Clenndenning tiptoed back. "All's well," he whispered. "Nobody in sight. You get his shoulders, I'll try to manage his feet."

We half lifted, half dragged the too, too solid flesh into the dim corridor that stretched into endless shadow. There was a clang, then a steady creak from the elevator shaft. We both stood still. The car rose wheezily nearer, reached our floor, gave a rusty gasp, then continued to rise. I realized that my forehead was drenched with sweat.

We shuffled along the corridor with our burden till we came to an open door. "This is it," whispered Clendenning. "Can you see, all right?"

"Uhuh." There was just enough light in the corridor to outline a big, square tub in the small room. We dragged the heavy form inside and hoisted it painfully over the tub's stone edge, then slid it into a half-recumbent position on its back.

The doctor dusted his hands, then glanced at the door. There was a key on the inside. "We might as well lock it," he said. "But why am I making all these suggestions? I want no part of this."

I locked the door and we walked, still on tiptoe but fast, back to my room. Griselde was in the armchair, smoking. "Is everything hokey-doke?" she asked.

"Momentarily," said Dr. Clendenning. "I'm going to bed."

"So am I," said Griselde. "I am very tired."

I coughed. "This is rather awkward, Miss Miratour," I said, "but I have a possible solution. This is a good big bed, and if Doctor Clendenning is willing, perhaps you could take his room, and he and I—"

Dr. Clendenning also coughed. "There is a couch in my room," he said, "in addition to the bed."

"Fine," I said. "Then Miss Miratour can stay here and I—"

Dr. Clendenning coughed again, rather sharply. "That wasn't exactly what I had in mind. If Miss What's-her-name needs a place to sleep, she may have my couch. I welcome the opportunity to study her tactics. And to resist them."

"Oh, Dock-tor, you are so cute," said Griselde. Her eyes looked at me, cool and faintly malicious. "That will be lovely."

"Good night, Miss Miratour," I said. "I don't suppose you'll need this but you might as well have it." I gave her the pearl-handled revolver.

CHAPTER EIGHTEEN

I WAS AWAKENED by the telephone. Sunlight streamed through the lace curtains and gave a roseate glow to the gaunt red ruins outside. It was seven-thirty.

"Good morning." The voice on the wire was vaguely familiar. "This is Watkins. Did I wake you up?"

"Gosh," I said sleepily, "don't tell me you're at the Embassy already."

"Hell, no, I'm the same place you are, in bed. But I thought I'd better alert you. The clerk I told you about will come by the hotel for you in half an hour. To register. I just spoke to him on the phone and he says there's a cable there for you."

"Where?"

"At the shop. The Embassy. He'll bring it along. And Chelinski—that's the guy in the Foreign Office—will meet you back at the Embassy at eight-thirty and take you to meet General Gritska. Okay?"

"Fine."

"After you've seen General Gritska, I'll expect you in my office. The car should be ready and you can pick up Clendenning—did you see him last night, by the way?"

The question brought back with a chilling rush the recollection of the night's goings-on. "Yes," I said. "I saw him."

"Mousy little fellow, isn't he? I've got a sneaking suspicion, though, that there's more to his mission than meets the eye. Well, see you later."

He hung up, and I climbed out of bed. The morning had a crisp buoyancy to it, and below my windows, the wide street was a-bustle, the red-and-cream streetcars crowded. I could almost convince myself that this was the start of a brisk and normal day, but not quite. Cautiously I opened the door to the corridor and peeked out.

It was quiet and deserted. Then a man in a bathrobe, carrying a towel and whistling, came out of a room and approached the public bath. I held my breath and watched. He tried the door, rattled it, frowned, said something undistinguishable, rattled it again, shrugged, and went back to his room.

I closed my own door and got dressed.

The phone rang again. "Mr. Rockwell? A gentleman from the Embassy is waiting for you downstairs."

The corridor was still peaceful. In the lobby, a plump youth with yellow hair parted in the middle approached me. "I am George Czanowski, from the consular section," he said, and we shook hands. "I have brought a telegram for you."

I thanked him and tore it open. It was signed *Breen* and it said:

WHAT COOKS QUESTIONMARK LES BALDWIN HAS SUDDENLY DISAPPEARED HIS FOLKS THINK HE MAYVE GONE EUROPEWARD BETTER CHECK WHEN YOU PLANNING FILE FIRST STORY MAKE IT SOON

I read it again. The news about Les Baldwin was disturbing. It was inconceivable that any tentacles should have reached all the way into Ohio, but a lot of inconceivable things had been happening. And if he really was having a crack at Europe on his own, the chances were he'd be more of a hindrance than a help.

"I hope it is not bad news," said George Czanowski.

"No. I ought to answer it though."

He waved toward the desk. "You can send your answer here if you wish."

The desk clerk produced a telegraph pad and I scribbled quickly: *Arrived Warsaw yesterday still going through formalities beginning legwork shortly hope file soonest.* That should hold the fort, I thought as I followed George Czanowski through the plate-glass doors into the street. He had a Ford sedan waiting and we drove down the street a little way, then swung left into another wide thoroughfare, lined with cheerful shops and gay with flower stalls—unless you happened to look at the sightless walls above the ground floors.

"This is Marshalkovska," said George. "The main drag."

"Named for Marshal Stalin?"

"No," said George firmly. "Marshal Pilsudski. There is another street named for Stalin. Aleje Stalina."

"He doesn't sound so bad, does he, when you call him Stalina?"

"Bad enough."

We turned right into a considerably narrower street, partly blocked by heaps of rubble, and stopped in front of a gloomy building of yellowish stone. George led the way into a small bleak office that smelled of stale cigarette smoke. There were posters depicting the industrial glories of Poland and Russia, and a bare counter. I was given a long form which George filled out for me, then I signed it, and a man in uniform stamped my passport. He didn't seem happy about it, though—he spoke in surly monosyllables and ignored George's good-by when we left.

We drove round the block—the fact that I could think of our passage through these towers of rubble as going round the block showed I was getting used to it—and recrossed Marshalkovska. Ahead of us, blazing against a row of whitewashed buildings, appeared a battery of American flags. Just beyond them, a traffic cop stood on a podium—it was a lady cop and she wore a white jacket and a white skirt that didn't quite reach to her knees. In her boots and cap, she looked like the drum majorette of a Legion parade.

"This is part of the Embassy," said George. "The information service and consular section."

"And the lady cop? Is she part of it?"

George grinned. "Some people think so. She is not so bad, eh?"

"She certainly brightens the corner."

"It is an interesting corner in many ways," said George as we approached it. "It is the intersection of Ulica Piusa and Aleje Stalina—Pope Pius Street and Stalin Avenue."

"Stalin rates the avenue, does he?"

"Naturally," said George. He sounded the horn lightly, and the lady cop twirled on her podium, her white skirt flying. She signaled us to come on, grinned, and saluted.

"She is very nice," said George, swinging to the left around her and waving. "She likes Americans. Some day she will be liquidated—unless she is a U.B. agent. She may well be. Here we are."

Ahead was another American flag, and on the broad sidewalk in front of iron palings a pretty girl in nylons and a yellow linen dress—in contrast to the bare legs and mannish suits of most Polish women—was talking to a young man in an American captain's uniform. The building behind the palings looked solid and well-scrubbed amid blooming chestnut trees and lilac bushes. It was something to catch you in the throat, this chunk of America, clean and crisp and friendly, in the midst of a shadowy hostility. The girl and the captain both waved to George as he turned the Ford into the driveway.

We got out and went up some steps and entered a huge room, paneled in light wood, with broad stairs rising to a second-floor balcony. There were doors all around on both floors and people coming in and out, and the blessed sound of the American language floating everywhere. I never thought a nasal twang could sound so good, or "oh, yeah?" like poetry.

On a brown-leather sofa at one side of this room was sitting a small, rather dapper man with neat, pleasant features and smooth dark hair. He rose and walked toward us. "Good morning, George," he said.

"Good morning, Mr. Chelinski," said George. "This is Mr. Rockwell, whom you've heard about."

"It is a great pleasure, Mr. Rockwell," said Chelinski. His English was relaxed and easy. We shook hands.

"General Gritska will see you at nine," he said. "So we have a few minutes. Perhaps you would like a little chat here; my own office is apt to be"—he paused and glanced at me—"sometimes a little crowded."

"Whatever suits you," I said.

George Czanowski said he would see us later and disappeared through one of the many doors. Chelinski offered me a Chesterfield and we both sat down on the sofa.

"I presume there is no secret about your mission," he said, "as I understand it has been published in the American papers."

"That's right."

"Naturally, you must concentrate on your objective, but I hope you will find time to write a little about Poland herself, about the miracle of reconstruction that takes place daily before our eyes."

"What little I've seen has been very impressive."

"I am very glad," said Chelinski earnestly. "We are, of course, anxious that you should succeed in your mission, but we are even more anxious that you should write something nice about Poland."

"I'll try to write what I see."

"That is all anyone can ask. Meanwhile, you may count on our full assistance in your efforts to find Miss Nita Romaine."

"Thank you. Have you any idea of your own as to what may have happened to her?"

"I do not wish to be uncharitable—I have never seen the girl—but it is my belief that she is simply having a little affair of the heart. I admire the American press, Mr. Rockwell, but it sometimes tends to sensationalize trivial things. Forgive me."

"Of course. However, I have some reason to believe this is not as trivial a matter as you suggest."

"So?"

"If it were trivial, why should several attempts have been made to prevent my coming to Poland?"

"Have there been such attempts?"

"Rather violent ones."

"No!" He looked genuinely amazed and troubled. "I can assure you, Mr. Rockwell, that my government could not possibly be involved in such a thing. Unless—"

He stopped, and I waited. He puffed on his cigarette, rather nervously. "Unless?" I said presently.

He remained silent for a moment. Then he said, "Unless, I, myself, have been deliberately misled. All I know is that I have been instructed by General Gritska to be fully co-operative."

"Why should anyone mislead you, Mr. Chelinski?"

He stared at his cigarette. "Perhaps I should not say this, but we are in the American Embassy and no one will hear. You see, Mr. Rockwell, I am not a Communist. I am a Socialist, and in the past I have opposed the Communists. I am not completely trusted by them. They use me for—I have heard an American say it—for window dressing."

"But you go along with them?"

"I have made that decision. I do it for the good of my country and, believe me, Mr. Rockwell, there are many things about this government that are very good for the country. Above all else, above all parties, I am a loyal Pole."

The words found a familiar echo in the back of my mind. "Tell me," I said casually, "do you happen to know a courier in your service called Wiktor Lepski?"

He glanced at me sharply. "Yes," he said. "Quite well. Do you know him?"

"He was on the *Queen Jadwiga* with me. We became very friendly."

"And did you last see him on the *Queen?*" The question was as casual as my own had been.

"No. In Paris."

"You saw him in Paris?" There was nothing casual about the question this time. It was eager.

"I didn't exactly see him. I spoke to him on the phone."

"And was he well?"

I made an equivocal gesture. "Have you any reason to

be worried about him?"

"No, no, of course not. One does not worry about a courier. He is here, there, everywhere. It is merely that—"

Again he paused, and again I waited.

"—Merely that Wiktor is sometimes a little curious. And for people like Wiktor and myself, that is not always good. Look, it is almost nine o'clock. We must hurry."

CHAPTER NINETEEN

WE DROVE TO THE FOREIGN OFFICE in a government car, another black Zis. Like the Embassy, it was a completely reconstructed building, large and spreading and of white stone that looked austere in spite of vivid flower beds and window boxes. Soldiers with Tommy guns stood at the gateways in the high iron fence that surrounded it.

Chelinski's office was very small and cluttered, but bright with sunlight, and its lone window looked over the bluff on which the building stood. Beyond a stretch of green trees and truck gardens lay the broad, brown-blue expanse of the Vistula. On Chelinski's littered desk was a vase of petunias and a framed photograph of a placid looking woman and a child.

"My little family," he said, smiling at the photograph. "I shall now go and see if—"

He was interrupted by the unceremonious opening of the door. A self-assured young man in horn-rimmed spectacles entered. "You are late, Mr. Chelinski," he said in English.

"I am very sorry, I—"

"General Gritska is not pleased. Is this the American journalist?" His English was stiff and labored, a palpable affectation, designed perhaps to let me see that Chelinski was being humiliated.

Chelinski nodded. His face had grown slightly flushed.

"This way, please," the young man said to me. "General Gritska is waiting."

I followed him into the corridor and along it to another door which he opened and went through ahead of me. I found myself in a long room with chairs against the walls that seemed to converge upon a distant desk in front of tall windows. In the laddered light and shadow of Venetian blinds, I couldn't, for a moment, see more than the outline of the figure hunched behind the desk.

He rose as I walked toward him and leaned forward on his hands. He was heavily built, his hair long and yellow. I stopped short. Even without the dark glasses, there was no mistaking him. And there was a patch of court plaster on his cheek.

"Mr. Rockwell?" His voice was smooth and cool. "How do you do?"

I couldn't speak.

"Have you had a pleasant voyage?"

I glanced around. The young man in spectacles was only a few feet behind me. "Yes, thanks," I said.

"You came on the *Queen Jadwiga,* did you not?"

"Only as far as Calais. I came from Paris on the Orient Express." I watched his face, but there wasn't a flicker.

"I see," he said. "The *Queen Jadwiga* is a beautiful ship, is she not?"

"Very comfortable."

"I said 'beautiful.' "

"Yes. I heard you."

His eyes glowered. "You did not find her beautiful?"

"Okay, she was beautiful."

"I hope you will mention that fact in your articles. I hope you will not be like other American journalists and mention only the bad things you discover, or imagine that you discover, in Poland."

` I was getting tired of this. I leaned forward and lowered my voice. "If you will ask your secretary, or whatever he is, to leave, we might be able to talk."

His eyes remained cold and uncomprehending. "Why should he leave?"

"I thought it might save you embarrassment."

"Why should it?"

He was a cool one, all right. I took another sharp look at him. There was no doubt, no possible doubt, as to who he was.

"I have instructed Mr. Chelinksi," he was continuing, "to extend to you every assistance. I do not expect that you will find this lady whom you seek, but you will be given every opportunity."

I took a breath. "General, you know exactly where she is, don't you?"

He stared, outraged, incredulous. "What you say?" His English failed in the moment of stress.

"I think you heard me."

"I do not think it possible. You would not dare say such a thing."

"I merely asked a question."

"Listen, young man," said the General or whoever he was, "I can withdraw your credentials in a matter of minutes. I can order your deportation in a matter of hours. You would be well advised to control your tongue."

"I'm sorry. The *Queen Jadwiga* is a beautiful ship."

He drummed on the desk for a moment. Then he said, "I think that will be all." He sat down.

The young man was at my elbow. "This way," he said.

I turned and followed him the length of the long room and into the corridor. He remained a step or two ahead of me, as if to make it clear we were not walking companionably.

"The General has been away, has he not?" I asked.

"I do not know," said the young man. "This way."

I had stopped in front of the open door of Chelinski's office. "Aren't we going to say good-by to Mr. Chelinski?"

"It will not be necessary."

"Maybe not. But I'd like to."

The young man frowned. I stepped into the small sunny office. There was no one at the desk. I glanced round and saw the young man in the doorway, a look of amusement on his face. "Mr. Chelinski is not here," he said.

"Where is he?"

"I do not know. Please come." The "please" was impatient, not polite.

I stood where I was, looking thoughtfully at the framed photograph on Chelinksi's desk. "You know," I said to the young man, "I don't think I like you."

"That is not important. Come. The car is waiting."

He was mistaken about that. When we got outside, there was no sign of the car I had come in. The young man said something to one of the sentries who made a shrugging reply. The young man turned to me. "The car is no longer available. But you will quite easily find a taxi."

. He walked back into the building, his pale face impassive. Behind him the sentry to whom he had spoken gave me a cheerful wink. Somehow, it made me feel immeasurably better.

It wasn't so darned easy to find a taxi. I walked along the street, which hummed with reconstruction, for perhaps a quarter of a mile before one came along. And then I didn't know what to tell the driver. He was pleasant and patient about it, smiling and offering suggestions in Polish—or in Hindustani, for all I know. Then I had an inspiration.

"Piusa Stalina," I said.

The driver laughed and tapped his eye to show he understood. Then he held up a correcting finger. "Stalina Piusa," he said, and we both laughed.

Five minutes later we pulled up in front of the comforting sight of the Embassy.

CHAPTER TWENTY

WATKINS WAS WAITING for me in the paneled hall, and a good thing, because I hadn't any Polish money for the taxi. He sent an office boy out with a handful of zlotys. "It's funny they didn't bring you back in a government car," he remarked.

"I have a feeling General Gritska dislikes me."

Watkins glanced at me. "Was he the guy on the train?"

"Yes, he was. He didn't let on, though."

"You're sure?"

"Positive."

Watkins shook his head. "Your description sounded like him, and we knew he'd been out of town lately, but I just can't understand a man in his position going through all those shenanigans."

"What beats me," I said, "is why a man in his position couldn't have found some simpler way to keep me out of Poland. If he's really a big shot, that is."

"He's an even bigger shot than he seems," said Watkins. "Quite the power behind the throne is Gritska, and he certainly could have stopped you if he'd wanted to. Except that—" He paused and snapped his fingers. "By George, he wasn't here when your application went through. I'd forgotten that. It went straight from Chelinski to the Foreign Minister. Gritska may well have been in Paris at the time."

"And the time," I said, "was very shortly after the disappearance of Nita Romaine."

Watkins nodded thoughtfully. "Your hunch about a connection there is looking better every minute," he said.

"I trust you didn't mention it to Gritska, though."

"I'm afraid I did."

"Ouch! How did he take it?"

"With displeasure."

Watkins couldn't help chuckling. "I'm afraid that was a mistake," he said. "The General has quite a reputation as a chaser, and he's sensitive about it." He glanced at his watch. "Car should be here any minute. We'd better get some money changed for you."

He steered me through one of the hall's many doors into a corridor. "Tell me," I said as we walked along, "do you suppose all this could be explained by Gritska's fear of personal scandal?"

"No," said Watkins. "He could brazen out a scandal. In fact, it's partly because of that ladies' man reputation that he's such a popular figure."

"Is he popular?"

"With the public, yes. They don't know how ruthless and brutal he is at close range. To them, he's one of the few figures in this government that has any real color to him. He's got that robust lustiness that Goering had, and that Tito's got. What's more he's a real Pole. A lot of these boys aren't. They've no home except their spiritual one in Moscow."

We had reached the end of the passage, and Watkins paused. "No," he said, "Gritska could stand a scandal a lot more easily than he could stand a newspaperman's murder. If he really tried to put you out of the way, he's playing for bigger stakes than we know about."

He opened a door to a busy office full of adding machines and clacking typewriters, and we dropped the subject while a crew-cropped young man gave me a huge wad of zlotys in exchange for a traveler's check. "Printing-press money," said Watkins, "but it seems to buy stuff. How are you fixed for cigarettes?"

"I could use some."

He led me down a near-by stairway into a dark room of endless shelves laden with canned goods and soap and toilet paper and lord knows what all, and I bought a couple of cartons of cigarettes and some chewing-gum.

Back in the main hall, Watkins peered out the front door and frowned. "Car's not there yet," he said. "Still, it's just ten o'clock." ·

Waiting, I said, "One thing that bothers me is this. If our friend, the General, was so anxious to stop me before I got here, what kind of odds would a life insurance company put on me now, do you suppose?"

"A natural question," said Watkins. He smiled, but his eyes were somber. "If Gritska was really prepared to have you done away with, the chances are he hasn't changed his mind. But now that you're in the country, the Polish Government has a certain responsibility for you. And Gritska, whatever he may be up to, is part of that government."

"That sounds reassuring."

"Not necessarily," said Watkins. "If something happened to you that looked like an accident—or that looked as if robbery was the motive—well, the government couldn't be held accountable. Or there might be an effort to maneuver you into some kind of a jam that would force the Embassy to disavow you."

He paused, and I decided I wouldn't say anything just then about last night's incident in the hotel.

"That French girl," said Watkins, "if she really is French, she may have been some kind of decoy. I think you're well rid of her. There's something mighty funny about the way she slid across those borders. Ah, there's the car."

In the driveway outside a maroon Chevrolet sedan had drawn up. "Hello," said Watkins, "you've drawn Red Emma."

A large brick-faced woman sat at the wheel. She wore the same sort of gray uniform that another chauffeur had worn.

"The one lady driver that's been wished on us," said Watkins. "It's a compliment to you, in a way. She's a definite U.B. agent. Good driver, though."

"I don't quite get it," I said. "Can't you hire your own drivers?"

"We do," said Watkins. "But the U.B. makes good and sure that any driver we hire takes the pledge, you might say. We've got a few we can trust, or think we can, but for a job like this, which is strictly unofficial, we have to take whoever turns up in the pool."

"I don't want to look a gift horse in the mouth," I said, "but couldn't we drive ourselves?"

"You'd be stopped in no time. They've got road blocks every hundred miles or so and even with your C.D. plates—"

"What kind of plates?"

"C.D. *Corps diplomatique*. They help, but you still have to show your license. You needn't worry too much about Red Emma. Her job is to make sure you don't go monkeying around any military installations, and to report it if you try."

"I don't expect to try," I said, "but I was thinking of what you said a few minutes ago. About something that might look like an accident."

"Hmm, yes—still, Doctor Clendenning will be with you."

"You also said something about there being more to him than meets the eye."

"I didn't mean anything sinister," said Watkins. "Scarcely could be, could there? All I meant was that he works for a privately endowed international outfit and isn't necessarily vouched for by any American authorities.

Neither are you, for that matter."

"I'll begin to suspect myself if I'm not careful," I said.

Watkins grinned. "Just in case Red Emma gives you trouble," he said, "you might as well have a spare set of keys. Let's see, which car is that?"

He took another look, then went out through the same door we had taken before. In a moment, he was back with a couple of keys on a ring. "She won't know you have these. Presumably, anyway. All set?"

"Guess so. Does Red Emma speak any English?"

"Couple of words. And some German, if that helps. Her real name is Zofja, if you want to address her. Same thing as Sophie. She'll answer to Sophie."

I thanked him and he wished me luck and we shook hands.

In the back seat of the jouncing car, the comfortable assurance I had felt in the American atmosphere of the Embassy evanesced. My mind began to brood on what might be waiting for me at the hotel. To my relief, the lobby of the Polonia was its gloomily tranquil self as I entered.

Dr. Clendenning was sitting beside a potted palm, looking wispier than ever. "Ah, there you are," he said with a trace of reproach. "Where have you been, anyway?"

"Police, Foreign Office, Embassy. Has anything happened?"

He shook his head. "I don't think anybody has tried to take a bath yet. At least, there has been no alarm."

"That must have been an awfully powerful dose you gave the guy."

"I suppose it was," he admitted. "I never gave it to an adult before."

"You don't suppose he's dead?"

"Goodness," said Dr. Clendenning, "isn't it a little late in the day for you to be so solicitous? However, I'm quite sure he's not. Not from what I gave him, anyway."

"Where is Miss Miratour?"

"Upstairs, packing your things. She's already packed mine." He nodded toward a suitcase near his feet. "She's really a very kind, helpful girl."

I frowned. "How did she get into my room?" •

"She's registered as your wife, isn't she?" He smiled. "We're going to be quite a little—what's that phrase?— *ménage à trois,* aren't we?"

"What do you mean, going to be?"

"I naturally assume that she's coming with us. And she certainly does."

"Doctor," I said, "I'm against it. It strikes me as simply looking for trouble."

"Humph," said Dr. Clendenning. "You didn't mind looking for trouble last night. Or letting me in for it, either."

"Well," I said, "we'll see." I went to the desk and asked the clerk to get my bill ready, then took the elevator to my floor. In the wide, dim corridor, a chambermaid was standing in front of the door to the public bath. She gave the knob a rattle and called something. I waited, my mouth suddenly dry. Then she shrugged and trudged on down the corridor.

My knees felt a little shaky as I went on into my own room. Griselde Miratour was standing beside the bed, upon which my open suitcase lay. She glanced up, unconcernedly, and said, "I have almost finished with your luggage. Am I not a good girl?"

"Mm, yes."

"The little dock-tor thinks I am," she said and suddenly laughed. "Oh, that dock-tor, he is so funny. Last night, I am very tired, so I wish to go straight to sleep on the couch. But he keeps saying, 'Tempt me, you must tempt me.' 'Oh, go to sleep,' I say. But finally, I say, 'Oh, very well, I tempt you, come to my arms, my adored one.' And what does he do? He says, 'Ah, I fool you, I resist!' Then he begins to snore. He is crazy, I tell you. But cute."

She continued to chuckle for a moment, then she sobered and gave me a curious glance. "Do you think there is something peculiar about him?"

"Most people would think so, from what you've just told me."

"No, no, that is not what I mean. Do you think he is what he says he is?"

I stared at her. "Why shouldn't he be?"

Griselde hesitated. "I have found something in his luggage—quite accidentally, you understand—that makes me wonder a little."

"What did you find?"

"Perhaps it is not important. I only wonder a little. Do you think he is altogether American? What you call hundred per cent?"

"He has an American passport."

"Ah." Griselde smiled. "But so do I. Half of one. And you must not frown at me like that."

"What did you find in Clendenning's luggage?"

"I have told you it is not important. I do not wish to discuss the matter further."

"I do. Why were you going through his luggage in the first place?"

"Because he has asked me to help him." Her eyes were cold. "And if you say things like that, I will become angry. I do not wish to become angry. There are more important things to consider. *Par exemple,* what is to be done with the clothing of the chauffeur?"

"Might as well leave them, mightn't we?"

"Do not be a fool," said Griselde. "The chauffeur, he will be afraid to tell the police what happened. But if the clothes are discovered here, it will be trouble for us.

We must hurry, too. Because there is already curiosity about the bath."

"There's no room for them in my bag."

"I am aware of that," said Griselde impatiently. "The best thing, I think, will be to wrap them in newspapers. There are newspapers in the bureau drawers."

She pulled open a drawer. "What is this? Ah, you have taken these things from his pockets. We must not leave them. I will put them in your bag, so. Except the wallet; put that in your pocket. Now then. Take your typewriter and your bag and go downstairs. I will bring the clothes. Hurry."

"Miss Miratour," I began, then I stopped.

"Well?"

"Nothing." I closed the suitcase and picked it up, along with the typewriter, and went out. In the corridor, the same chambermaid went past with an older woman who looked like the housekeeper. I didn't wait to see where they went.

There was no sign of Dr. Clendenning in the lobby. Then I saw him, through the plate-glass door that was wedged open that balmy morning, standing beside the Chevrolet. Red Emma was lounging against a fender, her muscular arms folded. They seemed to be conversing, and I wondered in what language. The desk clerk had my bill ready and was very polite. Had everything been satisfactory, he asked, and I said yes, fine. A bellhop took my bag and went ahead of me toward the door.

Just as I reached it, a piercing scream came from somewhere up above. It was a woman's scream, and it came again. Outside on the pavement, Red Emma snapped alert. There was a patter of footsteps high on the stairs, and an instant later, Griselde came running down the broad marble sweep. She carried a bundle wrapped in newspaper.

Her heels tapped across the lobby, and she caught my arm. "They have found him," she said quietly. "Waste no time."

Dr. Clendenning, blinking through his pince-nez, opened the back door of the car, and she climbed in. He followed her. Red Emma stood motionless on the sidewalk. "We go now," I said.

Red Emma gave me a scornful look. *"Nie,"* she said crisply. She swung around to the car and pulled open the front door, reached inside and yanked the key out of the dashboard. Then she strode past me and into the hotel.

"What is the matter?" cried Griselde. "Where is the driver?"

I reached into my pocket and turned with one of the shakiest grins on record. "Right here, lady," I said.

Then I jumped in, jammed the spare key into the switch, threw her into first, and swung out into the dusty stream of traffic.

CHAPTER TWENTY-ONE

I THANKED MY STARS that the car was a Chevrolet, and not a Zis or something peculiar, and that Griselde was there to shout directions into my ear. It was bad enough as it was—the unexpected heaps of rubble, the holes in the streets, the droshkies and horse carts and buses and cops— and then, quite suddenly, we were bowling through a lane of poplar trees and into open country. Far off to our left, across the flat yellow fields, we could see the bluish bluffs that marked the course of the Vistula.

"We had better stop," Griselde said presently.

"Why?" I asked.

"I have some ideas which I think should be discussed."

"Couldn't we put some more miles between us and

Warsaw first?"

"No. We might come to a barricade."

"We'd better do as she says, Stonewall," said Dr. Clendenning. "That's what we brought her along for."

"Okay," I said and pulled over to the side. "What's on your mind, Miss Miratour?"

"I think that I should do the driving."

"What!"

"Oh, you need not look so offended. Although you are cute when you look that way. In the first place, I drive very well and I know the country a little. In the second place, we shall soon come to a barricade. The guard there will have been warned, no doubt, that an American Embassy car with a lady driver will pass that way this morning. If there is no lady driver, he will become suspicious."

"If you're the lady driver, he'll become suspicious, anyway."

"Not of necessity. I will be able to speak to him in quite good Polish. Also, I will be in uniform. It will not fit very well but it will be a uniform." She undid the bundle on her lap and shook out the rumpled gray coat and black-visored cap. Then she stepped into the road and put them on. The dangling sleeves and rakish cap had a fetchingly gamin look.

"That coat won't fool anybody," I said.

"It will be better when I am sitting down. The important thing is that it will look official."

"Are you going to put on the pants, too?" asked Dr. Clendenning with interest.

"That will not be necessary," said Griselde coldly.

"Suppose the guard asks to see your license," I said.

"Was there not a license in the wallet?"

"Yes, but it states pretty plainly that it's a man."

"Never mind," said Griselde. "Give it to me. If anyone asks for it, I will try to bluff. I will show it very briefly.

Like American detectives in the movies."

I thought of something else. "Won't these guards get an alarm for a stolen Chevrolet?"

Griselde shrugged. "It is not really stolen. It is an American Embassy car, is it not? It has *corps diplomatique* plates, has it not? Anyway, we take a chance, eh? Move over."

She slid in behind the wheel and tilted the cap. "Ah, I love American cars," she murmured, and sent the Chevvy forward with a merry spurt that almost threw Clendenning and me to the floor.

Mile after mile clicked past on the macadam road. On either side stretched fields of grain, threaded with the reds and blues of poppies and cornflowers, splashed here and there with the deeper, richer yellow of mustard.

A little before noon, there loomed ahead two small white-painted sheds and a towering pole, red and white striped, that, as we neared, lowered across the road like an old-fashioned tollgate. The soldiers in khaki appeared, one on either side, each with a Tommy gun. Griselde skidded to a halt with the front bumper practically touching the barrier. She leaned out of the window and pointed toward the license tags, pouring out a stream of half-angry, half-jocular Polish.

The soldier looked sheepish and said something conciliatory. Griselde softened slightly, but the retort she shot back was still sharp. The soldier called to his mate, who said something that plainly indicated he wanted no part of it. Griselde shouted something impatient. The soldier wiped his forehead, then turned and went into the little shed. A moment later, the barrier slowly rose. It was barely above our radiator cap before Griselde sent us hurtling on.

"You see," she said, turning with a pleased smile, "it was not so difficult."

"I told you she'd be helpful, Stoney," said Dr. Clendenning.

Griselde gave me a chilly glance. "Were you arguing the point?" she asked.

Around one o'clock we rolled into a pretty little town of yellow- and cream-colored buildings with red roofs, overlooked by a great church with an onion-shaped dome. It was called Kielce, Griselde said, and if things hadn't changed, there was an excellent spot here in which to eat. We had a fine lunch of smoked eel, cold ham, some sort of casserole, and a bottle of Dr. Clendenning's favorite water. We all felt a good deal better about everything when we climbed back into the Chevvy.

In the middle of the afternoon, we hit another road block, and again Griselde talked her way blithely through it. Toward dusk, against the deepening blue of the sky, set among gentle hills, the glowing red towers and spires of Kraków appeared.

It was a lovely city. I suppose that any reasonably intact city would have looked good after unhappy Warsaw, but Kraków, in the golden light slanting across the remains of the ancient wall that once surrounded it, had a quality of slumbering enchantment. A charming park, in which fountains shot their spray high in the air, now circled the inner city where the great wall had stood, and everywhere were chestnut trees and lilacs and big, solid buildings and churches with onion spires. In spite of the urban bustle in the streets, the place had the feeling of a college town, and I remembered, out of some dim store of useless knowledge, that the University of Kraków was the oldest, or maybe second oldest, in Central Europe.

I mentioned the fact to Dr. Clendenning. "I am aware of it," he replied. "In fact, I expect to be taken on a tour of the university tomorrow morning."

"Someone is meeting you, then?"

"I certainly hope so," said Dr. Clendenning. "Grand Hotel, please, driver."

Griselde snorted and turned into a comparatively narrow street of modern shops, then brought the Chevrolet to a halt in front of a glass marquee. "Grand Hotel, sir," she said with a touch of bitterness. "No doubt you wish me to await you, sir."

"Somebody has to stay with the car," said Dr. Clendenning mildly. "Remember what happened to the last driver."

Griseldé shrugged moodily, and I followed the doctor into a gilt and red-plush lobby. Again, the desk clerk spoke English and said we were expected—he had a double room all ready.

"With a bath?" asked Dr. Clendenning.

"Unfortunately no, sir. This is a very old-fashioned hotel. But there is a public bath near by which I am sure will be convenient for all practical purposes."

Dr. Clendenning winked at me. "He doesn't know all the practical purposes we put public baths to, does he?"

The clerk looked puzzled.

"Never mind," said the doctor cheerfully. "We'll manage. Next question is, has anyone been inquiring for me?"

"I was about to tell you, sir. That gentleman by the window, he has been waiting for you. I will call him."

It wasn't necessary. A short, bald-headed man with a silky pointed beard rose from a leather chair at the front of the lobby and came toward us. Dr. Clendenning trotted forward, and I could hear the bald-headed man greeting him in English.

"Also, I have a telegram for you, sir," the clerk said to me.

I felt a vague uneasiness. He handed me a bluish folded slip, and I tore it open and read:

HAVE TIP YOUR FRIEND WITH DARK GLASSES HAS SUDDENLY
LEFT TOWN THOUGHT YOU BETTER KNOW ALSO HOTEL POLONIA
INFORMS US PARIS HAS BEEN TRYING TO REACH YOU BY
PHONE REGARDS

WATKINS ·

The clerk was saying, "Do you wish to go to your
room, sir? The page will bring your bag."

"What?" I scarcely heard him. "Oh. Yes. Yes, by all
means."

"The doorman will take care of your car. He will also
show your driver to a room in the employees' quarter."

"Good. Look, I'd like to put in a call for Paris right
away. To Mrs. Rockwell at the Hotel Lutetia."

"Right away, sir? If you wait for two hours, it will be
much cheaper."

"Right away, please. I'll be in my room."

As I turned away from the desk, Dr. Clendenning
buttonholed me. "I want you to meet Doctor Jarowski,"
he said. "Do I pronounce it right, Doctor?"

"It is close enough," said the bald-headed man, smiling.
We shook hands.

"Doctor Jarowski is chief of staff at the hospital I'm
going to," explained Dr. Clendenning. "And he has very
kindly asked me to have dinner with him tonight. Do
you mind?"

"Not at all. Enjoy yourself."

"Thank you. What are you going to do?"

"I don't know yet. Don't worry about me."

"Just so you don't go to sleep in that public bath." He
chuckled.

"Pleased to have met you," said Dr. Jarowski.

I followed the bellhop upstairs to a large room with
two wooden beds. Through the windows, beyond a stretch
of red roofs, I could see the greenery of a square and the

soaring towers of a church. It was a pleasant view, but after I had looked at it for a while, I decided that my nerves needed something more bracing than a view. I phoned down and asked if there was any whisky in the house.

"I am sorry, sir," said the clerk. "There is only vodka. Vodka and beer. Also some Polish vermouth that I do not recommend."

"Send some up, anyway," I said, "and some vodka. I'll see if I can make a Martini. Have you any ice?"

The clerk said he would see. Presently, a boy came up with a tray and an ice bucket—for champagne, I supposed, in the old days—and I tried to distract myself with the experiment. The result wasn't good, exactly, but it could have been worse. At least it was bolstering, and I told myself that Jane undoubtedly was returning my sociable call of last night. Was it only last night? It seemed a week since I had heard her voice.

The phone rang. The clerk's voice was apologetic. "I am very sorry, sir, but I have spoken to the Hotel Lutetia in Paris and there is no Mrs. Rockwell staying there."

I stared into the monthpiece. "But damn it, man, I know she's there. Did they say she'd checked out, or what?"

"The hotel said only that they had no one of that name, sir."

"Thank you." Slowly and bleakly I hung up. Perhaps she and Mrs. Pickett—that was an idea, I would try Mrs. Pickett. Except that she wasn't Mrs. Pickett. What was that silly name she was using? For a panicky moment I couldn't think of it, then it came to me. Lovejoy. I picked up the phone again. "Will you have another go at the Hotel Lutetia," I said, "and ask for a Miss Lovejoy? And if she's not there, see if they know where she is and anything else you can find out. It's very important."

Waiting, I poured another Martini. One thing about

the experiment, it carried authority. The phone rang again, and I leaped for it.

"There is a lady to see you, sir," said the clerk.

"A lady? Who.is she?"

"I do not know, sir. She is already on her way up."

I heard the smart tapping of high heels in the corridor. As I hung up, the door opened and Griselde Miratour came in. Her eyes were crackling.

"Because my name is Griselde," she snapped, "you need not think I am always patient. I do not like it that you treat me like a servant."

"I'm sorry."

"It is not nice that you should leave me with the chambermaids. It is not grateful."

"Something came up," I said. "I had to make a very important call. I'm waiting for it now."

"Very important? It must be your wife."

"You're quite right."

"Oh." She sounded mollified, but not entirely. "What is that you drink?"

"A Polish dry Martini. Like to try one?"

"But certainly." She watched my hands as I poured. "You are nervous."

"Anybody would be nervous trying to make a Martini out of this stuff."

She took a sip and made a face. "I see your meaning. But that is not why you are nervous."

"I'm a little worried about this call, that's all."

"You do not need to keep looking at your watch. In a moment you will find out the time in a very beautiful way."

Even as she spoke, the deep rich strokes of an old bell came from the square, from one of the towers that stood black against the twilight sky. Seven strokes.

"Wait," said Griselde. "Watch the tower. Do you see?"

High in the nest of spires that surrounded one slender needle a sliver of light appeared. Then the clear, lovely notes of a bugle floated out upon the air, and the whole city seemed to fall silent. Then suddenly it stopped, in mid-note, and the light went out. The sounds of the city started up again.

"Did you never hear of the Bugler of Kraków?" asked Griselde.

"I'm afraid not."

"It has been made into a children's story. But it is true. In the long ago times the bugler played a pretty little tune. Then, in the war against the Turks, an arrow struck the bugler and he fell dead in the middle of the little tune. So, ever since, the bugler must always stop at the place where the arrow stopped his fellow bugler of the long ago. It is quite beautiful, is it not?"

"It is very beautiful, Griselde," I said, and strangely, the simple story, told while the notes still lingered, seemed to lighten my own troubles.

Once more, the phone's jangle rattled the room. The clerk's voice said, "I have the Hotel Lutetia on the wire. They say that Miss Lovejoy has departed and has left strict instructions to give no information. However, if it is very important, they will attempt to give her a message. Do you wish to do that?"

"I certainly do."

"It will be necessary to charge for the call."

"Never mind that. Tell her to call me here and if I'm not here to leave her number. Got that?"

"Yes, sir." The clerk hung up.

Griselde stared over the rim of her glass. "You are unable to reach your wife, yes?"

"If you must know, yes."

"Do not worry," she said soothingly. "She is in Paris, the most civilized city in the world."

"How do I know she's in Paris?"

"She cannot go very far without a passport."

Miserable as I was, I had to smile. "That's an interesting thought, coming from you."

"See, you are feeling better already. Now I will take you to a very nice place for dinner and you will feel better yet. We will have the *spécialité de la maison* which is called 'Adventure with a Sardine.' Really."

"I'd better stay here. In case my call comes through."

"It may take a long time," said Griselde. "And it is not good to sit and wait for the telephone. It is bad for the morale. Besides, the restaurant is very near and you can ask the hotel to send a chasseur if your call arrives."

"What's a chasseur?"

"One who chases, I suppose, but that does not sound like the same thing."

"It sounds like a former friend of yours."

"Do not speak of him," said Griselde. "And after dinner we will go for a little while to a night club. There is a very good one here and it is also close to the hotel."

I sat up. "Would it be called the Monte Carlo?"

"How did you know?"

"Oh, I get around. You're sure the hotel could reach me there?"

"Quite sure. I know the manager there. I will speak to him and tell him you expect the call." She looked at me curiously. "You appear pleased. Do you like night clubs so much?"

"Not in general, but I'm anxious to see this one. I'd like to have a talk with the manager, too."

"What about?"

"About material for a story."

Her eyes were dubious. "Listen, be careful if you talk to him. Do not ask him too many questions. He is not a very nice man."

"I'll be careful."

She gave me a shrewd glance. "No, you must tell me the truth. Do you expect to do anything that will make trouble?"

"Well, to be perfectly honest, he may not like the questions I want to ask him."

"I thought so." She walked to the window, then came back. "Very well, but I must tell you something. If there is trouble, you must not go to the police. Do you understand? Whatever happens, I must not become involved with the police. Do you promise me?"

"Okay," I said. "They probably wouldn't be on our side anyway."

"You must seal the promise," said Griselde. She was standing in front of me, her face tilted toward mine. Her lips came closer, and she put her arms around my neck. "Do not look so worried. It will be the kiss of a sister."

Maybe it was. I never had any sisters, so I wouldn't know.

CHAPTER TWENTY-TWO

THE MONTE CARLO was not far from the square, but it was hard to believe that the gentle notes of the bugle could pierce its smoky, scented, strident interior. It belonged to another world, a world as ancient, no doubt, as the church in the square, but as far removed from it as Broadway and Fifty-Second Street. Not that it was tawdry—it was big and well lit and there were cloths on the tables, and the people looked respectable enough. A few wore evening clothes. But the whole feverish atmosphere struck me as anomalous in that crenelated old city.

An unctuous headwaiter led us to a table on the low balcony that surrounded the dance floor on three sides. At the fourth side was a stage, across which a crimson curtain was now drawn. It seemed to me that the headwaiter was staring curiously at Griselde, but she didn't notice, apparently, and we sat down and ordered the inevitable carafe of vodka.

"You like it?" asked Griselde.

"It's all right, I guess. Are there places like this in Warsaw, too?"

"No. Oh, there are *boîtes*, but they are smaller than this, not so nice. And they do not have the cabaret. Perhaps they think it is bad taste to have the cabaret among the ruins. I do not know. These Communists do not wish people to have fun."

"Insofar as fun means night clubs," I said, "I agree with them."

She looked surprised. "But you have wished to come here, have you not?"

"Yes, but not to have fun."

Griselde looked at me thoughtfully. "Perhaps you had better tell me why you have wished to come here. And what are these questions you wish to ask the manager."

I hesitated, and Griselde added, "He does not speak English. In what language will you ask these questions if I do not help you? The language of flowers?"

She had a point. And as long as everybody else and his brother seemed to know what I was up to, it could scarcely hurt to tell her. So, briefly, I did.

"Is that why you think your wife is in danger?" she asked then.

"I didn't say she was in danger, exactly, but—"

"I think perhaps she is," said Griselde. "And you, too. Ah, here comes the manager."

A thickset man in evening clothes, with sleek black hair and oily features, was threading his way through the tables toward ours. There was a broad smile on his face, a smile that had a touch of the Oriental about it.

"Mlle. Miratour, *n'est-ce pas?*" he said and held out his hand.

Griselde extended ladylike fingers and said something in French. They talked back and forth for a minute or two, then Griselde turned to me. She looked pleased. "He remembers me very well," she said. "He says everyone in Poland remembers me because of the film I have made here. He wishes to introduce me to the audience during the cabaret if you do not mind. Do you?"

Somewhat ruefully I said, "I was hoping not to attract attention."

"You have already attracted attention. Everyone recognizes an American. Besides, it will be good for both of us. For my reputation as an actress, and for you, it will help with your questions. So I shall say yes, eh?"

"I guess so. When do you think I should pop these famous questions?"

"After the cabaret. It starts very soon."

She turned back to the manager and spoke again in French. Then she nodded toward me, and he and I shook hands. His smile had grown perfunctory and his little eyes, under heavy lids, were obviously sizing me up. Then he bowed and went away.

The orchestra, which had been playing "Lady Be Good," stopped with a long-drawn blare. A thin, pale man, also in evening clothes, stepped from behind the crimson curtain and began to talk in rapid Polish.

"What you call the M.C.," whispered Griselde. "He is quite good. Quite witty."

People were laughing.

"He makes a risqué remark," said Griselde. "Too complicated to explain."

The man went on talking. Suddenly he interrupted himself by clapping his hand to his mouth, and there was a ripple of delighted tittering.

"He makes a little joke about the government," whispered Griselde. "Everybody loves it."

He signaled offstage and skipped away as the curtain was drawn back, revealing a man and woman in the costumes and attitudes of an Apache dance. It was like all Apache dances, I guess, but they were pretty good, at that. And they got a big hand. They were followed by a dumpy woman in country-cousin clothes, who sat down on a straw suitcase and began to sing a song which I gathered was a comic one. In the dimness I saw the manager coming toward us again. He bent over Griselde and whispered in her ear. Griselde rose.

"I go now," she said, "to make my appearance."

I frowned. "Can't they introduce you from the table?"

"It is much better from the stage. Perhaps they will ask me to sing. Do not fret yourself, I will be back *tout de suite.*"

She patted my shoulder and followed the thickset manager among the tables and behind a silver-painted screen at the end of the balcony nearest the stage. I stared after them uneasily. I couldn't help wondering if this was a gag by which Griselde hoped to see the manager before I could question him.

The comic singer left the stage, and the M.C. stepped out again. From his tone, I guessed that he was saying something like, "We interrupt our show for a moment to introduce a celebrity who—"

Griselde stepped out into the spotlight. So far, at least, it wasn't a gag, and gazing at her slim form, her flowerlike face as she smiled gaily at the audience, I felt half-ashamed of my suspicions. She wasn't asked to sing, and I thought that she looked a shade disappointed as she walked off the stage.

I waited for her to reappear but she didn't. The spotlight turned blue and an Egyptian belly dancer moved into it, a swarthy, sinuous woman with a heavy headdress, transparent pantaloons hanging from her loins and metal breastplates. The music became low and throbbing.

The minutes went by to the undulating rhythm. Then, from behind the silvery screen, came the figure of a woman and for a relieved instant, in the half-darkness, I thought it was Griselde. But it wasn't. It was a girl in a low-cut evening gown, and I couldn't think why she looked famil-iar. Then I realized it was the girl who had taken part in the Apache dance.

She came straight to my table and sat down in Griselde's chair. She reached for my hand and patted it. "I speak a little English," she said. "So M'sieu Theopolis has sent me to keep you company."

"I've already got company," I said and took my hand away. "Who is M'sieu Theopolis?"

"The *patron*. The manager."

"And why does he think I need company?"

The girl's voice was teasing. "Because the company you have had before has gone away. Now, now, you must not become.angry. Someone in the audience has admired her, someone very rich, and she has gone away with him. Who can blame her?"

I stared at her, aware that I was breathing hard. "I don't believe you," I said.

Her face darkened slightly. "You are not very polite."

"No," I said, "I'm not, and M'sieu Theopolis is going to find it out." I pushed my chair back and got up.

"You had better stay here," said the girl. "M'sieu Theopolis will not be pleased."

"I don't expect him to be pleased," I said, and started for the far end of the dim, smoky room. Like a figure in a nightmare, the belly dancer continued to gyrate and weave. Behind the silver screen was a swinging door and beside the door stood a man, a very large man, in waiter's clothes. He put his arm across the door and shook his head. *"Nie, nie,"* he said gruffly.

"Tak, tak," I said, thereby virtually exhausting my Polish, and tried to push past him. His hand, which was huge and bristled, came down flat on my shirt front and shoved me back. There was no sense trying to sock him. He wouldn't have felt it. So I did the next best thing—hauled off and kicked him as hard as I could in the shin. He gave a yelp and began to jump up and down on one leg, grasping the injured tibia—or is it the fibula in front?—with both hands. Quickly I ducked past him and through the swinging door.

I found myself in a long corridor, from which one door opened into a steamy kitchen and another onto the stage. I saw the thin M.C. standing in the wings, his back toward me. There were other doors along the corridor but they were all closed. At the far end, perhaps fifteen yards away, was a patch of darkness from which came a welcome smell of fresh air—apparently the back entrance.

I started slowly along the passage, then I heard a door open behind me. I swung round and saw Theopolis standing there, his arms folded over his powerful chest, his face dark with anger. He snapped something at me in French.

"Où est Mlle. Miratour?" I snapped back.

"Elle est partie." The words were cold.

"Où?"

I didn't catch his reply, but it pretty plainly said it was none of my damned business. The swinging door opened and the waiter I had kicked came through it. He put a plaintive question to Theopolis, who nodded with an unpleasant smile. The waiter took a step toward me. I glanced around and saw that another waiter, or more likely bouncer, had appeared just in front of the back entrance. And he, too, started in my direction.

A sickening sense of my position swept over me—here I was in precisely the kind of fix Watkins had warned me against. A fight over a girl in the back of a rowdy night club, a couple of professional thugs to work on me, a body tossed into the alley—and what could the Embassy or anybody else do about it?

The first waiter was almost upon me, coming slowly, his fists clenched, his eyes bright with anticipation. Theopolis grinned that Oriental grin of his. I half turned and saw the other waiter coming closer. He was almost as big as the first one, with dangling apelike arms.

There was only one chance that I could see. Nobody ever called me a star on the football field, but one thing I'd always had was a good stiff-arm. I swung around and plunged full tilt at the oncoming waiter. The stiff-arm, I guess, is a strictly American institution—at least, this fellow didn't seem to know about it. I caught him squarely on the side of the jaw, twirled all the way round as his long arms tried to tackle me high, then I was out of his grasp and had a clear field to the back door.

In a moment I was outside, in a murky, ill-paved alleyway. Trees rose from behind a stone wall opposite. I wasn't sure which way to turn—it might be a cul-de-sac. Then in the darkness, I saw a car moving slowly away down the narrow street, almost filling it. As it passed a crooked street light, the only one in sight, I saw that it was a black limousine.

I started to run after it. Behind me, the two waiters had stopped uncertainly in the doorway. I could hear Theopolis's angry voice. I kept on running. The limousine was picking up speed by now—maybe whoever was in it saw me—and pursuit was quickly hopeless. I couldn't even spot the number. It swung around a corner and disappeared, and when I reached the same corner it was gone.

High above me, in the stillness, a bell began to toll. Eleven times it struck, then a pause, and there floated out upon the night the liquid strains of the bugle. Then the sudden stop—the stop of unseen death striking out of nowhere. I shivered and kept on going until I recognized the street on which the hotel stood.

CHAPTER TWENTY-THREE

I WAS AWAKENED by the telephone. Outside the window the sun was well above the red roof tops, and Dr. Clendenning's rumpled bed was empty.

The desk clerk's voice said, "Paris on the wire, sir. One moment."

There was a brief colloquy in Polish, then another and fainter one in French, followed by a succession of tinkling sounds as of a great many coins being deposited. Then suddenly there boomed into my ear the hearty and welcome voice of Mrs. Pickett.

"Rocky? Thank goodness I've got hold of you at last."

"Amen," I said. "Tell me quick, is anything wrong?"

She hesitated. "Well, not wrong exactly, but there's a couple of items I thought you'd better know about. In the first place, we've changed hotels."

"So I gather. Why?"

"Nothing to worry about," said Mrs. Pickett, "but apparently we were being shadowed at the other hotel. I assumed at first that it was some unknown admirer of mine and didn't say anything to your Jane about it, but she happened to spot him herself. Seems it was the same man who caused all that commotion at the café that night. So I thought it might be a pious idea to move, and we did."

"Without being followed?"

"I can't be sure, but I was mighty cagey about it. If I do say so I shouldn't. I had a Thomas Cook man move us with great fuss and feathers to one of the big hotels on the right bank, and meanwhile Jane and I slipped off to a little pension that I knew about. Next day I had our bags sent to the Gare St. Lazare and had them picked up there that night. We kept our toothbrushes with us, in case you're fretting about that. And we haven't seen our shadowy friend since."

"Where is this pension? What's the number?"

"I don't think I'd better mention it on the phone," said Mrs. Pickett. "Not if certain people are as interested in you as they seem to be. You can always get a message to me through the Lutetia, or through young Baird at the Embassy."

"Where are you calling from now?"

"My old stamping-ground, the Deux Magots. It's a deuce of a business from a call box, but it's safer. I've got tokens running out of my ears."

"Is Jane there with you?"

"Well, uh, no," said Mrs. Pickett. "Not at the moment."

Something in her voice gave me a sinking feeling. "Mrs. Pickett," I said tensely, "has anything happened to Jane?"

"Look," said Mrs. Pickett soothingly, "it was something that happens every five minutes in Paris, especially to visiting Americans. She was in a very minor taxi accident, that's all, and she got a bit of a shaking up and she's gone to the American Hospital for a day or two of observation. There—that's nothing to give you the jimjams, is it?"

"You swear she's not seriously hurt?"

"Honor bright. In fact, Jane herself thought it was rather silly to go to the hospital, but it seems that the driver of the other car was a male nurse, by a happy chance, and he was very professional about the whole thing. It was his fault, he said, and he wanted to be absolutely sure she was all right. At first, he wanted to take her to a private nursing-home that he apparently is on the staff of—tsk, tsk, of which he is on the staff—but Jane held out for the American Hospital."

"I'm glad of that."

"Yes, I thought it was a good move. Except that the hospital's awfully crowded these days, mostly with Americans who never ate snails before."

"Was Jane alone when it happened?"

"I hope that isn't reproach I detect in your voice," said Mrs. Pickett. "Although maybe I shouldn't have let her go without me, at that. Anyway, she wanted to do some shopping, and I was hard at work on a powerful piece of prose for the paper, so off she went. To buy hats. You'll be relieved to know the accident occurred before she bought any."

"Don't be heartless, Mrs. Pickett."

"I keep trying to tell you that it was a very minor accident. This other car simply happened to ram her taxi from behind and—"

"Are you sure?"

"Sure about what?"

"That it simply happened that way? You don't think it could have been deliberate?"

"What would anybody have stood to gain by it?"

"I don't know. Did you see this male nurse?"

"Of course. I bounced straight off to the hospital the minute I got word. He seemed quite a decent young chap. And he insists on paying all expenses. I suppose he's had experience with lawsuits from that kind of thing. Anyway, the main point is that everything is all right, Jane is perfectly comfortable and you've nothing to worry about. Except your own affairs. How are they coming?"

"Not so good."

"A pity. Well, do your best. Look, there's one more item.

That poor youngster Les Baldwin has turned up in Paris."

"I'll be darned," I said. "It's not a complete surprise, though. Breen cabled me that he'd suddenly left town."

"It was sudden, all right," said Mrs. Pickett. "Somebody must have put up his passage. He came by air, which isn't cheap in spite of all those ads about how you can save three dollars by doubling up with the stewardess. What's more, he won't talk about it."

"You've seen him, then?"

"Briefly. He's in a terrible stew, can't get a visa for Poland, can't get ice water in his hotel, doesn't know what to do. Know what I think? I think some other newspaper put him up to this, probably our opposition. Which is very encouraging."

"Why?"

"Why? Because it means that the *Record's* sending you over here has been a sufficiently successful piece of promotion to worry our rivals, that's why."

A metallic voice speaking French broke in on the conversation. "Time's up," said Mrs. Pickett. "I've still got some tokens, but I want to try 'em in a pinball machine they've got here. So long. Take it easy."

"Give Jane my—" I began, but I was talking to nobody, unless to someone who was listening in.

I sighed and started to get dressed. A terrible loneliness took hold of me and, despite Mrs. Pickett's calm assurance, I was far from easy in my mind about Jane. That accident smelled decidedly fishy to me. I remembered Griselde's curious remark of last night—"perhaps she is in danger"— and that got me to brooding about Griselde. One ugly suspicion couldn't be overlooked—that she herself had baited the trap from which I barely escaped. But I just couldn't believe it.

When I went down to breakfast, I asked the clerk to

check the servants' quarter on the off-chance that she had turned up. Her jacket and cap were there, he reported, but her bed had not been slept in. Had I reason to suspect anything wrong? Perhaps he had better check up on the car as well. The car, it turned out, was safe and sound—otherwise, said the clerk, he would have advised me instantly to notify the police. "But when it is a person that disappears," he added, "it is no use to go to the police."

After breakfast, I went back to my room and had a stab at compiling some kind of story of my experiences to date. But it was a sorry jumble that came out of the typewriter, and I was gazing at it hopelessly when Dr. Clendenning reappeared, looking wispily bright and bushy-tailed.

"Know where I've been?" he chirped. "Doctor Jarowski's been showing me all over the university. They've got a statue of Copernicus with a Latin inscription about his being their most distinguished alumnus. I liked that—I could picture him coming back to class reunions."

In spite of my troubles, I laughed.

"Jarowski thought that was funny, too," said Dr. Clendenning, looking pleased. "Nice chap, Jarowski, except that he gets up too early. I'm spending the week-end with him at some health resort in the mountains before we go to the hospital. Have you seen the temptress this morning? I'd like to say good-by to her."

"The temptress," I said, "seems to have vanished."

"What!" His eyes opened wide behind the pince-nez. "You mean she's flown the coop?"

"She may have flown it, or she may have been plucked out. I don't know."

"Merciful heavens! What happened?"

He twisted his hands nervously as I told him. "Most peculiar, most peculiar," he said. "What d'you suppose her game could be, Stoney?"

"What makes you think she has a game?"

"Most people do that come traveling to these parts. I dare say you have one."

"Mine isn't much," I said. I paused and took a plunge. "I'll tell you what it is if you'll tell me yours."

The pale eyes fluttered behind the pince-nez. "Mine?"

"Yes. There is something in your luggage, Doctor, that would suggest you are not quite what you say you are. No doubt you know what I am referring to."

Dr. Clendenning looked puzzled. "What in the world could it be?"

"Also," I said, "I'd be interested to know in what language you were talking to our original chauffeur yesterday."

"German," said Dr. Clendenning promptly. "I speak a little German, and so did she. You see, I—" He stopped and a smile of comprehension appeared on his face. "That item in my luggage, could it be this?"

He reached into his bag, which was lying open on the floor, and fumbled around till he found a folded scroll. He undid the ribbon that bound it and spread it out for me. It was an elaborate sort of diploma in German script letters.

"Can you read it?" he asked. "It's from the medical school of the University of Munich and it certifies I am this word of two hundred letters here, which I believe means one who has completed their course in anesthesia. I spent a year at Munich back in the twenties."

"Oh," I said.

His eyes hardened a little. "Why were you going through my luggage, Stoney?"

"I wasn't. Miss Miratour happened to notice it while she was packing for you. Quite by accident, she said."

"Hmm," said Dr. Clendenning. "I suppose the French are always suspicious of anything German. Can't really blame them. But I don't like this business of fellow-Americans suspecting each other."

"Neither do I."

"But you're wondering why I've brought this certificate with me?"

"Well—"

"I'd better tell you. It's not a matter of any great shakes, but it just might become necessary for me to prove that I was at Munich at this particular time." He touched the date on the certificate. "You see, I'll be visiting a number of hospitals while I am in Poland, and the War Department has asked me to keep an eye out for a Nazi war criminal that's never been tracked down. Name of Nachtwitz. Karl Nachtwitz. Seems he was one of those chaps who carried out a lot of experiments with drugs on the inmates of concentration camps."

"Why would he be in Poland?"

"He was last heard of at the big concentration camp of Oswiecim, which isn't far from Kraków. They think he might possibly have made a deal with the Russians, trading his knowledge for his life. He might have managed it under some other name."

"How in the world would you be expected to recognize him?"

"Ah, that's precisely the point," said Dr. Clendenning. "I am one of the very few Americans that ever met him. We were at Munich together."

"And you think you'd remember him?"

"To be perfectly frank, I doubt it. But I might. There was something odd about him, a limp or a twitch or a tail, something odd. I can't quite remember it now, but it might come back if I saw him. The main thing is that having this extra little mission makes me feel important."

He paused and smiled modestly. Then he said, "You were going to tell me what your game is."

"It's nothing secret," I said. "As I told you, I'm a newspaperman and I'm trying to find out what I can about that American singer who disappeared recently. You've probably read about it."

He wrinkled his forehead. "Girl singer?"

"Yes. Very pretty girl singer."

"I seem to recall something about it, yes. Hmm. You don't suppose that could be the girl Jarowski mentioned, do you?"

I sat up. "What girl did Jarowski mention?"

"It probably isn't," he said, "but it struck me as curious at the time. And Jarowski seemed to be rather sorry he'd said anything about it."

"What was it he said?"

"Well, it seems that at this health resort where we're spending the week-end, there's a spendid new government sanitarium that they're all very proud of. As good as any American sanitarium, he said, and then he just happened to add that, in fact, they had a young American lady as a patient. That was all."

"You didn't ask him anything more?"

"I didn't like to, he could so obviously have bitten his tongue for saying that much. And it was none of my business."

I got up and took a turn around the room. I began to feel excited again after my low spell. "There must be mighty few American girls in Polish sanitariums," I said.

"We prefer sanitaria," said Dr. Clendenning mildly. "But otherwise, I should think you're quite right."

"How far is this place?"

"I'm not sure. In some mountains. I think he said the Sudetens."

"I thought the Sudetens were in Czechoslovakia."

"Don't look accusingly at me," said the doctor. "I didn't put them wherever they are."

"How are you getting there?"

"Jarowski has a car from the hospital. We're driving up this afternoon. In fact, he's supposed to meet me here any minute."

"Do you think he'd be willing to take me along?"

"Frankly, no," said Dr. Clendenning. "Not if he knew you were a reporter looking for that girl."

"He wouldn't have to know. I could be a reporter who wanted to write a glowing piece about their wonderful new sanitarium. In fact, that's just the kind of thing they want me to do."

Dr. Clendenning drummed nervously on the bureau. "Wouldn't that be abusing his hospitality?"

"Maybe it would. But the stakes that are involved would more than justify it."

"In that case, gentlemen"—a voice came from the doorway—"should I not at least be told what those stakes are?"

The door had opened silently, and silky-bearded little Dr. Jarowski stood there smiling.

CHAPTER TWENTY-FOUR

AS HE STEPPED into the room and closed the door, the bugle sounded from the church tower. Dr. Jarowski glanced out at the square. "After forty years," he observed, "that bugle gets on a man's nerves. On the other hand, it is a pleasing custom. No doubt the government will put a stop to it one day." He cleared his throat and looked at me, making it plain that this was a momentary digression and not a change of subject.

Still, that last remark struck me as encouraging, encouraging enough to play it straight. "Doctor," I said, "how much of our conversation did you overhear?"

"More than either you or I intended," he said. "I am not a professional eavesdropper. There are too many of them in this country."

"All I can do, then, is to repeat the suggestion I made to Doctor Clendenning. May I go with you?"

Dr. Jarowski stroked his beard. "Because you wish to see this American girl that I have been so indiscreet as to mention?"

"Yes."

"Who do you think she is?"

I reached for my wallet and brought out two pictures of Nita Romaine, one from the newspaper, the other the snapshot Les Baldwin had given me. Dr. Jarowski studied them both. "Nita Romaine," he read aloud. "I have heard something about this. On the Voice of America. There has been nothing, of course, in the Polish press."

My throat felt dry. "Do you recognize her, Doctor?"

He cocked his head and looked at the two photographs. "I have had only a glimpse of her," he said carefully. "This one, from the newspaper, I would not recognize. The other one, I am not so sure. It is something like her. But the girl I saw appeared thinner, more—more ethereal."

"Do you know why she is there?"

"No. I do not have close connections with the sanitarium. The director is a political figure, not a medical man. However, we sometimes send children from our hospital to this sanitarium, and I make occasional visits to see that everything is well for the children. On my last visit, I have chanced to hear a patient speaking English, a patient in the special section for unusual illnesses, also for people who are a little—" He paused and tapped his temple. "And the nurse who is with me tells me, 'Oh, that is an American girl. A special case.' That is all I know."

"Didn't it strike you as unusual?"

"Very. But I have told you, the director is a political

man. One does not ask him questions if one is prudent."
He glanced at me thoughtfully. "I do not think it will
do you much good to ask him questions. Still—"

My heart jumped. "You mean I can go with you?"

Dr. Jarowski held up a finger. "I have not said so. I
am thinking." He walked to the window and folded his
hands behind his back. "It is dangerous. It is dangerous
for me. But it is not of myself that I am thinking. It is of
the children. If I get into difficulties, they will remove me
and put another political director in my place."

"I'd have a word or two to say about that," interposed
Dr. Clendenning. "After all, I'm here by government invitation. It wasn't my idea, the dear lord knows."

Jarowski smiled. "Yes, that might help."

"Also," I said, "I had a personal interview with General Gritska yesterday in which he not only promised his
co-operation but specifically urged me to write about
things like this sanitarium."

"General Gritska is not a recommendation to me," said
Dr. Jarowski. "However, it would help with the director."

"At least, it gives you an out."

Dr. Jarowski smiled sadly. "Is it not a pity," he murmured, "that a man like myself must think of such
things? But it is for the children. If I can do this without
risk to them, I will try it. You may come with us."

"Doctor," I said, "you're a brick."

Again he held up a finger. "Wait. You may be followed.
Here is what you must do. Go downstairs alone and tell
the clerk that Doctor Clendenning is about to leave the
hotel but that you are staying. Leave your things here. It
would be wise to give the impression that you do not know
Doctor Clendenning very well, that you were companions
only by chance."

"Which is the simple truth," said Dr. Clendenning.
"In a way, it takes some of the fun out of it."

Dr. Jarowski frowned. "You will then tell the clerk," he continued to me, "that you are going to take a stroll, to look about the city. You will proceed, slowly and like a sight-seer, to the Church of Our Lady, from which the bugler blows. Pass through the church and out the door on the far side where we will be waiting. Understood?"

"This is more like it," said Dr. Clendenning.

"Please, my dear colleague," said Dr. Jarowski, "do not joke about these matters. If you had to live in this country, as I do, you would not think it so funny."

"I would either think it funny or cut my throat," said Dr. Clendenning. "Get a move on, Stoney."

As I walked up the street of shops toward the green square, I was suddenly sure that someone was trailing me. In the fairly crowded street, it was only a feeling, but a strong one, a feeling that among the many footsteps behind me, someone was moving steadily and purposefully.

I crossed the huge, sunlit square to the church, with an elaborate show of leisure and interest. After staring upward for a genuinely awed moment at the two medieval steeples, I passed inside, into the deep shadows of a hexagonal sort of foyer, beyond which the long nave glowed with dusty beams of stained-glass light. Someone was immediately behind me. Instead of continuing into the church itself, I stepped into one of the dark recesses just inside. A woman in a shawl came in, paused to dip her fingers in the holy water, genuflected, and moved on. I started to smile at my fears, then on her heels came a man, short and broad in the gloom, who didn't bother to genuflect. He seemed to be peering into the church, then with soft, quick steps he moved on to the far side and down the aisle, toward my intended exit. I saw his figure pass a candle-lit chapel, then stop, looking around.

I stayed where I was for a moment, then took a quick peek through the door by which I had entered. Around the periphery of the square, a little car was bumping over the cobblestones. It looked like an Austin or Morris. As it came nearer, I could make out the two doctors in the front seat, appearing uncommonly large for their size. It came abreast of the church, and I ducked fast out of my shelter and across the sidewalk. Dr. Jarowski saw me, slowed to the briefest of stops, and I jumped into the back seat. The car bounced on, out of the square.

"Why have you not gone to the side door?" demanded Dr. Jarowski rather sternly.

"I think it was being watched."

"Oh," he said. The monosyllable was grim, and he drove on in silence.

Once out of the city, we bowled along for the next hour. or more within intermittent sight of a sluggish little river that I could hardly believe was the Vistula. Dr. Jarowski said it was, though, and later, he pointed out a sign that said *Oswiecim, 15 kilometers*—the fearful camp that had lain among these gentle hills, somewhere beyond those lines of murmuring poplars.

Soon afterward we came to a road block. Dr. Jarowski's credentials seemed in good working-order, but the guard insisted on examining Clendenning's and my passports. He noted our names painstakingly and it occurred to me that he would almost certainly report our passing to his superiors, an uneasy thought.

As we drove ahead under the uplifted barrier, Dr. Clendenning asked in a quietly sardonic voice, "Who is running the concentration camp now, Doctor?"

"It is a museum," said Dr. Jarowski. "For the time being."

In the early afternoon we entered the so-called recovered territories that used to be German Silesia and, in the first fading of light, passed through the shattered city that once was Breslau. With dusk, the country grew wilder, the road steeper. Around seven, we reached the hill-perched town of Jelenia Gora, with twinkling lights among winding streets; then the road began to climb more steeply than ever, constantly twisting.

"We are almost there," said Dr. Jarowski. He didn't say much else; he was thoroughly occupied with driving along that narrow, hairpin-curving road. Presently it leveled out briefly, and Dr. Jarowski halted the car. We appeared to be on the rim of a deep cup-shaped valley, in which lights were sparsely dotted. Ahead, under brooding, amorphous mountains, a few glowing patches were visible in what apparently was a long, rambling building.

"The sanitarium," said Dr. Jarowski. "Is it not beautifully situated?"

"No doubt," said Dr. Clendenning, "but are we?"

"I beg pardon?"

"I mean, are we likely to be received with open arms at this hour?"

"Oh, we do not stay there," said Dr. Jarowski. "There is a very pleasant little mountain pension near by."

We climbed for maybe another mile, leaving the dim sanitarium behind and below, then crunched into the steep driveway of a three-story building with a big porch and a cheerful lamp over the door. A dog began to bark, then a woman came out and called to us in Polish. "She makes us welcome," said Dr. Jarowski.

We entered a parlor that looked well scrubbed, and the woman, who proved in the light to be ruddy-cheeked and motherly, led us to our various rooms. Mine was on the second floor, with a big bed on which lay an eiderdown almost as high as it was wide and long. The window looked out on the valley far below and there was a fragrance of pine in the room.

It felt like a fine place to sleep. After an impromptu but hearty dinner, I climbed into the soft bed and drifted off, in the cold, pine-scented night.

Then suddenly I was wide awake. It seemed as if I had been asleep only for a moment, but the faint beginnings of gray light were visible outside. I hadn't awakened of my own accord, I was sure. I lay tensely still and listened. There was a murmuring outside that might have been wind in branches, or low voices. Then I heard footsteps on the porch, which was in front of my window—the footsteps of several people, and no effort made now to hush them. The loud, harsh clanging of the bell shattered the silence of the sleeping house.

CHAPTER TWENTY-FIVE

I SLIPPED OUT OF BED and walked the cold tile floor to the window. All I could see at first was a vast swirl of white mist filling the endless valley below. Then, beyond the edge of the porch roof, I made out the driveway and the shapes of two automobiles. I remembered that Dr. Jarowski had parked his around in back.

I could hear the front door opening, then voices, loud and peremptory, followed by the resonant stomping of feet on the floor below. Other voices, querulous, curious, frightened, joined and swelled the disruption of the stillness. Outside, the dog began to bark.

I pulled on my clothes fast. It didn't take long, as I'd been sleeping in my underwear and I didn't bother to put on my shoes. On the floor below, a door had opened and a voice that sounded like Dr. Jarowski's could be heard among the others. Then I heard the creak of stairs.

I picked up my shoes and climbed through the window, onto the porch roof. It slanted pretty steeply, but my stockinged feet clung to it and I eased myself along to the edge. The light was a little clearer now, and I could see that it was a long drop to the driveway in front. Too long.

Behind me, inside the building, I could hear footsteps on the second floor, a loud pounding on my door, an impatient rattling of the knob, then more pounding. I edged crabwise along the roof and peered over the side. It was a more promising angle. The pension was perched against a sharp slope that came almost level with the porch roof, separated from it by a distance of maybe ten feet. The ground, in the hazy dimness, appeared to be a soft mass of bushes or furze.

Inside, a series of heavy blows sounded against the door. There came a splintering crash, and I jumped.

I was wrong about those bushes being soft. They were as stiff as military hairbrushes—must have been sumac—but at least they had some give to them. I bounced and began to slide. I let go of my shoes, which for all I know are there to this day, and clutched frantically at the springy whipping brambles all around me, but I kept on sliding, rolling, and pitching. It was a much steeper hillside than I had realized, almost a cliff, and I also realized that it plunged a lot farther down than I had thought. In no time at all, I was well below the driveway, and it became rapidly apparent that I was on one of those descents around which the main road hairpinned. It was a nightmare sensation, enhanced by the clammy whiteness of the mist around me.

From far above came voices, and a beam of light swinging way to the left, then way to the right.

Suddenly the bushes closed, and the declivity ended in space. For a fraction of a second, I thought I was going over a precipice, then with a good, hard bump, as grateful just then as a nurse's cool hand, I landed on familiar macadam. I had hit the road, evidently at a lower bend of its spiral up to the pension.

I lay there for a bit, dazed and bruised. And yet with a certain fierce clarity of mind. Through the mist, I could see the lights of the pension, ablaze by now, and they looked to be the best part of half a mile above me. If that were so, then the long, sweeping turns of the road must cover a good four times that distance, which meant that pursuers, unless they took the same hard way I'd taken, would be quite a while getting there. Even if they came in a car, they'd be a good five minutes on that corkscrew road. I breathed easier and made an effort to sit up.

Nothing seemed to be broken. After a moment I tried standing—keeping well under the overhang—and that seemed to work pretty well, too. I ached, but all joints functioned. My hands felt wet and I realized that they were both bleeding. But only from bramble scratches.

The sky was growing steadily lighter, the mist dissolving into fleecy shreds. I could see now that the road took another dip a little way to my left and I could make out the entrance to a gravel drive just at the curve. That had to be the driveway to the sanitarium, and now I could see it, the long, sprawling outline against the graying hillside.

My brain began to work fast. If those intruders at the pension were a bunch of strong-arm boys, they probably wouldn't know I had any interest in the sanitarium, wouldn't look for me there. I was a torn and bleeding figure—surely the sanitarium would grant me healing shelter.

An ominous sound came from above—the starting of a car. I strained my ears. It was only one car, I was sure of that. I waited a moment, listening, then ducked across the road and peered over the farther edge. There was another sharp descent, but it was easy enough to lower myself cautiously over the rim, into a clump of bushes that received me as if into a hammock. A hammock with brambles.

The sound of the car grew fainter for a moment, then louder as it came round a bend, fainter once more, then steadily louder. The sweep of headlights struck the road I had just left, and with them came the dancing beam of a spotlight. Then all three lights flashed past me, and behind them the dark shape of the car, round the next bend and out of sight. An instant later the lights reappeared fifty yards below me, vanished again, reappeared once more, then I didn't see them.

Apparently that car wasn't looking for me except on spec. The men left behind were probably doing that. Maybe Jarowski was in the car that had just passed, maybe Clendenning, too. I pulled myself back over the edge of the road, ears alert for the second car, and started along the macadam toward the near-by driveway. It occurred to me, ingeniously it seemed, that the sound of the auto having passed would lend substance to my appearance at the sanitarium door. It would be assumed that I had fallen out of it, or been struck by it. I remembered that victims of auto accidents often were knocked out of their shoes.

I turned into the driveway. It rose steeply, then leveled out under an old-fashioned porte-cochere, from beneath which wide wooden steps led to a long, glassed-in veranda. A single light, made pale by dawn, burned inside the glass door. The door was locked, and I began to beat on it, with what was intended to sound like feeble desperation, and gave out with a couple of moans.

Presently, the main door beyond the glass one opened, and an old watchman—judging from his rumpled alpaca coat—poked his head out. I beat a couple more times on the glass, made sure he noticed me, then gave one good, loud moan and dropped in a graceful collapse on the steps.

The glass door opened and the watchman turned a flashlight on me. I raised a clutching hand and let out a few gasps. The stage, I was beginning to think, had lost a great actor when I went into journalism. Then I wasn't so sure. The glass door closed and the watchman disappeared into the other one. I sat up, feeling disgruntled, then quickly resumed my huddled position. The watchman was coming back with an elderly, grumpy-looking nurse in blue and white stripes. The watchman held the light on me, and she came down a couple of steps and gave me a distasteful inspection. Then she said something in Polish. I replied with a couple of gasps and a moan, and they both went away.

This time several minutes passed. Then the nurse and the watchman came back, accompanied by two orderlies, or so I assumed—sleepy-looking men in white coats. They had a stretcher which they proceeded to lay out at the foot of the steps, then they half lifted, half eased me down onto it. Grunting, they trundled me up the steps, across the veranda, and into a lofty room which, like the pension, had a clean, piny smell, but with overtones of antiseptics. It was lighted now by an ironwork chandelier that dangled from the beamed and whitewashed ceiling and had a little row of weak bulbs around it. Ceiling and chandelier were just about all I could see. The orderlies deposited me on some kind of sofa; then they both lit cigarettes.

Presently I heard footsteps; then a very young and pink-cheeked man in a white coat was bending over me. An intern, I assumed. He spoke to me in Polish. I shook my head and he said, "Amerykanski?" I decided my best bet was to stick to gasps and groans.

The intern gave the nurse a questioning look, then shrugged, and unbuttoned my shirt. He applied a stethoscope, then ran his hands over my arms and legs. He said something to the nurse and looked at his watch. The nurse's reply sounded brusque and unencouraging. If I was any judge, the intern was debating whether he should wake some superior, and the nurse was taking a decided negative. Then the intern, with the air of a man who has found a happy compromise, said something to the two orderlies and they sighed and put out their cigarettes and picked me up again.

I couldn't see much except whitewashed walls and brown wooden doors as I was carried down a long corridor. Then I heard a clang, and was carried into a spacious elevator, with the watchman taking the helm. We rose very slowly, three stories; then I was in another corridor that ended, suddenly, at a pair of heavy, bolted doors. I could hear the watchman fumbling around with keys, and a thought struck me, a thought at once exciting and frightening. As a foreign stranger, was I about to be left in the section for special cases?

A key turned in a lock, a bolt slid, then the doors opened and we passed into another corridor, like the last but with a difference: in the upper part of each door—there were half a dozen on either side—was a small aperture, like the old speakeasy entrances. The watchman unlocked one of these doors and I was carried into a square, whitewashed room and tipped over slightly out of the stretcher and onto a bed. Except for the bed, the room was completely bare. I saw something else—there were bars at the lone window.

The intern touched my forehead briefly, then dusted his hands and walked away with the look of a man who had done his best. The nurse and the orderlies followed. The watchman hesitated and called something after the intern. I could hear his answer—a casual oh-don't-bother sort of answer. If the question was what I thought it was—namely, should he lock the door?—I could hardly believe my luck. The watchman shrugged and followed the others into the corridor. The door remained ajar.

I heard the double doors down the corridor close with a loud click. It was a somewhat dampening sound; on the other hand, it meant I would have plenty of warning if anyone came. Unless somebody had been left on watch in the corridor.

That I had to find out. I got off the bed, tiptoed to the door, and very cautiously peeked out. The corridor, into which pale daylight seeped through a small barred window at the far end, was empty. All the doors except mine were shut and there was no sound anywhere.

Twelve doors—and behind one of them, I was almost certain, was Nita Romaine, though why, for what sinister reason, heaven only knew. I padded along the corridor, looking at each door. All were alike, each bolted and locked. I tried applying my eye to the little apertures, one after another. Each one commanded a good view of the room beyond, all of them rooms like mine with barred windows, and I could see slumbering forms in white iron beds under gray blankets in eight of the twelve rooms. Of the eight, I was reasonably sure that four were women, and of those four, two were fair and two were dark. That reduced the odds considerably in my favor. But if I tried knocking and got the wrong one, the jig was up.

I stood in the center of the dim corridor, trying to think. Then, in a voice that has never been noted for tunefulness, I began to sing softly but, I hoped, loud enough: *"Oh, say can you see."*

Nothing happened.

I moved close to one of the two magic doors, peering through the aperture and tried again.

"Oh, say can you see."

The sleeping form stirred and turned. A face, deathly white in a mist of dark hair, lifted from the pillow.

"Oh, say can you—"

A voice, dazed and thin, joined mine.

"—see, by the dawn's early light—"
I tapped gently on the door.

CHAPTER TWENTY-SIX

IT TOOK HER A LONG TIME to get out of bed. To me, standing with my eye pressed to the aperture, it seemed an
agonizingly endless process. Once or twice she seemed
to feel the effort too great and sank back again. Then
I'd tap and hum, and she'd make another try. Finally
she got her legs out from under the gray blanket, with
a brief glimpse of white flesh under a coarse, gray gown.
She sat on the edge of the bed, then, staring dully at
the door. Finally, she rose and came toward me, moving
with trancelike slowness.

Mentally, I compared the photographs of Nita Romaine
to this white and floating face. I remembered the word
Dr. Jarowski had used—ethereal—and I could see why
he hadn't been sure about the photo. This could be the
same girl, but if it was, God only knew what she had been
through. It was not only an ethereal face, it was a haunted
one, a face living in some terrible dream. It swayed toward
me, then loomed big against the aperture. I could hear
a muffled, feeble voice saying, "Who is it?"

"It's another American," I said, trying to make my voice
penetrate without rousing the whole corridor. "I've come
to get you."

"I can't hear you." And I could just barely hear her.

I tried again. "Are you Nita Romaine?"

"What?"

"Are you Nita Romaine?"

"I can't hear you."

I risked a bellow. "Are you Nita Romaine?"

My voice seemed to reverberate throughout the wing.

Somewhere, somebody banged on the inside of a door. The face on the other side of the aperture continued to stare blankly. Then suddenly white hands covered it, and the girl turned away, half lurched toward the bed, and sank down on it.

Beyond the double doors that blocked the corridor, I heard footsteps. Then the sound of a key in the lock. Quickly I ducked back into my own room and threw myself onto the bed, my mind in a turmoil.

I heard the double doors open and close, then shambling footsteps on this side. They didn't sound like alarmed footsteps, more a matter of routine. Then, through the little space where my door stood ajar, I saw an attendant in gray with a huge tray of dishes. I heaved a sigh of relief. This, evidently, was the breakfast hour. I glanced at my wrist to see what time it was, and realized I had left my watch in the pension. Well, couldn't be helped.

In the corridor I could hear keys jangling, then the sound of a door opening, and a few words exchanged. Then that door closed, and the same thing happened at the next one. I slipped off the bed and took a squint through the crack between door and jamb. I could see the attendant, who appeared a weary little fellow, opening the third door across the way from mine. He set down the tray, took a dish from it, and placed the dish inside the door. Then he said one of the few Polish words I recognized "Dziendobry" — *good morning* — and closed that door.

The fifth door on that side was the American girl's. The fourth room was empty. He passed it and unlocked the fifth one. He opened it and stopped to put down the tray, and in that instant, I was across the hall and on top of him from behind. I clapped my hand over his mouth and spun him round and back across the hall and into my room, without a sound other than one quick gurgle of fear.

Then I closed my own door in his face and slid the outside bolt. For a moment he was silent, stunned I suppose, and I raced back to the dark-haired girl's room.

Even as I stepped inside, I could hear the flailing of fists against the other side of my door, and muffled cries. But neither sound carried very far. I closed the door of the girl's room behind me.

She was still half lying on the bed, her face buried in her thin hands, her dark hair hanging loose and straggly. She wasn't exactly sobbing, but a queer sound, a lost, bewildered sighing came from her.

"Miss Romaine," I said.

She didn't move.

I crossed the little room and shook her shoulder. "Sit up," I said almost roughly. "Listen to me. I'm an American. I'm a friend of Les Baldwin's."

A shiver ran through her and she sat up, taking her hands away from her face. "Who?" she said, and she sounded frightened.

"Les Baldwin," she repeated. "Why do I know that name?"

"Because you're engaged to marry him."

Her eyes turned full on me, wide, incredulous, groping for something. "Oh, no—" she began, "but—Les Baldwin— Les Baldwin—" She sank back, pressing her fist to her mouth, and in those deep, wide eyes, light flickered.

Outside, in the corridor, I heard the double doors flung open, hard, authoritatively.

"You are Nita Romaine, aren't you?" I shook her shoulder again. "Aren't you? Nita Romaine?"

The eyes were pleading. "I—I don't know who I am. I—"

The door flew open behind me and I turned. General Gritska was standing there, his hands on his hips, his sensual mouth tight, his eyes blue lumps of ice.

CHAPTER TWENTY-SEVEN

HE DIDN'T SAY ANYTHING for a while, just looked at me. He didn't look at the girl at all. Presently a sardonic smile appeared on his moist lips, as if the situation, outrageous though it was, had its amusing aspects. I wished I knew what they were.

Behind him, faces shimmered in the corridor, faces of men in white coats, of nurses in blue and white stripes. General Gritska turned and said something to one of the nurses, then stood aside for her to enter the room. Remaining aside, he bowed slightly toward me with heavy ironic courtesy.

"Please return to your own room," he said.

I looked down at the dark-haired girl. The eyes sunk in the white face had turned blank again, moving from me to the nurse.

"Good-by for now," I said to her. "Try to remember—"

Gritska's voice cut across the room like a whip.

"Please."

"Coming," I said. I walked past him into the corridor. Across the way, an orderly was unfastening the bolt of my own room. The breakfast attendant staggered out, stared wildly around, then pointed at me, babbling in Polish. Then he saw the General and scuttled for his tray. I felt Gritska's beefy hand on my back. "Please, to your room."

I walked into the whitewashed box. The bars at the window looked thick in the light that poured between them. Behind me I heard Gritska's voice speaking coldly in Polish, then the sound of the door closing.

I glanced around. Gritska was standing inside with his

arms folded.

"Sit down," he said.

I sat down on the bed, not entirely out of obedience—my knees had gone to water. "Sorry I can't offer you a chair," I said.

"Do not apologize," said Gritska. The little smile reappeared. "It is a very nice room. You will like it when you get used to it."

My stomach took a cold drop. But I made myself say, "I don't intend to get used to it."

"You as well might."

"You mean I might as well?"

The smile vanished. "I have not come here for lessons in English," he snapped. "My English is quite sufficient to tell you that you are going to remain in this room for some time."

"Until the Embassy hears about it."

The smile came back, mockingly pitying. "My poor fellow. What do you think your Embassy can do for you now?"

"Plenty." But I had my doubts.

"Perhaps you do not understand your position," said Gritska. "I will try to explain. In my poor English." He paused to glare. "You have come to this sanitarium of your own volition. Your condition was plainly abnormal. During the short time that elapsed before proper treatment could be arranged, you have assaulted an attendant and you have broken into the room of a woman patient. These are facts to which there are many witnesses. If it becomes necessary, these facts will be placed before your Embassy. It will make no difference. You will remain here until our excellent medical staff certifies that your condition is such that you may safely be released. It will probably be a matter of several months."

"What!" I sat up straight on the bed. "What do you

mean, several months?"

"I think it is quite clear," said Gritska. He showed his teeth. "Or have I made another mistake in grammar?"

"You've made a mistake in something."

"No," said Gritska. "But you have. You have made a severe mistake. And let me tell you this. You are very lucky. If I were not a kind-hearted man, you would not disappear merely for a few months. You would disappear completely."

"Why?"

"Because you have interfered with matters that are of grave importance."

"Because I've found out where you're hiding Nita Romaine?"

"I do not understand."

"Oh, yes, you do."

His brow wrinkled, as if he were making a genuine effort to think. "Perhaps you are suffering from a delusion," he said. "Perhaps you think that the patient whom you recently disturbed is the woman of whom you speak."

"I know damned well she is."

"She happens to be the daughter of a government official. She speaks a little English. She has been undergoing treatment for a mental disorder for a period of months."

"I see."

"I am glad that you do," said Gritska. "You may even come to believe it." He paused and let the next two words sink in. "In time."

He smiled and turned, opened the door, and stepped out. Automatically I lunged across the room, then began to beat my fists on the closed door. I heard the bolt slide, then a key turn. "You can't do this to me," I yelled. From the corridor came only the sound of heavy, receding footsteps.

CHAPTER TWENTY-EIGHT

"YOU CAN'T DO THIS TO ME," is one of the most hopeless phrases, I guess, that there is. When the user knows perfectly well that it isn't true is about the only time it's ever used. In my days as a police reporter, I used to wonder why prisoners went on saying it, long after the reverse had been thoroughly proven. Now I knew. That phrase was hope. I shouted it for maybe half an hour that morning.

I hated to stop doing it. It had been something to do. Now there was nothing to do. I felt in my pants pockets, then in the pockets of my torn coat, but there weren't any cigarettes.

I tried looking out of the window. The bars didn't help, but the view was all right. My room was at the front of the building, apparently on the top floor, and it looked down on the whole magnificent sweep of valley. I could see our road, a thin black strip appearing and disappearing among the trees. Here and there on the long slopes, the dark green of pinewoods parted for the paler green of grassy hillsides, dotted with the white trunks of birch, lindens in yellow bloom, mountain ash with its ruddy clusters. The valley itself was a great bowl, though the hills that formed its farther rim were considerably lower. Down there were great stretches of pastureland and the tawny squares of grainfields, and a string of glittering blue ponds. Far across the valley rose the red roofs and towers of a town—must have been Jelenia Gora that I'd thought was so pretty the night before. It was still pretty, but my approach was different. The difference between a pretty girl in your arms and one on a magazine cover.

After a while the door was unlocked and a nurse came

in accompanied by two burly attendants. She was carrying a coarse gray nightshirt, like the gown worn by the American girl, and it was made plain to me that I was to put it on. I didn't see much use arguing, or in standing on my modesty, especially as the nurse was elderly and warty.

I slipped on the scratchy garment, then asked in somewhat indelicate sign language what the sanitary arrangements were. The nurse and both attendants laughed and the former pointed under the bed to an old-fashioned chamber pot. I made more signs indicating I'd like to wash as well. They all laughed again and shrugged and went out, taking my own clothes with them.

Later—close to noon, I judged by the sun—the door was unlocked again and an attendant slid a dish quickly into the room and banged the door. I caught a glimpse of one or more figures in the corridor. The stuff in the dish was some kind of meat stew, tasty enough, and I gulped it down. There wasn't any spoon—God knows what they thought I could have done with a spoon—and I licked my fingers when I was through. There was something unpleasantly animal about the whole feeding process.

Presently I began to suspect that there was something worse than animal about it. A heavy lassitude came over my limbs and my head began to feel light. For a while I clung to the bars and tried to concentrate on the shifting shadows in the valley, but it was no use. I could either lie down on the bed or slide to the floor. So I lay down on the bed.

The door opened again and a young man in a white coat came in, alone for a change. He sat on the edge of the bed, felt my pulse, then slipped the loose sleeve of my nightshirt back. I realized he had a syringe in his hand. I was too torpid to protest. I felt a sharp sting, then the feel of the needle inside my skin, and a little twinge as it came out. The young man patted my shoulder and went away.

I lay there wondering what this was going to do to me. And then, strangely, I began to feel fine. Wonderful. The strength flowed back into my arms and legs and my mind grew beautifully crystalline. Why, I'd be out of this place in no time. What was I worried about, anyway? If nothing else, I could tear those bars out by their roots and jump. I walked across the room, my stride springy, and seized the bars gaily in my hands. How ridiculous that they **didn**'t give way. What was wrong with them? I shook them hard, and slowly realized that nothing was going to happen. Cold doubts crept into that crystal mind— why had it seemed so crystal? It certainly wasn't now. It didn't even feel like mine. It seemed to be floating around the room watching me. My knees, those fine, springy knees, began to buckle. I stumbled back to the bed.

Almost at once I began to feel good again. I sat up, and the feeling ebbed at once. It was simpler to stay lying down and feel good.

Outside the window the afternoon was beginning to fade. Once more the door opened and two men came in. The first was an attendant who crossed the room and reached up between the bars. A metal shutter fell into place with a clang. For an instant the room was totally dark, then a bleak, bluish light suddenly flooded it. I couldn't tell where it came from at first; then I saw it emanated from a square hole in the ceiling that had been invisible in daylight. The orderly went out, closing the door, and I twisted my head—carefully, so as not to disturb that lovely clarity—for a look at the second man.

He was middle-aged and he didn't wear a white coat, just ordinary dark business clothes. He had a little mustache and his face was lined and rather kindly. But there was something about his eyes that troubled me. I tried to remember where I had seen eyes like that before, and into my crystal mind, the recollection flashed. One of our reporters once, a good one, had made a deal with the opposition paper to give them our page-one layout before every edition. If he had been some pipsqueak, it would have been different, but he was a good man and he had sold out. I remembered his eyes when we caught him. This man's eyes had the same unhappy look.

He stood there silently, staring down at me. Then in labored, guttural English, he said, "You are feeling better, yes?"

"I feel queer."

He pursed his lips and nodded. "You have had a very bad fall. You remember that, yes?"

"That isn't why I feel queer."

He repeated, "You have had a very bad fall. You have perhaps struck the head."

"I didn't strike my head."

He appeared to ignore me. "You have had a very bad fall. That is why you have come here. Because you have had a bad fall."

Although it was guttural, his voice had a deep resonance, almost a melodious quality. It was soothing.

"That isn't why I came here," I said.

"You have had a very—"

"I came here to find the American girl in that room across the hall." I was conscious of my own voice rising a little hysterically.

"—a very bad fall. That is why you are here. There is no other reason. There is no American girl in the room across the hall."

"You know there is. She—"

"A very bad fall. There is no American girl here." His voice sank to a drowsy hum. He leaned over me and said it again and again. The way he said it, it sounded all right. It sounded true. I knew it wasn't, but it was easier and pleasanter to pretend that it was. Once I made an attempt to sit up, to shake it off, but immediately the sense of drowsy well-being turned into dizziness, and I sank back. He went on repeating, "A very bad fall—no American girl here—"

I realized I was saying it with him. It was pleasant to say it with him, like reciting poetry with someone who shares your tastes. And pretty soon I was asleep.

When I woke up, the room was empty, but someone was still murmuring, "A very bad fall—no American girl here—" The words were coming from my own lips. I clamped them together and the sound stopped, but not the rhythm of it.

I tried sitting up. It wasn't so bad now. In fact, after one short spell of dizziness, I felt almost normal. I wondered how long I had been asleep. There was no way to tell in the bluish light. But it must have been quite a long time because I was ravenously hungry.

Near the door sat another bowl, this time full of bland-looking porridge. I thought about it for a while. Undoubtedly there had been some sedative in the other one that prevented my struggling against the hypodermic later. But they'd get the hypodermic in by force if they had to. And I was getting hungrier by the minute. I picked up the bowl and ate, scooping the porridge up in my fingers.

The same routine followed: the lassitude, the visit from the young intern, the hypodermic, the sense of strength and well-being and clarity, the weakness and dizziness when I tried to rise.

In due time the doctor with the mustache and the guilty eyes returned. He began as he had the first time. "You are feeling better, yes?"

I stared up at him, at the lined face and at those eyes. "Doctor," I said, "where did you learn English?"

He started to ignore the question. "You have had a bad

fall—" he began, then he stopped. The temptation to answer was apparently too great. "I have studied at your University of Pennsylvania."

"No kidding!" I exclaimed. "What year?"

"Many years ago. Nineteen twenty-four. But you must not ask me questions. You are the patient, I am the doctor. You—"

"What kind of a doctor are you?" My voice was suddenly bitter. "What are you trying to do to me?"

He stood there silently for a moment, twisting his hands together. They were slim, delicate hands. His eyes seemed faraway and his mouth worked. Then he came back to earth. "You have had a bad fall. A very bad fall."

"Doctor! Answer me!"

"A very bad fall. That is why you are here. There is no American girl here."

I tried to interrupt, but my brain was already wearied with the effort to speak on my own. I lay still, and the voice drifted monotonously, rhythmically, into my consciousness. Soon, as before, I was saying it with him, and I slept.

When I next awoke, I felt as if I had been asleep only a short while. There was no sense of being refreshed and the rhythm of the doctor's voice still rippled through my brain. But something had changed. It took me several seconds to realize that the shutter had been opened, that the room was full of daylight. At the same time I realized that there was a knocking at the door. A voice was calling, "Mr. Rockwell, Mr. Rockwell." It was the same doctor's voice. I sat up and blinked.

"You have a visitor, Mr. Rockwell," came the doctor's voice. "May we come in?"

I nodded wonderingly. The door opened and the doctor entered, then bowed to admit a familiar-looking man in a pin-stripe blue suit. I knew him perfectly well but I couldn't for the life of me remember his name.

"Rockwell," he exclaimed, coming toward me. "How are you?"

"All right." My voice sounded strange and dull. "I have had a very bad fall."

"So I hear," the man said. "The Embassy was notified of it last night. The Foreign Office said we could see you and I got down here as soon as I could. We're worried about you."

"Thank you," I said. I remembered who he was now. Watkins, of course. Silly of me.

"I wanted you to know we're doing what we can," Watkins was saying. "However—"

"Can you get me out of here?"

The words were an effort. Behind Watkins's back, the doctor caught my eye and held it. His lips moved soundlessly.

"It's an awkward situation, Rockwell," said Watkins. "As I understand it, you came here voluntarily after your fall. The chief doctor here has certified that you are not in any condition to be removed. We've asked permission to have you brought back to the Embassy but they say you must remain under observation a while. There's nothing more we can do for the moment."

"Thank you."

"Maybe you'd like us to notify your wife in case she's worried at not hearing from you."

"Thank you." Then some dim protest stirred in my mind. "No, no, it would be better if you notified Mrs.— Mrs.—" The name was gone. Feverishly I groped for it in hazy swirls of memory. "Mrs. Pickett." I came up with it triumphantly.

"Oh, I see," said Watkins. "Where do I reach her?"

I put my hand to my forehead, trying to think. "Your man—your man in—the other city. He will know."

"Baird?"

"Yes. Baird."

"Right-o," said Watkins. "So we'll take that load off your mind." He glanced toward the doctor hesitantly. "Would you mind very much if I saw the patient alone for a moment?"

"Not at all," said the doctor graciously. Again his eyes caught mine briefly, his lips moved, then he stepped out of the room and closed the door.

Watkins bent over me anxiously. "Tell me, boy," he said, "are you sure you're all right?"

My whole being wanted to tell him *no, no, no,* but my lips—I could hear them—said, "Yes, thank you."

"You don't seem normal. I suppose that's your fall."

"Yes. It was a very bad fall."

He glanced at the door, then at me again. "What about the American girl you thought was here?"

Tell him, tell him, tell him, my inside fairly screamed. But I could hear a voice saying, "There is no American girl here."

"I guess that's that, then," said Watkins. "Chin up. We'll get you out of here as soon as we can." He gave my shoulder a friendly little shake, then walked to the door.

I tried to cry after him, to call him back, anything, but no words came. He gave me a worried smile, then the door closed behind him. Footsteps died away in the corridor; then complete, dead silence.

CHAPTER TWENTY-NINE

THE NEXT TIME I WOKE UP it was to the bluish light of the shuttered room. It must have been a long while later, because I felt completely rested and relaxed. Except for the maddening sameness of the light, the loss of any sense of time, it might have been any ordinary awakening. I tried sitting up and there was no dizziness. I tried standing and it went all right.

There was a fresh bowl of stew by the door, and I noticed also that the chamber pot had been emptied and replaced. I was hungry, but not so hungry as before, and I decided to think things over for a while before I succumbed to appetite, and to the same routine.

One thing seemed fairly certain, whatever drug I was being given hadn't taken more than a superficial hold as yet. I was also reasonably sure that the same drug was being administered to Nita Romaine. But why? Why to either of us? What sort of drug was it? Could it be—

It had to be. It had to be the drug that lay behind all those Iron Curtain political trials, the drug of whose existence western science was virtually sure but at whose nature it could only guess. The drug that produced those smoothly flowing confessions—Mindszenty's and Rajk's in Hungary, Kostov's in Bulgaria—would Nita Romaine and I be standing in the dock some day, admitting to espionage and heaven knew what skulduggery?

But, in her case, anyway, forgetfulness seemed to be the aim—a confession wouldn't be much good from somebody who didn't even know who she was. Maybe that was the first step. Or maybe she knew something—had found out something—that was being deliberately driven from her mind. Just as she was being driven from mine. But what could she have known? Had she really been having an affair with Gritska, caught him in some dreadful indiscretion? The date of an attack on Yugoslovia, maybe? Some plot against the bad old imperialists?

I abandoned that murky line of thought. What I had better be thinking about, while this period of lucidity lasted, was how in the name of all that was holy I was going to get myself out of this mess. There had to be a way; there was always a way. People got out of Alcatraz, and that was a tougher proposition than this.

I considered the bowl of stew. Presumably, I had to get that down before the intern with the syringe would come. He would hardly come alone otherwise. I stopped and snapped my fingers. Alone, he came alone. There was the weak point, the frail link in their chain.

Probably he, or someone, checked through the aperture on whether the bowl was empty or not. Maybe someone was watching now. I went to the door and pressed my eye to the little square, but I couldn't see anything. It was that one-way kind of glass. In any event, it wouldn't hurt to act things out.

I slid the chamber pot part way under the bed, as if casually getting it out of sight. Then I grabbed greedily for the bowl and sat down with it on the bed, hunching over it with my back half turned to the door. I scooped the stew out, slowly as if mouthful by mouthful, and dropped each soggy lump into the pot. Then I replaced the bowl near the door, stretched and yawned comfortably and lay down.

How much time went by, I'll never know. Probably half an hour, but it seemed like half a day. The blood was racing through me. I felt as I had when a child, lying endlessly awake in the early hours of Christmas.

Finally I heard footsteps. There was a long pause, then the door opened. I forced myself to relax, to get the tension out of my muscles. The young intern was standing there. He glanced at me casually, then closed the door. He strolled toward the bed and sat down on the edge. My eyes measured him. I guessed I had maybe ten pounds on him. He felt my pulse, then touched my forehead. Ten pounds on my side, plus surprise.

Gently he slid back my right sleeve. His left hand held my forearm lightly; his right hand came toward it with the syringe. This was it.

My free hand came fast across my chest and grabbed his right wrist, and my own right shot straight up and belted him under the chin. He slipped part way off the bed and I hurled myself against him, my fingers digging into his wrist, holding that damnable syringe out of harm's way. He was half on the floor now, on one knee and swaying backward, and I was over him. I sent my fist smashing into his face with all the strength I had, and he keeled over, suspended only by his right wrist, which I still gripped. His fingers were tight on the syringe. I shook his wrist fiercely, but he didn't let loose.

Up till now he hadn't made a sound. Too surprised, I guess. But suddenly he let out a whoop, and I picked up the chamber pot with my free hand and smashed it to shreds over his head. After that, he didn't make any more noise, or move, either. His fingers loosened on the syringe and it dropped with a tinkly clatter to the floor. I kicked it beyond his reach, then I let go of his wrist, and his arm fell limply with a squashy thud.

I stood still for a moment, getting my breath, and then I heard footsteps. Running. I cursed that one yell he'd let out. Quickly I stooped and picked up the syringe, and at the same instant, the door flew open and an attendant bowled into the room. He was a big, hulking man, with a heavy red face and stupid little eyes. For a moment, he stared down unbelievingly at the prostrate body, then he turned. His little eyes gleamed.

With a snort like an angry bull's, he came at me, his big hands poised to crush. I did the only thing I could think of. I leveled the syringe at him, and he stopped dead. Into those eyes crept a look of fascinated horror, the look of a primitive savage suddenly confronted with some awful magic of a strange god. I took a step toward him, and he cringed back. I could hardly believe my luck. I took another step, holding the syringe like a tiny rapier, and he threw up his hands, those hands that a moment before had been clutching at me, and cowered behind them. "*Nie, nie,*" he cried, his voice fearful and pleading.

Boy, I thought, *this is some heap big medicine they've been shooting into me if it scares the hired help like this.*

The corridor was quiet. Apparently, this man alone had been assigned to backstop the intern, chosen for brute strength and luckily for me, brute brain. Without taking my eyes off him, I closed the door, then I pointed down at the intern and made undressing motions. It took a few seconds to make him understand what I wanted, but once he did, he couldn't obey too fast.

While he pulled off the intern's white jacket and trousers, and undid his shoes, I slipped out of my nightshirt, sliding first one arm and then the other out of the loose sleeves so that only for a second was the syringe out of play. Then, keeping its point an inch from his face that was mottled now with fear and dripping sweat, I made him kneel and put the intern's shoes on my feet, then hold the trousers for me to step into, pull them up and fasten them. The white jacket was harder, but I managed by putting one arm through a sleeve, then changing the syringe from one hand to the other, keeping the needle steadily on him, then the other arm in the other sleeve, and he buttoned it. I was all set—all dressed up with God knew where to go.

I turned the poor quaking devil around and touched the back of his wet, red neck with the needle, then gave him a slight knee in the rump. He understood that quickly enough—forward march. We moved together to the door and into the corridor. The small barred window at the far end showed black sky, stars, and the dim shapes of treetops. That was a piece of luck and it explained why only one attendant had come. At the other end, the double doors stood a trifle ajar, presumably for the intern's entrance. There was no sound beyond them.

I gave my guide a light prick and steered him across the hall to the dark-haired American girl's door. As well be hanged for a sheep as a lamb. The man might have a key —he must have had a key to my room. He came face up to her door and stopped. I kept the needle touching his neck and reached round him and pointed to the lock. He turned his head a little and gave me a look of despair. I increased the pressure and he groaned. The sweat was pouring off him now and the back of his neck glistened greasily in the dim light.

Then the known evil of future punishment yielded to present unknown fear. He reached in his pocket and pulled out a ring of keys. His hands trembled as he selected one and fitted it into the lock. He undid the bolt and pushed the door open.

The American girl's room was lighted like mine, bleakly and bluishly from the ceiling. She was sitting on the edge of her bed, in her gray gown, staring blankly toward us. I suppose that, like me, she had no idea whether it was day or night, time to sleep or time to eat or time to sit and stare.

"Nita," I said softly. "Nita Romaine. It's me. Your American friend."

She gave a frightened little gasp and didn't move. I didn't dare move, either. "You'll have to do it yourself," I said. "Make yourself do it. Remember Les Baldwin. Think of him. Make yourself get up. We're going away."

For a moment she clutched at the bed's edge, then, slowly she swayed to her feet.

"Walk," I called softly. "You can do it. Walk. Walk toward me."

She glided across the room like a sleepwalker, her thin hands held uncertainly in front of her.

"You're doing fine," I said. "Keep coming."

She reached the door. I gave my tame Cerberus a spot of needle and he stood aside for her, then she fell against me. I caught her with my free arm and twisted the slack in the back of her gown into a knot and gripped it. "You've got to stand up," I said. "I can't do it. I'm busy."

She straightened and then she saw the syringe in my hand. Her mouth fell open and suddenly she began to giggle. It was the kind of giggle Topsy might have given if she'd found Uncle Tom holding a whip over S. Legree.

"Close the door, Nita," I said, "and get a grip on yourself. We've got a long way ahead of us."

Maybe it was the lingering effect of that hypnotic drug, but I practically believed what I said. And yet my mind knew that it was hopeless. Almost. There was a chance, just a bare chance, that only the old night watchman would be downstairs. I wondered if it was close to morning or early evening or what. Well, nothing like finding out.

A light jab with the syringe, and the three of us moved forward. The girl still clung to me, but she managed to walk more steadily now, the effect of gliding heightened by the noiselessness of her bare feet. Up till now, she hadn't spoken a word. Then she said, in a faint voice, "Where are we going?"

"Home," I said.

"Home?"

"Home. Keep moving." I wished I believed it.

We passed through the double doors and into the main section of the corridor beyond. It looked endless, the brown doors in the white walls dwindling into the dim distance like one of those optical illusion problems. The whole place was deathly quiet except for the sick sound of someone coughing somewhere.

On our right, I saw the grillwork of the elevator shaft.

The attendant stopped and, turning his head cautiously, gave me a questioning glance. Obviously, we couldn't ring for the lift, but where in the devil were the stairs? You'd have expected them to be near the shaft, but they weren't in sight. Maybe one of these anonymous doors led to them. Maybe they were at the far end. I hadn't any idea and—the unpleasant thought struck me—the attendant would soon know it. He could lead us wherever he chose.

He was still looking at the elevator shaft. I shook my head and nudged him on. I thought that a sly gleam appeared in his eye, but we kept walking. On and on, down that endless nightmare corridor. Then I saw a space between two of the doors and, to my limp relief, the head of a stair rail. It was a short-lived relief. Just as we came abreast of the stairs, footsteps sounded, coming up. Slowly.

I looked around. There was no place to hide, unless we tried doors at random. There was a better chance than that, but not much better. In my white jacket, it was just possible that I could pass muster in the dimness as an intern taking a patient somewhere, with the help of a meek attendant. Anybody whom I'd fool ought to have his head examined, but it was the only thing I could see to try. And it would be better on the stairs, where the light was dimmer yet, and where we might be able to brush past quickly.

The footsteps were coming closer.

I gave the red neck a flick and nudged him toward the stairs. He took one step downward, and then a figure emerged into the gloom of the landing below. It was the doctor with the mustache.

Well, Rockwell, I thought, *it was fun while it lasted.*

"Look," whispered the girl beside me.

"Ssh."

The doctor paused on the landing, wheezing a little.

Then he looked up and stared. I could see his face clearly enough for its puzzled frown to be visible. He came up a few steps, his hand on the rail, and said something in Polish to the attendant.

My hand had gone fluttery, but I kept the needle where it was. No use throwing my aces away yet.

The attendant waved his arms helplessly and made a few frightened squawking noises in his throat. The doctor said something impatient, something like "Stuff and nonsense, my good man." Then he came up another couple of steps, took a good look at me, and gaped. He steadied himself on the railing and something approaching an incredulous smile touched his face.

"It is you," he said in a stunned voice.

"Yep," I said wearily, "it's me."

He shook his head. "How did you do it?"

"Doesn't make much difference now, does it?"

He didn't answer. He continued to stare, plucking thoughtfully at his mustache. Then he said, "I will send this man away."

"No you don't," I said.

"It will be better."

There was something in his voice—something I couldn't believe—but it was there.

"Okay," I said.

The doctor spoke in Polish to the attendant. The latter glanced round nervously at me. "Let him go," said the doctor.

For a moment, I debated whether to give the attendant a mighty heave forward, and hope to heaven it would send both him and the doctor into an unconscious heap—and all in complete silence—or to trust in what I had heard, or thought I had heard, in the doctor's voice.

I let my arm drop.

The attendant gave a huge, exhausted sigh of relief, and

started down the stairs. *"Nie, nie,"* said the doctor sharply and pointed upward. Clumsily the attendant halted and turned, came back up, past the girl and me, and down the corridor. His footsteps grew fainter.

"Come with me," said the doctor.

I put my arm around the girl's waist and helped her to descend. The doctor turned and led the way, down into the gloom of the stair well. The floor below was like the one we had left, except that a door opposite the stairs was larger than the others and had some official lettering on it.

The doctor put his finger to his lip. "Wait here a moment," he said. He crossed the corridor to the official-looking door, opened it, and disappeared.

"Guess we've had it," I said. "He's going to call help."

The door reopened and the doctor came out with a worn trench coat. He placed it around the girl's shoulders. "It is cold out," he said. "You will need something."

Then he led the way down the next flight.

At the landing he stopped, and again put finger to lips. "Remain here till I tell you," he said, and went on down the stairs. From where the girl and I stood, I could see that he had descended into that same big room into which I had been carried so long, long ago—how long ago, I couldn't guess. I could see the iron chandelier dangling from the beamed ceiling. And I could hear the doctor's voice, low and businesslike, and another voice meekly saying, *"Tak, tak."* I understood—or hoped I did. He was getting rid of the watchman.

A minute later he was back at the foot of the stairs, beckoning. The girl leaned heavily on my arm as we made the final stage of the descent, into the huge, wainscoted room.

"Come," said the doctor. We followed him across the tiled floor, he and I on tiptoe, the girl's bare feet soundless. He opened the front door, beyond which the same pale light burned on the veranda. We crossed though its glow to the outer glass door, and the doctor pulled that open, too.

"I will go with you to the driveway," he said stiffly.

The three of us went down the wooden steps, under the porte-cochere. "A little farther," said the doctor. "Away from the light. Then I must leave you."

The gravel of the driveway crunched loud under our feet. Wind rustled the pine boughs all around, and it was cold. There was no moon, but the stars were bright. And now we stood in darkness.

"I can do nothing more," the doctor said quietly. "I do not know what you will do now. Maybe you will be lucky. Have you any money?"

"No."

"Here is a little something." I felt a few notes being thrust into my hand. "God go with you."

"And God bless you, Doctor," I said, "but why—"

He interrupted. "I only ask God to forgive me. Go now, you have not much time."

Then, as we started down the driveway, he called, "Wait. There is something important. If you are lucky—if you get away—there is something you must do for Miss Romaine."

"She is Miss Romaine, then?" I'd been sure, but I was glad to have it confirmed.

"Yes. But she herself no longer knows it. You must take her to the man who has invented this devil's instrument. You yourself will be all right—you have had only a little—but you must take Miss Romaine to this man."

"Where is he?"

"In Paris. I do not know how you will find him, but you must do it."

"What is his name?"

"It is Doctor Edelweiss. Now go quickly."

CHAPTER THIRTY

WHERE THE GRAVEL ENDED at the hard macadam of the mountain road, I drew Nita Romaine into the shelter of the bushy overhang while I tried to figure out our next move. The notion of pushing upward toward the pension had its attractions—the woman there had been friendly. On the other hand, she would know that I was a fugitive. It might be worth her life to take us in. And it would be a logical place for pursuers to search.

No, I decided, our best bet was to head down into the valley. Maybe some peasant would give us a lift—the peasants were supposed to be anti-regime. If we could just get as far as Jelenia Gora, which I judged to be about twenty miles away, we might find sanctuary. I took Nita Romaine's arm. "We're going to walk for a while," I said. "Feel up to it?"

In the darkness, I could sense her trying to steady herself. "I don't know," she murmured. "I feel better though. In the air. It's been a long time. A long time without air."

"Just take it easy. The walk will do you good."

She put out a hand and said, "Wait. A little while ago—you said a name—what was it? Lewis—was it Lewis?"

"Les. Les Baldwin."

"Yes, that's the name. But you—you are not—"

"No. I'm a friend of his. Keep thinking about him. Come on."

"Wait," she said again. Unexpectedly she put both arms around my neck and clung to me, burying her face on my shoulder, "Hold me," she whispered. "Hold me for a moment. It brings things back. Like that name. It makes me strong again."

I held her for a moment. Then she took her arms away

and stepped back. "I am better now," she said and stood erect. "I will walk as long as you tell me."

"Atta girl," I said, and we started. It was hard going. The road was so steep, despite the long turns, that you had to keep holding yourself back, and it wasn't too easy to see it. On our right was the shadowy overhang, on our left vague shapes that masked unknown declivities. Behind us, all was silent. I glanced around now and then, but in the great sanitarium, only the lone light at the front door showed. No alarm yet.

The intern's shoes were tight and began to hurt. I paused after a while and took them off. That was better. "Now we're even," I said to Nita, smiling. "Both barefoot. Pretty funny pair we must look, huh?"

"Funny," she repeated. She sounded puzzled, as if trying to find some hidden meaning. "Funny. Ragged and funny." Then suddenly she began to sing, in a soft, husky voice:

> "Oh! we ain't got a barrel of money,
> Maybe we're ragged and funny,
> But we'll travel along
> Singin' a song
> Side by side . . ." *

She sang it all the way through, with an easy rhythm that set our feet to moving briskly along the steep macadam. She had been holding my arm as she sang, then, as the song trailed off, she let it fall. "Did you hear?" she cried. "Did you hear?"

"I sure did, and I'd like to hear more."

"That isn't what I mean. I remembered. I remembered

the words. They just came."

She was almost breathless with the excitement of it. I patted her shoulder. "Sing some more."

"Tell me a song. Quickly. While I'm remembering."

"Long, Long Trail A-Winding."

She began to sing that, and her deep, warm voice mingled with the wind that sighed in the lonesome pines above us.

I became aware presently of faint, gray light coming over the towering hills. The wind died. Down in the valley, a rooster crowed, then another, and another. Somewhere a cow mooed, and the tinkling of a bell came across the slopes. The darkness was paling into wispy white mist, rising from the depths all around.

Somewhere far below us, in the stirring valley, I heard the chug of a motor. I strained my ears. It sounded as if it were coming toward us, but that was nothing to worry about. Then I stopped short. It wasn't, eh? What would the sanitarium's logical move be when we were discovered missing? To phone the nearest police station, of course. And the nearest police station would be down in the valley undoubtedly. Who else would be driving up this lonely road at this hour, in this country of few private cars?

"What's the matter?" asked Nita.

"I think I hear a car coming."

She listened. "It can't be coming after us, can it?"

"No, no," I said easily, "of course not. Just the same, I think we'd better duck till it gets past."

Even as I spoke, I saw the car's headlights piercing the mist. I couldn't understand how it had got so close so quickly, then I realized it was on a lower bend of the road, that it would still have a wide sweeping turn to make before it reached our level. But I wondered if that long, powerful beam had revealed us.

"Quick," I said to Nita, "over here."

There was a deep ditch under the overhang, littered

with leaves and twigs. We crouched down against the dirt bank, deep in shadow, burying into the loose brush. If they hadn't already seen us, we would be all right, I thought—unless their headlights should hit us as they rounded the curve.

The car was in second gear, chugging manfully upward and nearer. I could see the beam cast away from us, dissolving in the valley's mist, then the car came around the bend and the beam swung in our direction, closer and brighter, and the sound of the motor was loud.

The beam went past. And then the car stopped. So did my heart. The motor shut off and the car backed a foot or two as the gears checked it. I tried to see what kind of car it was. In the growing light, through the white wisps, I thought I saw—was it possible? Were those the letters C.D. on the license plate?

From the back seat, from someone apparently peering through the window came a booming voice. "Thunderation! I could have sworn I saw somebody. Well, we might as well shove on."

"Mrs. Pickett!" I yelled and leaped out of the ditch like a gazelle.

CHAPTER THIRTY-ONE

"Bless my soul," said Mrs. Pickett with majestic calm. "Driver, we need go no farther."

"So I see." The driver's voice was familiar, too. Griselde Miratour sat at the wheel, her elbow over the window edge, the same chauffeur's cap aslant on her dark head.

I stumbled across the road and almost fell against the side of the maroon Chevrolet. All I could see, for a moment, was Mrs. Pickett's broad, comfortable face, and I kissed her through the window with a loud smack.

"Really," said Mrs. Pickett. "We are not alone, you know."

I realized that someone was sitting beside her in the back seat. It was Dr. Clendenning, looking small and worried and bewildered. "Water," he said. "Give the man some water. Both men."

"Later," said Mrs. Pickett. "Do I hear a voice over there?"

Nita Romaine was calling thinly from the ditch. "Who is it? Don't leave me! Please, don't leave me."

I pattered back across the road to her side. Behind me I heard Mrs. Pickett saying, "Great heavens, he's in his bare feet."

I had to lift Nita out of the leaves and brush. The sudden fear, the cessation of effort, the strange voices, all had left her limp and unstrung. When I set her on her feet in the road, she started to collapse, her hands groping wildly for support. I caught her around the waist and half carried her to the car.

"She's in bare feet, too," said Mrs. Pickett. "Who is she? Who are you, young lady?"

"I don't know," gasped Nita weakly.

"I see," said Mrs. Pickett. "Typical friend of Rockwell's. Later on, no doubt, we shall—"

I interrupted. "This is Nita Romaine."

"Who?" said Mrs. Pickett blandly. Then her mouth fell open and her eyes bulged. "You don't mean the young lady you were looking for in the first place?"

"I sure do," I said, "and this is no time to stand around gabbing about it. We've just busted out of that miserable hell-hole up there and—"

"Ah," said Mrs. Pickett, "we were on the right road, after all."

As she spoke, the dawn stillness was shivered by the clanging of a bell far up the hill—though not far enough.

It sounded like a school fire alarm.

"Let's get going," I said grimly.

"I can't turn around here," said Griselde.

"Splendid," said Mrs. Pickett. "Then we can either meet the enemy head on, or race away from him. Backward."

"I can't help it," said Griselde with a touch of pique.

"I think I can," replied Mrs. Pickett. "Seems to me that when I was a girl riding around in cut-down Fords, it was possible to turn a car by having everybody swing the front bumper around. I forget just why we did it, but I'm sure we did. Shall we try? All out, then."

She hoisted herself with dignity into the road, and Dr. Clendenning followed. "Now," she said to Griselde, "back her around as far as you can."

"Watch out for the ditch," I said. "It's deep."

"Watch it for me, please," said Griselde. She backed across the road, till the rear wheels were on the crumbling edge of the macadam.

"All hands to the bumper," called Mrs. Pickett briskly. "Except the young lady. Get her out of the way."

I helped Nita to the side of the road, then along with Mrs. Pickett and Dr. Clendenning bent to the bumper and lifted. "Get it bouncing," ordered Mrs. Pickett. "That's the way. Now, then, swing, and swing again. That's the ticket. Once more, boys. Almost there. I think that's got it."

"I will try it," said Griselde. "Watch my wheels."

She cut them sharply and inched forward. They cleared the brink of the misty steep by an eyelash, and the car was headed downhill.

"Everybody in," cried Mrs. Pickett merrily. "Rocky, you put your young woman in back with the doc and me, and you climb in front with Miss Folies Bergère. *Chez nous*, James!"

Griselde snorted. She glanced around to see that everybody was settled, then shot the car forward, a precarious business on that corkscrew road, but not as precarious, for my money, as dawdling. Far up the hill, that hideous bell continued to clang.

Griselde skidded around one curve after another. Her lips were clenched, her eyes fixed on the sinking road, and nobody spoke. The mist was lifting fast now, and pastures and grainfields emerged on either side. The red roofs of farmhouses appeared among clumps of trees. When we reached the floor of the valley everybody breathed more easily. The bell could no longer be heard, and behind us were no signs of pursuit. They were probably beating the bushes in the immediate vicinity.

"Ah, this is better," said Griselde. "I am a little tired. I have been driving all night."

"Would you like me to take over?" I asked.

"Not now. Later perhaps."

"Where did you drive from?"

"Warsaw. Ask your large friend. She will tell you."

"Large friend, large friend?" repeated Mrs. Pickett indignantly.

"Your *grande amie*."

"Humph, that's more like it," said Mrs. Pickett. "At least, it sounds better. Yes, young man, we drove all the way from Warsaw all this night simply to get you out of a pickle."

"How did you propose to get me out?"

"Well, we didn't know exactly. But we knew, in a general way, what the circumstances were."

"In a pig's eye, you did." I couldn't keep the bitterness out of my voice.

"All right, we thought we did," replied Mrs. Pickett equably. "And we also thought that Doctor Clendenning here could throw his weight around and demand to see you. He's got more weight than you'd think."

"I don't really," said Dr. Clendenning apologetically, "but it does happen that I am in a position to hold up a quantity of medical supplies and equipment that the Ministry of Health hopes to get from the United States. In fact, that's probably the only reason I'm not in jail, like poor Doctor Jarowski. They arrested both of us, but they let me loose."

"Let's not go too fast," I said. "No, not you, Griselde, the conversation. Where did Mrs. Pickett come from?"

"I?" said Mrs. Pickett. "From Paris, of course."

"But how?"

"By army plane."

"Any particular army?"

"I assumed it to be ours," said Mrs. Pickett. "I didn't ask. From Paris to Berlin was a cinch, of course—plenty of flights—and I was lucky enough to connect with one to Warsaw. It's only a hop, skip, and jump by air. I was in Warsaw in something less than eight hours after I got word that you were in one of your usual jams. The Embassy said it was powerless to act—in its own words—and I figured somebody had better act and I took off."

"How did you get a Polish visa?"

"Well," said Mrs. Pickett, "I seem to have overlooked that little formality. Haven't you noticed my costume, by the way?"

I hadn't, and I twisted around for a look. She seemed to be wearing an ordinary tan raincoat; then I saw that her substantial legs were clad in khaki stockings.

"The boys were kind enough to lend me a WAC uniform." She grinned complacently. "I'm a member of the crew. Jolly useful one, too. I enlivened the trip for all concerned."

"I'm sure you did, Mrs. Pickett," I said, "but tell me, first, where—how—is Jane?"

"Perfectly fine," said Mrs. Pickett. "Nothing to worry about. You don't think I'd go traipsing across Europe after you if Jane wasn't all right, do you?"

"I suppose not," I said. "And you, Griselde, how did you get into the act?"

"I will tell you," said Griselde, keeping her eyes on the road. It was beginning to climb again as it entered the hills on the far side of the valley bowl. The roofs of Jelenia Gora loomed closer through the trees.

"If you laugh at this," Griselde began, "I will kill you, because my feelings are still very hurt. It was not because I was a famous actress that I have been asked to appear on the stage at that cabaret, that Monte Carlo. It was a trick, a trick against my *amour-propre*, my vanity. When I have walked off the stage, who is waiting there? That Stanley, that beast of a Stanley. He has arranged everything with that nasty manager. I am astounded. I have not dreamed he is not in Warsaw. Before I can do anything, he commands those pigs of waiters to carry me out to his big black car which is waiting. One puts his filthy hand over my mouth so I cannot scream. Then he takes me back to his beautiful flat in Kraków. Ah, they live well, these Red beasts."

I glanced around to see if Nita Romaine showed any sign of response. Perhaps she, too, had been abducted in that same way. But she had fallen asleep, her head pillowed on Mrs. Pickett's comfortable shoulder.

"You are listening?" said Griselde.

"Of course I'm listening. Go on."

"So for twenty-four hours I am his prisoner. Then suddenly he is called away, something has gone wrong with him, I do not know what."

"I think I had something to do with that," I said. "So?"

"So I am alone in this flat with only the servant. I wish to try the bribery. But I have no money. So with what can

I make the bribe?"

"Ah, what indeed?" said Mrs. Pickett.

Griselde threw a cold glance over her shoulder. "The servant, it is a woman. She is of the women's militia, very strong, very determined. Also, she is not so pretty. And that gives me the idea. I say to her, it is so boring when Stanley is not here, why do we not invite some young men and have some fun, eh? I see in her eyes she would like that. But she does not know any young men, she says, and I am not surprised. Ah, but I do, I say, I know two charming Frenchmen—if I may but use the telephone. When I say Frenchmen, I see her thinking to herself, ah, that would be chic. So she permits me to telephone. I call the French Consulate. And sure enough, two young Frenchmen come at once, with all their papers and credentials, and they say what is this? This is French citizen, you cannot keep her prisoner or we will make the trouble. Very much trouble, and the scandal, too. That settles it. And I go away with the two young Frenchmen from the Consulate, and that is that."

She smiled complacently.

"I must say," I remarked, "that your Consulate seems to move in where our Embassy fears to tread."

"Remember, though," put in Mrs. Pickett, "that you are not a rather good-looking young girl."

"There was another reason," said Griselde, "but that is not important now. After I am free, I go back to the Grand Hotel, and there I find the little doctor. He has been in jail. He is in a bad state of nerves. Were you not, Doctor?"

"I'm afraid I was," said Clendenning. "And the lord knows why I'm using the past tense."

"So," said Griselde, "the car is still there, the requisition for petrol is still there, and so we drive back to Warsaw."

"Frankly," said Dr. Clendenning, "I was scared. Scared

blue. I wanted to get back to the Embassy. And when we got back to the Embassy, we encountered—I'm sorry, ma'am, what was your name again?"

"Pickett. Mrs. Pickett."

"We encountered Mrs. Pickett and, uh, matters took an entirely different course."

"I'm sure they did," I said, not without sympathy.

"It was like this," explained Mrs. Pickett. "I'd arrived only a short time before, you see, and I was busting to go straight to this booby hatch you had somehow landed yourself in. But that chap at the Embassy—Watkins, is it? —he said the only chance I'd have of seeing you would be to pose as your mother. Well, I was everlastingly blowed if I was going to do that, and I didn't think much of that Watkins for suggesting it, either. At this point, the good doc here turned up, and he seemed to know all about this place you were in, and he volunteered to go back there with me, and Miss Miratour volunteered to drive, and here we are."

"I'm certainly grateful to all of you," I said humbly.

"As a matter of fact," said Dr. Clendenning modestly, "I wasn't being as altogether altruistic as you might think. Mr. Watkins at the Embassy was almost convinced you had been given some kind of drug and it happens that drugs are rather down my alley and—"

"Wait," I said. "You told me children were down your alley. Children don't take drugs, do they? They didn't when I left the States."

"I believe some marijuana addicts start very young," said the doctor, "but I was referring to my own specialty, children's anesthesia. It occurred to both Mr. Watkins and myself that, just possibly, you might be getting the drug that has been used in all those treason trials—if there is one. That, of course, would have been of tremendous interest to western science. I even let myself hope that by some miracle I'd be able to get a sample of it. Foolish, of course, but even we cold-blooded scientists have our dreams."

My hand went to the pocket of the white jacket. The syringe was still there. "Have a dream on me, Doctor," I said, and handed it to him.

Griselde glanced at me out of the corner of her eye. "I hope," she said in a low voice, "that what you have just done is not a mistake."

CHAPTER THIRTY-TWO

JELENIA GORA, in the full light of early morning, was bigger and more bustling that it had appeared in its postcard setting across the valley, or when seen hastily at night. Not that we didn't see it pretty hastily this morning—we sailed right through the place. It still looked friendly, but it proved a more calculated friendliness than I had realized. It was almost solidly composed of hotels, large and small, all with woodwork facings and glassed-in porches. In many cases, their former German names could be seen in script lettering, whitewashed over and with newly painted Polish names like *Zloty Vidok* and *Pod Limpani.*

The red roofs dwindled behind us, among the thick chestnuts and poplars, and we were again among the lonely hills, grown gentler now and gradually descending toward the plains which gave Poland its name.

Griselde, with a cigarette clamped in her lips, said, "The best road is to Breslau. But it may be watched. What do you think?"

"Nobody's watching for this car," said Mrs. Pickett cheerfully. "They may be watching for Rocky and his lady friend, but not for us. I don't think anybody's chasing us, either, and I for one would like some breakfast."

"At Breslau," said Griselde. "We will stop at Breslau."

Which we did, and had a hearty meal of Polish ham and coffee in an old German restaurant. Nita Romaine was only half-awake and scarcely ate, but Dr. Clendenning coaxed a good deal of coffee into her. She fell asleep again as soon as we were back in the car. Griselde looked tired, too, with deep circles under her eyes.

"Wouldn't you like me to drive a while?" I asked her.

"Not yet. There is a road block between here and Lodz. It may be necessary to speak firmly to the sentry."

"Road block?" said Mrs. Pickett. "What's all this?"

"We have passed through it last night," said Griselde, smiling faintly. "You were asleep."

"It's a kind of spiritual tollgate," said Dr. Clendenning.

"Oh," said Mrs. Pickett. "And we're counting on Miss Folies Bergère to get us through, are we?"

"We sure are," I told her, "and she's a whiz."

"Humph. I'm pretty good at that sort of thing myself. Call on me, Miss Folies, if you need me."

"It is nothing to laugh about," said Griselde coldly. "We are carrying, are we not, the hot cargo?"

"We certainly are," declared Dr. Clendenning. "It may mean a great deal to science to examine this attractive guinea pig, if Miss Romaine will excuse the term."

I shifted around and leaned over the seat. "Doctor," I said, "can you tell anything from what you've seen so far of Miss Romaine's condition?"

"Very little. The pupils are dilated, which suggests scopolamine. It's been assumed all along, of course, that scopolamine would play a large role in whatever compound is used. As you doubtless know, it's sometimes called the truth drug, and the question is, to what extent can it be a lie drug as well? You see, what scopolamine does in a broad general way is to lower the mind's defenses—the mind becomes incapable of the effort involved in a deliberate lie. A lie, basically, is an intellectual achievement. Mankind's discovery of the lie was a great step, although in what direction, I'm not prepared to say."

"How about the discovery of the fib?" asked Mrs. Pickett. "That's the thing we couldn't get along without."

"The distinction is a shadowy one," said Dr. Clendenning.

"Rubbish," said Mrs. Pickett. "I've never told a lie in all my thirty-nine years, but I've told quite a number of fibs. Everybody has."

"Shall we return to the subject?" asked Dr. Clendenning somewhat severely. "When the mind is in the defenseless state induced by scopolamine, it would be susceptible to any ideas that might be deliberately drilled into it. The mind would have no means of judging their falsity or truth."

I asked, "Could an idea, or a recollection, be removed from the mind as easily as it could be instilled?"

"More easily," replied Clendenning. "Just as it's easier for anyone to forget a thing than to learn it. For instance, I keep thinking that your name is Rock something instead of Stonewall. Silly, but there it is. Besides, the condition that scopolamine produces is primarily an amnesic one."

"If scopolamine fills the bill so neatly," said Mrs. Pickett, "why is there any mystery about what they use?"

"Because scopolamine by itself would leave the victim, or patient, in a palpably groggy condition. The trick is to produce your witness, or defendant, or whatever, in a calm and seemingly normal state. So you mix your scopolamine—"

"I wish you'd stop looking at me when you say 'you,' " complained Mrs. Pickett.

"Excuse me. So one mixes one's scopolamine, presumably, with a stimulant like Benzedrine, plus some kind of

217

sedative to maintain calmness. As a matter of fact, we know that such a combination was used by the German air force to—"

He paused and glanced around. Behind us, across the rolling fields, the great gray and pink masses of rubble that marked the outer shell of Breslau were fast receding.

"And that," he murmured solemnly, "was one of their great cities, solid, prosperous, contented. If they had never had an air force— However," he went on more briskly, "they did have one, and one of the things they did was give their aviators this combination of drugs. They could fight like devils, hopped to the ears with Benzedrine, and calm as Moses with barbiturates, and when it was all over, they had practically no recollection of fear or horror because memory was wiped out with scopolamine."

Griselde remarked out of the side of her mouth, "I would like very much some of that combination. It would make the driving much more pleasant."

Dr. Clendenning laughed ghoulishly and held up the syringe. "If you are willing to experiment," he said, "this might do it."

"On second thought," said Griselde, "I will have another cigarette instead."

"Probably worse for you," said Dr. Clendenning. "Anyway, the Germans had a number of drug compounds like that and, after the war, we got some and the Russians got some. Of course, some people think the Russians already had a lie drug at the time of the big purge trials, but in any event, they probably acquired a better one from the Germans. It's one field the Germans were way ahead in, if that's anything to be proud of. The Russians probably acquired a few German experts in the field, too. We did, so it's reasonable they did. Sometimes I think that we got a lie drug, too, and that we gave it to all our newspaper editors."

"I trust," said Mrs. Pickett, "that you are not including society editors in that brash remark."

"Is that what you are?" asked Dr. Clendenning with interest. "You certainly go far afield, don't you, in search of your items?"

"This particular expedition," replied Mrs. Pickett, "is going to supply me with half a column. 'Bare feet and Mother Hubbards are the latest thing for motoring, according to fashionable Nita Romaine, who recently completed an interesting auto trip stuffed to the scuppers with twilight sleep. Her opinion was echoed by that dashing young journalist, Mr. Stanley—' "

She was interrupted by Griselde. "There is a road block ahead. What do you think we had better do? Run for it?"

The Chevvy came to a halt. "If they insist on seeing my papers," I said, "or Miss Romaine's, we're sunk."

"I'm not overloaded with 'em myself," said Mrs. Pickett.

"Mon dieu," said Griselde to me, "have you not got your passport?"

"I've got nothing."

"Really!" exclaimed Griselde. "Have you forgotten that your passport is half mine? That is very careless of you."

"I'd offer you half of mine," said Dr. Clendenning, "if it included a wife. Unfortunately my wife is in Philadelphia."

"If she were here," observed Mrs. Pickett, "it would scarcely help matters."

"If she were here," said the doctor, "she would have assisted Miss Miratour in her driving with a stream of excellent advice."

"I wish advice now," said Griselde. "What shall I do? Go ahead and trust to luck?"

"I'll trust to my uniform," said Mrs. Pickett, "but I suggest that Miss Romaine lie down on the floor back here and maybe there's some kind of rug we could put over her."

"There is a rug in the luggage compartment," said Griselde.

"Splendid," said Mrs. Pickett. "Supposing you fetch it, Rocky, and while you're in the luggage compartment, why don't you stay there for the time being?"

I grimaced, but the idea made sense. It was a decidedly unpleasant sensation though, to hear the lock click shut and to feel myself cramped into musty, airless darkness. Especially for a man in a claustrophobic state, anyway.

I felt the car starting, then rolling bumpily along, and in a few minutes it stopped again. I could hear a brusque voice, then Griselde's impatient and haughty one. Then Mrs. Pickett's came booming into the conversation, and suddenly the car hurtled forward, so suddenly that my head banged against the top of the compartment. It still hurt when, after perhaps five minutes that seemed a lot more, the compartment was opened by Griselde and I climbed stiffly out.

"It went very well," she said. "Your *grande amie* is very good with soldiers."

"Thank you," said Mrs. Pickett. "I was rather pleased with it myself. You'd almost have thought he understood me."

"I imagine he did," I said, "for all practical purposes."

Griselde chuckled. "If you wish to drive now," she said to me, "I would like some rest."

"Okay," I said. "May I borrow your cap?"

"With that white jacket," observed Mrs. Pickett, "you look like a dentist who's joined the Foreign Legion."

It was good to be driving an American car again. It gave me a feeling of chauvinistic confidence, as if I were piloting a bit of the States, an enclave, through a hostile but impotent country. The road was good, except for an occasional fissure, and we spun along between fifty and sixty.

At some point or other, we crossed back into Poland proper—the boundary wasn't marked any more—and in the early afternoon we reached the good-sized town of Lodz and stopped for lunch.

"Now you must watch for signs to Lowicz," said Griselde. "When we get there, we will be only sixty kilometers from Warsaw. Near there, also, is Chopin's birthplace. It is beautifully preserved."

"It would certainly be insouciant," said Mrs. Pickett, "to do a little sight-seeing as we pelt for sanctuary with our hot cargo."

"A Frenchman would," said Griselde coolly.

Again we bowled along at a good clip. Griselde and Mrs. Pickett dozed, but Dr. Clendenning, who had had a glass of his lovable water at lunch, was bright-eyed and talkative.

He wanted to know all about my experiences in the sanitarium, which he constantly compared with experiences of his own in treating children. In fact, he had me feeling as if my escape from that purgatorial place had been a matter of hiding in the sandbox, then making a dash on a kiddy car. He kept asking me, too, about any lingering symptoms I might have and seemed disappointed when I said none at all.

"Of course," he said, "it takes a week or two before that stuff really begins to work. And the effect varies in individuals. This poor girl here, I'd say she'd had quite a dose."

"Is it natural," I asked, "for her to sleep like this?"

"It's not natural, no, but I imagine it's largely exhaustion."

"Her mind's exhausted," I said, "even when she's wide awake. Do you think it's going to be permanent?"

"Hard to say, Stoney. Plenty of rest and wholesome food

and a friendly atmosphere should bring her back to normal in time. But whether a lot of queer ideas have been permanently etched on her cerebrum is something else again."

"It's my guess," I said, "that something has been expunged, rather than etched."

"How do you mean?"

"I think she knew something. Something dangerous to the regime. And what I want to know is, if that's so, would there be any possibility of bringing it back?"

Dr. Clendenning whistled softly. "By George, this is interesting. It would largely depend, of course, on how much of the damnable stuff she's had. If only we had some notion of what it was she knew, we might bring it to the surface, fish for it, as it were, by association of ideas."

"There wouldn't be any antidote to the drug itself that might help?"

"There might be an antidote that would speed the process of normalization. But as for bringing back a lost memory, I doubt it. Still, it's conceivable. If we could find the diabolical mind that invented this soup, we might get someplace. But there isn't much chance of that."

"Maybe there is," I said.

"What?" he almost shouted.

"That doctor who helped us to get away told me to take Miss Romaine to a man in Paris. A man who, by an odd and unpleasant coincidence, I happen to know. His name is Edelweiss."

Beside me, Griselde Miratour sat up straight, eyes wide. "What was that? Did you say Edelweiss?"

She spoke so loudly that Mrs. Pickett also woke up, blinking. "Edelweiss?" she repeated. "Now why is that name familiar? Ah, yes, our little friend with the big head."

"You mean a swelled head?" asked Dr. Clendenning.

"No. I mean a head like an apple on a stick."

"That's most peculiar," murmured the doctor. "Very odd. A lot of people have big heads, I suppose, but—"

"Please!" Griselde's voice cut in sharply. "Let us speak no more of big heads. Stop the car."

"Why?"

"Because I wish you to concentrate on this matter which you cannot do if you must watch the wheel."

"Okay." I pulled over to the side of the road, which now was yellow brick. Near by some children were picking cherries.

"Good," said Griselde. "Now then, tell me what you know about this man called Edelweiss."

I hesitated. I still wasn't sure to what extent I should take Griselde into confidence. "All I know," I said, "is that he's a friend of your friend, Stanley."

Griselde stared at me with narrow eyes. "You are quite sure of that?"

"Quite sure."

"*Alors,*" she said, half to herself, "this would explain many things."

"Do you know him?" asked Dr. Clendenning with interest.

"I do not exactly know him," said Griselde, "but I know a little about him. He is a German doctor whom the Americans have turned over to the French after the war. He has told the French that he is an expert in the treatment of the nervous disorder, which I believe is true."

"I'd certainly like to meet him," said Dr. Clendenning.

"Please, do not interrupt. At least, he has been enough of an expert in something to be valuable to French scientists. They have persuaded the government to permit him to remain in Paris and to change his name. It is not easy to live among Frenchmen with a German name."

"Griselde," I said, "how do you know all these things?"

She hesitated, as I had done a moment before and perhaps for the same reason. "Among ladies of the stage," she said, "it is sometimes convenient to have discreet medical treatment. It is awkward for the glamorous reputation to have certain things become public. And this Doctor Edelweiss, or Doctor La Fleur as he now calls himself, conducts a very discreet and respectable little nursing-home in St. Cloud, which—"

A loud cry burst from the back seat. Mrs. Pickett, for once in her life, was dead white. "Edelweiss! Fleur d'Alpes. Oh, my God, what a fool I've been!"

My limbs went icy cold. "Mrs. Pickett," I stammered, "you—you—don't—"

Her lips were tight and gray. "Fleur d'Alpes is the name of the nursing-home that your Jane was urged to enter. It is in St. Cloud." She stopped, unable for a moment to continue. Then, very low, "That is where she is now."

Far away, I could hear the laughter of the children in the cherry tree, then Dr. Clendenning's voice saying, "It's a good thing he wasn't driving. The poor chap's blacked out."

CHAPTER THIRTY-THREE

THE VIOLET BEGINNINGS of dusk threw a kindly haze over the gaunt and jagged outlines of Warsaw in the distance. The suburban street through which we now rolled, with its rows of poplars, its red-and-yellow trolley cars, had a cheerful normality that gave little hint of the desolation to which it led.

But all the desolation of Warsaw was no greater than

that in my own heart. Mrs. Pickett, too, was crushed and inconsolable. Except for a few words of remorseful explanation, she had scarcely spoken throughout the remainder of the trip. It seemed she had gone to the hospital to say good-by, and the authorities there had asked her to have Jane removed—some American college boys had been in a crash and they needed every bed they could spare. Jane, they felt, had little if anything wrong with her, although a few more days of observation might be advisable. The offer of the nursing-home still stood, and the hospital knew of nothing against it, so, in the haste of the moment, Mrs. Pickett had decided at least to look the place over. An hour before her plane was to leave, she and Jane had driven out to St. Cloud. The establishment seemed perfectly proper and in pleasantly rural surroundings—there had, of course, been no sign of Edelweiss—and Mrs. Pickett, with only faint misgivings, had left her. She had even thought the name, Fleur d'Alpes, rather charming—and it was her failure to connect this with Edelweiss that she couldn't forgive herself. She rocked back and forth as she told me these things, and now and then, during the rest of the drive, a groan of self-reproach would escape from her lips.

As we neared the city proper, its crumbling walls and gaping windows seemed more ghostly than ever. I couldn't think why for a moment, unless it was my own state of mind; then I realized that the usual crowds whose brisk milling lent life to the wasteland were nowhere to be seen. The streets were almost empty. The trolley cars that we passed now were empty, too, and standing deserted on their rails.

Across the shattered roof tops came a strange, dry, crackling sound.

"Great Scott," exclaimed Mrs. Pickett, "that's gunfire."

"It is quite possible," said Griselde, who had resumed

225

the wheel. "Sometimes these soldiers run berserk with their *mitrailleuses.*"

Once more the crackling rolled over the city.

"By golly," said Mrs. Pickett, "an awful lot of 'em must have gone berserk."

Griselde didn't answer. Her face was tense, her eyes crinkled in puzzled thought.

We were bouncing through a rutted, narrow street, piled on either side with rubble. Suddenly, around a corner ahead of us, zoomed a huge military truck, loaded with khaki-clad soldiers. It came straight for us, full tilt. All of the soldiers had guns, some rifles, some Tommy guns.

Griselde cut the wheel sharply and the Chevrolet lurched over the curb, grazed a heap of rubble, and missed the truck by inches. It slowed, as if uncertainly, then picked up speed and rumbled on. Griselde drove calmly ahead.

"Wasn't that a bit close?" asked Mrs. Pickett.

"A bit," said Griselde. Her knuckles, I noticed, were white on the wheel.

"D'you think the whole militia is out after Rocky?" asked Mrs. Pickett.

"I do not know," said Griselde. "There is something strange."

The narrow street opened into a wide thoroughfare that I recognized as the Aleje Jerozolimskie. But even this normally busy avenue was eerily empty and silent. We passed the Hotel Polonia, and saw a couple of dozen soldiers out front. They stared at us, but that was all.

At the foot of the avenue, in the gathering dusk, we could see the huge bridge that arched the Vistula. A great crowd seemed to be clustered at its entrance. Soldiers, they proved as we neared, at least a hundred. Somewhere to our left, the sound of gunfire rippled once more through the air.

Griselde swung the Chevvy right into the Aleje Stalina,

and we passed another truckload of soldiers hurtling toward us down that stately boulevard. Some of the men raised their guns as it thundered past. Two minutes later, we could see the wonderful sight of a floating American flag and the grillwork of the Embassy gates. But it was disconcerting to see, then, that a dozen or more soldiers were drawn up on the wide pavement outside.

Griselde pressed her hand on the horn, loud and long, and turned sharply into the entrance to the drive. The soldiers hopped like rabbits out of the way, and one or two of them lifted their rifles angrily. Griselde sounded the horn again.

A tense thirty seconds passed. Then, beyond the gates, a young man came out of the big stone building, trotted down the drive, and peered out between the iron rails. "Who is it?" he called.

I leaned out of the window. "A bunch of beat-up Americans."

The young man grinned, but he still hesitated. "Name, please?"

"My name is Rockwell and this is—"

"Okay, okay." The iron gates swung open, and Griselde drove in. Behind us, the gates clanged shut.

The young man came up to the car. "Sorry," he said, "but we've got orders to be extra careful tonight. All hell's breaking loose."

"What kind of hell?"

"Darned if I know. Some kind of political hell, I guess. Everybody's up in the air but they don't tell us guards nothing." He looked rueful and held the big plate-glass door open for us to enter. Griselde and Nita Romaine stayed in the car for the moment.

The whole place seemed a-bustle, people walking along the balcony, doors opening and closing, phones ringing, typewriters clacking. There was the feel of a newspaper office when a big story breaks.

A trim girl sat at the receptionist's desk, tense and alert. I asked her if Mr. Watkins was around, and she said she would call him right away. A moment later his lean form in its neat pin stripe appeared on the balcony and he came clattering down the stairs.

"Thank God," he exclaimed, grasping my hand and Mrs. Pickett's at once, "they got you out of there."

"Credit where credit is due," said Mrs. Pickett. "He got himself out. Not to mention the young lady he was looking for."

Watkins stared at me incredulously. "Not the Romaine girl?"

I nodded. I felt too weak to talk, too despondent to find any pride or pleasure in this moment.

"Where is she?" asked Watkins excitedly.

"Out in the car," said Mrs. Pickett. "We ought to get her to a bed."

Watkins scratched his head. "This is certainly no place to bring her," he said. "The chargé d'affaires has gone to the Foreign Office, but I trust he won't object if we take over his house. He lives on the premises." He turned to the receptionist. "Call Mr. Brock's housekeeper and tell her I'm bringing some people over."

The chargé d'affaires's house stood some fifty yards behind the main building, in a garden fragrant with lilacs and syringa. A rosy-cheeked woman ushered the lot of us into a large, comfortable living-room. There were a couple of big sofas and several easy chairs, a tile fireplace, a long window curtained against the night, and a table covered with American magazines.

The housekeeper said in awkward English, "There is bed in next room. For lady."

Nita Romaine's eyelids fluttered open. "No, no," she whispered. "Let me stay here. I'm afraid to be alone."

"Of course," said Watkins soothingly. "We'll fix you up on one of these sofas." He and the housekeeper got her propped up among the soft pillows, and the housekeeper fetched a blanket and laid it over her legs.

"You might get some ice out, too," said Watkins. "I think these people need a drink and I'm sure Mr. Brock won't mind if we broach a little of his whisky. I don't think he'd mind, either, if you got a pair of his bedroom slippers for Mr. Rockwell."

I glanced down in surprise. I'd forgotten all about being in my bare feet. Another thing I'd forgotten was how good rye whisky tasted in a tall glass with ice and soda.

When everybody was settled, Watkins went to a cabinet radio in one corner and switched it on. "We've been having a little excitement of our own around here," he said. "Nobody seems to know just what it's all about, but I gather the government has uncovered some kind of plot against it. It may be a lot of hooey, or it may—"

He was interrupted, as the radio warmed up, by a sonorous voice saying, *"Uwaga, uwaga."*

Even I knew what that meant. We'd heard it often enough through the *Queen Jadwiga's* loud-speakers. It meant "attention please," and I remembered with a stabbing pain how Jane and I used to say it to each other. *"Uwaga,* where is the toothpaste?" Things like that.

The voice was going on, in smooth Polish that had the silky cadence of a commercial back home. Then it paused, as when an American announcer says something will follow immediately.

"My Polish is lousy," said Watkins. "Did anybody here catch any of that? Except *uwaga?"*

"I did," said Griselde. "He says there has been a little trouble but that it will very soon be over. However, everyone must stay off the streets until further notice. Everyone must be calm and keep their radios on."

"Guess we might as well do the same," said Watkins. He hesitated and looked at Griselde curiously. "I don't mean to be rude, but who are you?"

"My name is Griselde Miratour. I am an actress. If you are suspicious of me, you may call the French Embassy."

. "No, no," said Watkins hastily. "It's very convenient to have you here." The voice was coming out of the radio again, and he waited till it stopped. "What did he say that time?"

"Same thing."

Watkins sighed. "I wish I knew what the score was. That's why Mr. Brock's at the Foreign Office—trying to find out just what cooks. If possible, before the correspondents get it. It always makes us look foolish when the newspapers get a story before the Department knows about it." He smiled in my direction.

"I don't suppose there's any society angle," said Mrs. Pickett.

"Uh, look," I said to Watkins, "I hate to sound egocentric, but could all this have any connection with us?"

"I hardly think so," said Watkins. "As a matter of fact, we've had several hints of something in the wind. That's one reason why we couldn't go to bat for you as strongly as we'd have liked. It's something pretty big. This may be it."

The voice came out of the radio. *"Uwaga, uwaga!"* There was a new note to the words, a note of complacency bordering on glee. The voice surged on, sounding like an announcer who had seen with his own eyes a stream of housewives rushing to buy the large economy size.

"What's he saying now?" Watkins's voice shared the excitement.

"He says it is all over," replied Griselde. "The trouble is finished. Everyone may come out and rejoice that the foolishness of defying the people's government has been once again proven to the world."

The voice went on, sinking now to a more ominous tone, at once sorrowful and menacing—this was what happened to you if you failed to buy the product right away.

"I caught some of that," said Watkins. "Something about Trotsky and Tito."

"Yes," said Griselde. "He says that the plot was the work of Trotskyite, Bukharinist, Titoist, Fascist imperial-ist deviationists."

"Pretty tough ticket to popularize," remarked Mrs. Pickett.

"He says," continued Griselde, "that most of the plotters have been captured and will be given fair and just trials which will undoubtedly result in their being hanged."

"Does he mention any names?" asked Watkins.

"No."

"Damn," said Watkins. He tugged at his chin and looked thoughtful.

"Is this what you meant by 'it'?" I asked him.

"Could be," said Watkins. "But I thought they'd put up a better show than this. There were supposed to be some pretty big people among the ringleaders. We've no idea who, though. It's been a damnably well-kept secret. If this was it, their Tito must have gone off half-cocked."

"Tito." The word floated across the room from the sofa where Nita Romaine lay. "Tito," she said again. "Tito." Her eyes were wide and straining, as if the name had struck some chord among the dusty strings of her mind.

"There, there, young lady," said Dr. Clendenning. "Don't you bother your head with politics. None of my other patients do." He glanced at Watkins. "Did you say this was whisky?"

"The best," said Watkins.

"I've never tasted whisky before in my life. It's something like the lovable water they drink here, only better."

There was a crunch of wheels on the gravel outside. Then the slamming of a car door. "That'll be Mr. Brock," said Watkins. "Best behavior, everybody."

"Humph," said Mrs. Pickett. "Who were his parents?"

Footsteps sounded outside, rather weary ones, then the door opened and a tall gray-haired man of about fifty entered the room. His eyes looked tired and they moved around the room with mild surprise.

"These are the people I told you about," said Watkins. "The young lady on the sofa is the famous Nita Romaine."

Brock's eyebrows rose. "We-e-ell," he said. "That's a bit of a feat on someone's part."

"Mr. Rockwell's," said Watkins.

Brock shook hands with me and was introduced to the others. Then he sank into a chair by the fireplace. "I hope all of you will forgive me," he said, "but I've been through a very trying time of my own. Hang it all, Watkins, I still don't know what happened."

"Could I get you a drink?" asked Watkins.

"You certainly could. Has there been anything on the radio?"

Watkins paused halfway to the kitchen. "Yes, sir. They've announced that a Trotskyite, Titoist, Fascist imperialist deviationist plot has been put down and all plotters arrested."

Brock glanced at him skeptically. "Your Polish must be improving, Watkins."

"He left out Bukharinist," said Griselde.

Watkins coughed and went on to the kitchen. Brock gave Griselde a shrewd look, then his gaze wandered around to the rest of us. "I know you people must have problems," he said, "but the plain fact is I'm too fagged out to deal with them right now."

"Our only problem," said Mrs. Pickett, "is to get to

Paris as fast as possible."

"Paris?" said Brock. "That's not too easy, you know. Still, perhaps in a few days—"

"What about that plane I came in?" asked Mrs. Pickett. "When's it going back?"

"I don't know. That's up to our air attaché."

"You could order him to fly all of us back, couldn't you?" persisted Mrs. Pickett.

"Well, yes, I could," said Brock, "but I'd have to be convinced—"

Dr. Clendenning interrupted with a bright chirp. "You may not realize it, sir, but our mission is fully as important as any fly-by-night political dust-up. It happens, sir, that in the body of this young woman and in this syringe"— he held it up—"may lie the secret of how these satellite regimes and their master have wrung confessions from those who have opposed them."

"Good lord," said Brock. "I didn't realize anything like that was involved." He hesitated, interested and yet unable to shake his mind free of its other problems. "Still, I don't quite see why there's any great urgency."

"You don't!" cried Dr. Clendenning. "How long do you think Miss Romaine's body will retain its interesting condition? Every minute that passes, her value to science grows less."

I could have kissed him. I didn't give a hang just then about anybody's value to science, but any valid reason for speeding us back to Paris was all I asked.

Brock was stroking his chin thoughtfully. Watkins came back with a highball for him. "Uh, Watkins," he said, "give Colonel Morrow a buzz and find out what his plans are for the plane. We might have some passengers for him."

My heart leaped. Watkins moved toward the phone, which was on top of the radio, and as his hand reached for it, it rang. He picked it up, listened a moment, then turned to Brock. "You'd better take this."

Frowning, Brock got up and took the phone. "Brock, speaking." A short silence. Then, "What!" The word exploded out of him. "Are you sure?" Another silence. "This is damned awkward. I don't know what we should do. Is he alone?" Another pause. "You say he's wounded? Badly? Well—I suppose the Christian thing is to let him in. Make sure he hasn't got any weapons and bring him straight here to me."

He hung up and turned to the rest of us, a dazed look on his face. He said slowly, "General Gritska is here. He is seeking sanctuary."

CHAPTER THIRTY-FOUR

THE YOUNG MAN who had opened the gates for us and another guard entered the room, lurching with the weight of the figure they supported between them. General Gritska's lank blond hair fell over his beefy face, a beefiness grown blotched and sickly. A dirty old raincoat hung over his shoulders, over a powder-blue uniform which looked rumpled and stained. One stain in particular stood out—a large, wet, dark-red one over his massive belly.

Once inside, he straightened and threw back his arms, releasing himself from the supporting hands. "Mr. Brock," he said and gave a curt nod.

Brock who had arisen said, "Good evening, General."

Gritska's gaze went with an effort around the room. His eyes met mine and he gave a slight start. Then they fell upon the outstretched form of Nita Romaine and opened wide. Her eyes were open, too, and they stared back with troubled fear. Gritska started to speak, then swallowed, and let his gaze move on. He saw Griselde.

"*Mon dieu,*" he cried in a choked voice. "*Toi.*"

"*Oui,*" said Griselde coldly. "*Moi.*"

Then he caught sight of Mrs. Pickett and gave a feeble yelp. "The woman who sat on my hat!"

"*Oui,*" said Mrs. Pickett. "*Moi.*"

He continued to stare for a moment, then suddenly both hands clutched at his stomach. "I am shot," he said. "Would you—kindly—send for a doctor."

"I'm a doctor," said Clendenning brightly. "Of course, children are more in my line, but—"

"I must lie down," said Gritska. "Help me to the coosh." He staggered forward, then caught himself and gave me a wan glare. "To the couch."

Dr. Clendenning took the big man's arm and steered him to the sofa, across the room from the one on which Nita Romaine lay. "We'll just unbutton all those mean old buttons," said Dr. Clendenning in what I assumed was his nursery bedside manner.

Gritska groaned. There was something almost pathetic about him. Then I took another look at that brutal mouth, and I remembered that this was the man who had tried to have me killed, who had deliberately sought to destroy the mind of Nita Romaine, and who, above all, must be responsible for whatever unknown evils now surrounded the girl I loved.

Dr. Clendenning rose from beside the outstretched, burly form. "There," he said, "isn't that better? You just lie still and comfy for a while." His eyes behind his pince-nez looked at Brock and me, and he gave an almost imperceptible shake of his head.

Gritska's voice came faint but with a trace of contempt left in it. "You do not need to take too much trouble, Doctor. I know I am going to die. I wish only to live long enough to say a few things. I do not wish to die with these things on my mind."

"Would you like me to send for a priest?" asked Brock.

Gritska grunted a scornful negative. "I belong to the militant godless," he said. "Nevertheless—no matter. Mr. Brock, you have gone to the Foreign Office this night. If things had gone well, you would have found me there—as the new head of the Polish government." He paused dramatically. "I was to be the Tito of Poland."

The room was hushed. I heard Griselde catch her breath. Then from the other sofa, Nita Romaine's voice, almost as weak as Gritska's, murmured, "Tito. Tito of Poland."

Gritska tried to look at her, and his lips curled in a faint smile. "That explains," he said, "why things did not go well. It explains why we have had to act prematurely, before the uprising was properly prepared. It is my own weakness that keeps me from being the new leader of the people's democracy. My weakness for beautiful women."

His eyes moved from Nita to Griselde. Griselde blew on her fingernails.

"Some weeks ago," Gritska went on with an effort, "I have gone to the Monte Carlo night club in Kraków. There I have found singing a beautiful American girl. I am mad for her. I buy her champagne. I buy her jewels. But she remains cold. Finally, I tell her if she knows who I am, she will not be so cold. And then I tell her. 'I am the new Tito,' I say. 'In three months, I will overthrow the government, I will be the leader. Think what it will mean to you to be my'—I did not say mistress, but that was understood. And still"—a note of frustration entered his weak voice—"still she remains cold.

"The next day I realize what I have done. I have told to this American singer the great secret, the secret that places in danger the lives of all my collaborators. This is horrible. What shall I do? Shall I have her killed? But I am a kind-hearted man, I cannot do that. Besides, I am still mad for her, but that must wait. There is only one thing to do. I must arrange that she is given the drug, the precious drug that has been entrusted to us. In my position, I have access to this drug. The doctors obey my orders. They do not know it is something personal with me, they think it is the government and they are afraid. So it is arranged.

"Soon after, I must go to Paris. There is a man there, a doctor, from whom is obtained the drug. I have dealt with him before on behalf of the government. It has been a task I have assigned myself because I like the life in Paris, and others do not wish it because there would be great risk if the task was bungled. Also, in Paris, I make the contact with Polish exiles who will perhaps assist in my new movement.

"There, I get unpleasant news. An American journalist is coming to Poland to look for this Nita Romaine who has become so dangerous to me. In my absence, my government—that fool Chelinski!—has seen the chance to make the propaganda and has welcomed this journalist. Good God, what a position! As a member of the government, I must help this journalist find the girl who can ruin me. It is intolerable. I must take steps.

"Among my collaborators are officials of the Urzad Bezpieczenstwa. They have agents on the ship. The agents are instructed to throw this journalist overboard. But through some stupid error, he escapes. It is a great pity."

He paused to scowl at me. "Isn't it?" I said.

"So this journalist arrives in Paris. It is too dangerous to kill him there, so I instruct my agent to arrange that he is arrested. Again he eludes us. But now a very lucky thing happens. On the ship has been a courier, Wiktor Lepski. He has become interested in our movement. My collaborators in Paris arrange a meeting with him, and

I find he is become a friend of this journalist. Good, I tell him, you must bring your American friend to a rendezvous. He agrees. Then he finds out that the journalist will not leave the rendezvous alive. He tries to halt the arrangements, but it is too late. However, now this Lepski has become a danger to me. I do not dare have him killed, so I command the doctor to whom I speak to administer to him the drug also. He does not wish to do it—the coward does not even wish to deal with the journalist—but I command him. Otherwise, I will expose his dealings to the French authorities.

"Thus it happens. The journalist is lured to the rendezvous and then—then this woman"—he flung a feeble hand at Mrs. Pickett—"she not only spoils the rendezvous, she spoils my new hat."

He stopped, his breath coming shorter. The recollection of the hat seemed to have hurt him more than all the rest of his disrupted arrangements. Dr. Clendenning leaned over him.

Tensely I bent forward. "My wife," I said. "What have you done to my wife?"

His voice was very faint now. "After you have reached Poland, I have sent instructions to my agents in Paris to follow your wife. Once, they have almost lost her, when she changes hotels. But they find her again. Then I hear that you are getting close to my secret. I send new instructions."

Again he stopped.

"What were those instructions?" My voice trembled.

"To take her to Doctor Edelweiss. She must be a hostage. Also—"

I leaned close to him. "Also?"

"Also, she may know too much. She must forget—forget—"

His voice trailed off into nothingness, and his beefy,

blond head fell over to one side. Dr. Clendenning straightened slowly and solemnly. "I rather imagine," he said, "that the General is now changing his mind about godlessness."

CHAPTER THIRTY-FIVE

"DE MORTUIS NIL NISI BONUM," said Brock.

Griselde glanced coolly at the recumbent form over which a blanket had now been placed. "You did not know him as I did," she observed, "or you would not say that."

"Perhaps not," said Brock. "In fact, I was going to add that General Gritska had caused me a good deal of inconvenience in life, and he is causing me considerably more in death. It's going to be deuced awkward, having him found here. However, that's my problem, and I don't suppose any of you are greatly interested in it. What you're interested in is getting to Paris."

"But fast," said Mrs. Pickett.

Brock picked up the phone. "Get me Colonel Morrow, please," he said to the switchboard operator. Waiting, he remarked, "One thing in Gritska's favor, he's given me enough for quite a sensational dispatch to the Department. Almost too sensational." Then, "Hello, Colonel? Could you get that plane out of here tonight? I've got some passengers for you. Yes, I think you'd call it an emergency. Okay. Call me back."

He hung up and said, "That Colonel's a whiz. How are you people fixed for exit permits and such?"

"I'm fixed fine," said Mrs. Pickett. "I never had an entrance permit, so I just haven't been here."

"I don't even exist," I said glumly. "They took my passport."

"Hmmm." Brock rubbed his chin. "Don't suppose Miss

Romaine has anything, either. Think she's in shape to make the trip, Doctor?"

"I think so," said Clendenning. "She is not exactly ill. But I feel that she should be accompanied by a physician, even if he specializes in children."

"How are your papers?"

"In order, I believe, but I have no exit permit, either."

Brock sighed. "Well," he said, "you're all American citizens, and this is our own plane, and I'm going to take a chance on getting you out of here without any formalities. You and Miss Romaine, and Mr. Rockwell can apply for new passports in Paris. We'll notify the Embassy. But I'm afraid that you, Miss—" He paused and looked at Griselde.

"Miratour. Griselde Miratour."

"I am afraid that you, Miss Miratour, will have to remain."

"Why?"

"Because you are not an American citizen and I could get into serious trouble smuggling you out of here."

"If the French Embassy requested you, would you do it?"

Brock hesitated. "It would certainly put matters in a different light. But would the French Embassy make such a request?"

"I am quite sure they would," said Griselde. She smiled. "Sooner or later, you must know this anyway. I am an agent of the French Government."

The silence that followed was broken by Dr. Clendenning, who said admiringly, "So you really are a professional temptress?"

"In a way, perhaps, yes," replied Griselde. She continued to address Brock. "If you wish to telephone M'sieu La Porte at my Embassy, he will confirm what I have told you."

"Give him a buzz, Watkins," said Brock. "The switchboard has his number."

While Watkins phoned, I stared at Griselde, aware now of the taut competence in that flowerlike face. "Then you are not an actress?" I said.

She looked indignant. "Of course I am an actress. A very good one. But I am also a patriot. When my government asks me to do a certain job, I am happy to do it. Even when it means attaching myself to—to a man like this one." Her eyes flickered toward the covered body.

"Did your government know about his movement?" asked Brock with a hint of jealousy.

Griselde caught the note and smiled. "No, we have not been that clever. We have known only that there was something strange about his visits to Paris incognito. Also, we have suspected him of dealings with the mysterious Doctor Edelweiss. I was assigned to discover what was the purpose of his visits and what were his relations with this Edelweiss."

"So you knew all the time who Stanley was?" I said.

"Of course, but he did not know that I knew so I could not tell you. To my chagrin, he has left Paris before I have found out anything very much. So I have determined to follow him. And you, *mon cher autre* Stanley, have been most useful to me in arranging this."

"Why did you try to shoot him?"

Her lip curled. "It was with great difficulty that I have missed him, he was so big and clumsy. I wished only to persuade him a little to take me with him to Warsaw. But I was afraid he would begin to suspect me, so I have carefully arranged to have a place to run to if there is trouble. Because one in my position can easily be"—she stopped and slid her finger across her throat—"without one's government being able to act. So I have persuaded M'sieu Rockwell to let me stay with him at his hotel. It has not been easy. I have had to pretend to take sleeping-pills to show how serious I am."

Griselde paused and looked at me reproachfully. "Most men would have been very happy to have me stay, but he is in love with his wife, he says."

Mrs. Pickett stirred and, with a wan attempt at cheeriness, observed, "I'll be glad to report that back to headquarters, Rocky."

My smile was equally wan. "God willing," I said.

Griselde glanced at Watkins, who was still holding the phone. "To continue," she said, "the little dock-tor has now appeared upon the scene. I tell myself, uh-oh, he will know at once that you are making the fake. But he says nothing. Did you know, dock-tor?"

He nodded. "But I thought I'd wait and see what you were up to."

"I have thought the same about you," said Griselde. "Perhaps you, too, were a fake. Meanwhile, I go back to" —her eyes flickered toward the body—"to him, and as I feared, he is becoming suspicious. I am a little frightened. I am not yet made prisoner, however, so I slip away, back to the kind M'sieu Rockwell. In the morning—"

Mrs. Pickett cleared her throat. "I didn't quite get the transition there," she remarked.

Griselde smiled. "I have slept on the little dock-tor's sofa. In the morning, I tell him I will pack his things, and in his luggage I discover a German certificate. I begin to wonder. Stanley, the other Stanley, is interested in this Stanley"—nodding at me—"and this Stanley is connected with the dock-tor. I ask myself, is there something here related to Edelweiss? *En tout cas,* I do not dare return to the other Stanley, so I decide to find out what I can about the little dock-tor. Again, I have not found out very much. Perhaps, in future, I will devote myself only to my proper career."

She finished, with a deprecatory little shrug, and glanced

once more at Watkins, who had hung up some moments before. "Well?" she said.

"The French Embassy never heard of you," said Watkins.

Griselde gave a little moan, half of despair, half of resignation, and Watkins quickly put out his hand. "That's the official version. Unofficially, Miss Miratour, I am assured that you are not only an excellent actress but a most valuable servant of your government. *Brava!*"

Griselde passed limp fingers across her forehead. "*Mèrci*," she said.

"That seems to settle that, thank God," said Brock briskly. "Watkins, you'd better go to the airport with them. There'll probably be a lot of confusion there and you may have to do some bluffing. But you and Colonel Morrow between you ought to manage it all right. In a pinch, you can call Chelinski."

"Did Chelinski survive tonight's purge?" I asked.

"If you can call it survival," said Brock. "I saw him at the Foreign Office. Whichever side won out tonight would have kept Chelinski because he's useful. And when that usefulness is exhausted, he'll be thrown away like an old shoe. He knows it."

"Speaking of old shoes," said Mrs. Pickett, "have you got any that our Mr. Rockwell could have? I'm too old to run around Europe with barefoot boys with cheeks of tan."

"Mr. Rockwell's bag is at the Chancery," said Watkins. "Also his typewriter. Miss Miratour brought them back from Kraków. I don't know if he has any other shoes or not."

"One pair, luckily."

"I'll have 'em sent over," said Watkins. Which he did, and meanwhile Brock's housekeeper produced a platter of sandwiches and coffee, and presently Colonel Morrow called back to say everything was set. He would meet us at the main entrance to the airport, and he would have a pal from the Polish air force with him, a man for whom he had done some favors and who'd see that we got through all right.

The drive to the airport, in Brock's limousine, was an eerie one. It was almost midnight, and the whole shattered city seemed deserted, except for clusters of soldiers in the shadows here and there. There were more soldiers at the airport's outer gate, but they stood aside willingly enough for our C.D. plates, and we rolled up to the main building, from the tower of which a bright beam shone.

A wiry, hard-bitten little man in American uniform appeared in the doorway's light and came toward us. A tall, blond man in blue was behind him.

"This your gang?" the little man asked Watkins. "My boys are ready. Let's not waste time."

He looked understandably surprised as, one by one, we climbed out of the big, black car. Nita Romaine came last, in her rough gray gown with the raincoat thrown over it and bedroom slippers on her feet. "Some day," the Colonel said to Watkins, "I trust you'll tell me who these people are. Follow me and don't talk."

We followed him and the Polish officer into a spacious waiting-room, its lights dimmed, then through a side door into a corridor, another door, and we were on the airstrip. Nobody tried to stop us.

"So far, so good," said the Colonel. "There she is." He pointed across the ghostly pale concrete, among the shapes of a dozen or more planes, to one whose motors were humming. Our little cavalcade moved across the strip, then we were being helped up steps into the plane, a twin-engine Dakota. The pilot and co-pilot, a crisp pair in their early twenties, took their places, the door closed, and in a moment, we were taxiing across the field. The plane turned, the motors grew louder, we were moving faster and faster along the ground, then the motors opened full up and we rose. I've been told the take-off is the most dangerous part of a flight, but as we left the ground of Poland, I felt safer than I'd felt in a good long while.

"You can undo your belts now," called the co-pilot.

The whole, great battered city lay below us. Moonlight and shadow were kind to her, but the dark and jagged shape of endless ruin was still dreadful to behold. And yet the lights along her streets made a brave show of twinkling, the softness of many trees dulled the sharp edges of shattered walls and towers and, through the vast panorama of destruction, flowed the broad and tranquil Vistula, gleaming gently in the night. I thought of all the other conquerors this placid river had seen, Tartars and Mongols, Goths and Teutons, and still this city of the Polanie, the plain-dwellers, clung to the river's banks. She was a gallant city, regardless of all else, and I saluted her. Then lights and reflections and buildings and trees drifted swiftly into tininess, into nothing, and I went to sleep.

When I woke up, the plane was on the ground, the door open, and a voice saying, "What in tarnation is this outfit?"

"Special job for Warsaw," said the pilot. "Give 'em some coffee and stuff."

"Where are we?" I asked.

"Berlin," said the pilot laconically.

We were there for about an hour, a dreamy hour of artificial light, of American voices, a lunchroom that could have been a lunchroom in Ohio, then back in the plane and off again.

The next time I woke up, the light of dawn was flooding the green grass and white concrete of another vast airport.

"All out for Paris," said the pilot. "Last stop."

CHAPTER THIRTY-SIX

To my pleased surprise, two cars from the Embassy were there, and so was our old friend, Baird, looking neat but sleepy. "Warsaw phoned through that you were coming," he said, shaking hands all around, "and we thought you deserved at least a piece of red carpet."

"You will not go unrewarded, son," said Mrs. Pickett. "Any relatives that you or the Ambassador would like mentioned in my column, just tell me."

Baird grinned. Then he glanced at Nita and said, "I'd suggest that Miss Romaine be taken straight to the American Hospital. They're pretty jammed up, but we've managed a special room and—"

"Just a minute, boy," said Dr. Clendenning. "I'm her physician, you know."

"Oh," said Baird. "Sorry. What would you suggest?"

"The same thing," said the doctor, "but I don't like to feel left out."

"Perhaps you'd like to go to the hospital with her."

"I think it's advisable."

"All right," said Baird. "Now, as for the rest of you—"

I couldn't stand it any longer. "Baird," I said, "have you got any news of my wife?"

He looked surprised. "Why, no," he said, "I thought that she—I understood—"

Grimly Mrs. Pickett said, "Somebody blundered. Somebody named Amelia Lovejoy Pickett. And she's going to do her damnedest to set things right. If there's still time."

"Good lord," exclaimed Baird. "In that case—"

Griselde's voice cut in sharply. "I am sorry, *ma grande amie,* but you must permit me to take charge. This is a matter for the French authorities."

"Maybe so," said Mrs. Pickett, "but I don't propose to wait for a lot of red tape to get itself unwound."

"It will not be necessary," said Griselde. "But you must listen to me and do that which I tell you. The life of our friend's wife may be at stake. We are dealing with a very dangerous man."

"I'd still like to meet him," remarked Dr. Clendenning.

"I think you will," replied Griselde. "Please listen. I wish to go at once to the Palais de Justice. The rest of you may proceed to the American Hospital, where you will leave Ma'amselle Romaine. You must then wait for an hour. That you do not like, I know, but you must do it." She glanced at her wrist watch. "At half past eight, you will present yourselves at the nursing-home in St. Cloud. I think that you, m'sieu"—this to Baird—"had better not go. Too many may arouse suspicion."

"What will we do when we get there?" asked Mrs. Pickett.

"You will say you have come to inquire after M'sieu Rockwell's wife. You will ask to see Doctor La Fleur. You must be insistent, but not too insistent. The important thing is to avoid suspicion. Is all understood?"

"Up to a point, yes," said Mrs. Pickett, "but—"

"Beyond that point," said Griselde, "you must have faith in me."

It was a lovely drive through the sparkling morning, through leafy streets that fairly dripped with freedom, but I'm afraid I didn't appreciate it. Mrs. Pickett seemed oblivious to it, too. She and I accompanied Griselde in one car, while Nita Romaine, Dr. Clendenning, and Baird went straight to the hospital in the other. At the Ile de la Cité, under the towers of Notre Dame, we left Griselde, then were off again through the wakening city for Neuilly and the American Hospital.

Dr. Clendenning was waiting there, and the three of

us put in the next hour, that endless, nervous hour of in-
activity, with coffee and rolls at a near-by café. Clendenning seemed fidgety as I was, biting his nails and looking
constantly at his watch.

"By the way," said Mrs. Pickett, "has anybody told
Les Baldwin his good news?"

"Who's he?" asked Dr. Clendenning. "Never heard of
him."

"Your patient's fiancé," said Mrs. Pickett. "I'll call him
right now."

She came back from the phone looking a little misty
around the eyes. "Rocky," she said, "you should have
heard that kid's voice when I told him his girl was in
town and safe. If I can just hear your voice as full of joy
before the day's out, I'll be happy."

"Amen," I said devoutly.

On the dot of eight-thirty, we drove up in front of the
Fleur d'Alpes nursing-home. Among the gentle hills of
St. Cloud, it sat inside a white stone wall, a square, cream-
colored house surrounded by chestnut trees. The street on
which it stood was deserted, and an air of sleepy peace
hung about the place.

"You can see how respectable it looked," said Mrs.
Pickett sadly.

The iron gate in the wall was locked. There was a bell
pull beside it, and I gave the thing a yank. We could hear
its distant ring. Presently, the front door opened, and a
nurse appeared. She called something to us in French,
and Mrs. Pickett called back. *"Un moment,"* said the
nurse. She vanished, then a grumpy-looking old man came
out and down the path, and unlocked the gate. I gathered
that he was grumpy about the early hour.

We followed him inside. The same nurse was sitting
primly at a desk in a small chintzily furnished reception
room. An archway at the rear led into a polished hall, in

which I could see a staircase, and beyond it French doors that opened onto a sunny terrace.

Mrs. Pickett addressed the nurse, who answered with a few calm sentences, a shrug or two, and a regretful smile. Mrs. Pickett turned to me, looking puzzled. "She says your Jane spent a night here and was released the following morning. That was two days ago. I don't know whether to believe her or not."

I felt a cold nausea. "Does she know if Jane left alone?"

There was another exchange in French. Then Mrs. Pickett, her eyes worried, said, "Apparently Jane left with that confounded male nurse—if that's really what he is. It seems he isn't actually on the staff, but he handles special cases for Doctor La Fleur. I don't like the sound of it."

"Neither do I. Let's ask to see Doctor La Fleur."

The nurse caught the words and shook her head, pointing to her watch to indicate the unsuitability of the hour. Mrs. Pickett spoke to her firmly. The nurse's answer was equally firm. Their voices grew louder, Mrs. Pickett's insistent, the nurse's adamantine. Then suddenly I heard another voice, a voice that transformed the atmosphere like distant thunder on a summer's day. It was guttural and harsh, and came from the staircase.

"What is all this fuss about at such a time?"

There was a sound of small feet on the stairs. Beyond the archway, the misshapen form of Dr. Edelweiss appeared in the hall, in the light from the French doors. A dark dressing-gown covered his small body, above which his great head looked more grotesque than ever. His eyes glowered through the thick glasses as he came slowly into the reception room. "Well," he said, "what is it?"

"Don't you remember me?" I asked, trying to keep my voice calm.

He stared indifferently. "You are somewhat familiar."

His eyes moved to Mrs. Pickett. "You also." His gaze passed over Dr. Clèndenning and came back to me. "So?"

"I have come to inquire about my wife."

"Your wife? Ah, the American woman who was here. She has gone. She was released some time ago."

"Where has she gone?"

He spread his tiny hands and shrugged. "How should I know? It is your business to know where your wife is, not mine."

In spite of Griselde's injunction, I couldn't take it. "Don't try to bluff, Edelweiss," I snapped. "It won't do you any good. Either you tell me where my wife is, or I'll report you to the authorities."

He smiled contemptuously. "And what would you report to the authorities? I am a respectable doctor. The authorities know all about me."

"Do they know about your dealings with General Gritska?"

A brief frown crossed his face, but he answered easily, "General Gritska is one of my patients. People come to me from all over the world for treatment of nervous disorders."

I couldn't think of anything to say. I didn't want to give away too much—maybe I already had. The rasp of his voice cut through my indecision. "It is I, young man, who will call the authorities if you do not go at once. I do not wish the tranquillity of my patients disturbed."

I stood still, torn by a feeling of terrible helplessness. Where was Griselde? Was it possible that after all—

Then I heard Dr. Clendenning casually say, "What do you hear from the old bunch at Munich, Karl?"

Edelweiss's spectacled eyes turned on him. "What? What is that you say?"

"Don't you remember me, Karl? I was in your class."

Slowly, a hideous pallor spread over that huge and unholy face. "I do not know what you mean," he said, but his voice shook like trees in wind.

"Yes, you do, Karl Nachtwitz," said Dr. Clendenning. "And it looks as if you're going to be the first of the bunch to hang."

Edelweiss's features became contorted as they had the last time I'd seen him. A thin fringe of spittle appeared on his thick lips, his eyes burned. Then he took a step backward and his little hand went to the pocket of his dressing-gown.

"Grab him, Stoney," cried Dr. Clendenning, but Edelweiss was too quick.

The little hand came up with a revolver in it. "Very well, whoever you are," and his voice was shrill with an insane rage, "you will never see me again. Wherever I go, your friend's wife will go. If you try to find me, you will find her. And she will be dead. Farewell."

Rocking slightly on his small feet, he moved backward, through the archway, along the hall. While one hand held the gun level, the other pressed a button, and a panel opened beneath the staircase, evidently to another staircase leading down.

"You're not going any place," I said, and started toward him.

"Look out, Rocky," cried Mrs. Pickett. "He's crazy. He'll shoot."

"Let him shoot," I said and went through the archway. I could see the revolver trembling in his hand, but its muzzle stayed pointed at me.

"Stop," he said.

I kept coming.

"*Sehr gut,* you fool," he snapped, and the air was shattered with a single loud report. Someone screamed.

For a moment, I thought this was the way it was when you were shot. Then my head cleared, and I saw that Dr.

Edelweiss had dropped the gun, that blood was spurting from the hand that had held it. It was from his lips the screaming came.

My eyes went past him. Between the open French doors stood Griselde Miratour, calmly wiping her pearl-handled revolver.

Behind her appeared two men in dark suits and derby hats. I heard footsteps behind me, and two more men were coming from the front door through the archway. The four of them converged on the hunched, big-headed figure, who seemed to dangle as they grasped him.

Griselde came calmly toward me. "You have been very brave, but very foolish," she said, and her voice was almost severe. "I have told you not to arouse suspicion."

All I could say was, "Griselde, where did you learn to shoot like that?"

She laughed. "I told you it was not easy for me to miss that beast of a Stanley. I have practiced shooting very much. Do you know why? I have wished ardently to appear in the Paris success, 'Annie du Far West.' What in American you called 'Annie Get Your Gun.' "

CHAPTER THIRTY-SEVEN

THERE WAS NO FIGHT left in Dr. Edelweiss. All he could do now was blabber his willingness to help, to place everything he knew at the disposal of western science—if only they would spare his neck.

"That is for others to decide," said Dr. Clendenning. "What we want to know is, what have you done with Mrs. Stonewall?"

He fell over himself in his anxiety to tell us—she was all right, he said over and over, she had not been harmed, she was well taken care of at his secret laboratory, he would take us there at once. His frenzied eyes turned to me. "You know where it is," he babbled. "In the Rue Seurat."

It took half an hour to get there. Edelweiss was bundled between two of the Sûreté agents whom Griselde had brought with her, while Mrs. Pickett, Dr. Clendenning, and I followed in the Embassy car.

The narrow little street, with its flat walls and over-grown vines, looked lonelier than ever, and I felt an un-bearable tension as we entered the dark and musty hall of Number Twenty-Two. The grotesque doctor's little feet sounded like a child's on the gloomy, twisting stairs. The tread of the Sûreté men was heavy behind him. Then, above me, dusty light came from an opening door, and we entered the bare, high-ceilinged room, with its sky-light still jaggedly hanging.

Edelweiss crossed the room, between his guards, and opened the door to the smaller room beyond. He pushed the white operating-table back, and now it was possible to see in the floor the cracks of a concealed trap door. A spring in the wall released it, and it rose of its own accord, apparently on weights. A wooden staircase led downward into a murky corridor, along which were several closed doors. From the gloom, a man's voice cried out, answered by a sharp phrase from one of the agents.

"I know that voice," said Mrs. Pickett, descending the stairs behind me. "It's that wretched male nurse."

A man in a white jacket, that brought back to me all the horrors of the mountain sanitarium, was standing against the wall with both hands raised. Dr. Edelweiss said something to him, and the man, with trembling haste, opened one of the doors.

"No, no, fool," said Edelweiss, "that is the wrong one."

In bluish light that was all too familiar to me, Wiktor Lepski lifted himself from a white iron bed, his eyes startled and glassy. Dr. Edelweiss turned to me. "He is also a friend of yours, is he not?"

But another door was opening then, and that was all I could think about. I pushed past Edelweiss and the male nurse and the Sûreté men, into a small, bare room, lit by the same hellish glow. On the bed, under a white sheet, lay Jane, her eyes closed.

I fell to my knees beside her, grasping for her hand. It was warm, thank God, and as I held it, her eyes opened. "Oh, darling, darling," I cried.

Light flickered in the staring eyes, but remained puzzled.

Her voice was strange and faraway. "I do not know who you are," she said very slowly. "And yet—it is very queer—I know that I am in love with you."

We rushed her in the Embassy car to the American Hospital. In that comforting building of solid red brick among the green trees of Neuilly, I didn't feel too unhappy at leaving her. She couldn't have had much of that damnable drug, I was sure, and the American doctor to whom I talked was briskly optimistic. He patted my shoulder and told me to come back in the late afternoon.

Mrs. Pickett and I walked down the front steps and across the pleasant lawn together. A young man was pacing up and down one of the gravel paths, smoking furiously, and when he caught sight of us, he let out a yell and came charging across the grass. It was Les Baldwin.

He bit his lip nervously. "They say she'll be all right. They tell me not to worry. But, doggone it, she doesn't recognize me."

It was my turn to pat somebody else's shoulder. "She will," I assured him. "She knows your name. And if it makes you feel any better, she knows it very, very favorably."

"Gosh," said Les. "You sure?"

"Our Mr. Rockwell," said Mrs. Pickett, "is the outstanding authority on these matters."

"But they've told me I can't see her till this afternoon. I don't know how I'm going to wait."

"I'm in the same boat," I said.

"Oh, no you're not," said Mrs. Pickett. "You are going to be extremely busy between now and this afternoon."

"I am?"

"Sometimes I despair of you," said Mrs. Pickett. "Hasn't it occurred to you that you have quite a piece to send to our newspaper?"

It *was* quite a piece, the best I ever wrote, I guess. There was an awful lot of the first person in it, but Mrs. Pickett went over it with a blue pencil and said she could see no way to avoid that, much as she'd like to. I wrote it on her typewriter at her pension, and by the time I had finished it and put it on the wire, the afternoon had begun to wane.

When I got back to the hospital, Les Baldwin was coming down the front steps, his face one happy smile. "She recognized me," he said. "She called me Lewis the first time, but once I set her straight she got it all right. Some girl, isn't she, Rocky? I'd go to hell and back for her."

I started to say that certain other parties had already done that, then I thought better of it. No use having poor Les go through married life with the feeling of playing second fiddle.

The doctor I had talked to in the morning was waiting for me, and from the way he beamed, I knew everything must be okay. "She's practically back to normal," he said. "Even that other girl, Miss Romaine, has been showing splendid response to treatment."

"What kind of treatment?" I asked.

"It's a complicated story," he said, "and I don't have all

the details, but it seems that the German scientist who invented this drug has been arrested and he's given the French authorities a formula that he says will speed up the reaction process. I'd have thought twice about using it, but the ingredients seemed harmless, and the French tried some of it out on a Polish chap whom this scientist had apparently been holding prisoner—" He smiled apologetically. "I told you it was complicated. Anyway, it seemed to bring the Pole out of the stupor he was in, so we decided it was worth a try. Good thing we got the formula when we did, too."

"What do you mean?"

"Why, this fellow, this German scientist—apparently he was a war criminal on top of everything else—hanged himself in his cell early this afternoon."

A nurse came up and said if I was Mr. Rockwell, my wife was waiting for me.

Jane was sitting up in bed, her skin like peach bloom against white sheets, and her eyes were bright and blessedly normal. For a while, I just held her in my arms, making myself believe that we were both real.

Finally, she said, "Rocky?"

"Yes, darling?"

"I have a queer feeling I've seen you before today. Have I?"

"Yes. This morning."

"It's like a dream. What did I say?"

"You said you didn't know who I was but—well, you said you loved me anyway."

"Oh," said Jane. Then she asked, "What was I supposed to be full of, anyway?"

"Truth serum. I hope."

"If they ever want a testimonial for that stuff," said Jane, and she put her arms around me, "I'm their girl."